Bedding
the Enemy

Bedding the Enemy

MARY WINE

Kensington Publishing Corp.

www.kensingtonbooks.com

BRAVA BOOKS are published by

Kensington Publishing Corp.
119 West 40th Street
New York, NY 10018

All Kensington titles, imprints, and distributed lines are available at special quantity discounts for bulk purchases for sales promotion, premiums, fund-raising, educational, or institutional use.

Special book excerpts or customized printings can also be created to fit specific needs. For details, write or phone the office of the Kensington Special Sales Manager: Kensington Publishing Corp., 119 West 40th Street, New York, NY 10018, Attn: Special Sales Department. Phone: 1-800-221-2647.

Brava and the B logo Reg. U.S. Pat. & TM Off.

ISBN-13: 978-0-7582-3467-4
ISBN-10: 0-7582-3467-8

First Kensington Trade Paperback Printing: August 2010

10 9 8 7 6 5 4 3 2 1

Printed in the United States of America

Chapter One

Red Stone Castle, McQuade land, Scotland, Spring 1604

L aird . . .

He'd never courted the title. Never considered it something that might be his. Keir McQuade walked through the hallways he'd covered a thousand times in the last year alone but today it felt like he crossed the polished stones for the very first time.

Today he was Laird McQuade.

An uneasy peace had settled on his father's land. One that Keir did not trust. Everyone was watching to see what the new season would bring. His father had wielded power ruthlessly and his two elder brothers followed their sire absolutely— moonlit raids on their neighbors that had resulted in his only sister being stolen away.

Keir snarled softly. Bronwyn was the only member of the family that he held dear. He missed her now that she was wed and that was no mistake. He did not lament the loss of his father or brothers, only the fact that they had been so filled with greed that they could not remain among the living.

He'd run his brother Sodac through with his own hand after he'd tried to help their eldest brother poison their sister.

And for what?

To deny her a dowry that her mother had settled on her long ago. Keir shook his head. Three months later, he was still slightly amazed when he opened his eyes in the morning and recalled the events that had left him to inherit the title of Laird McQuade.

He neared his chamber and frowned. Footsteps scuffed on the floor and two younger lads came around the corner with a heavy trunk between them.

"Laird." They both ducked their heads, unable to tug on their bonnets or drop their burden. But they both looked at the top of the trunk, avoiding his eyes.

A maid came next with her arms full. "Pardon me, laird." She dropped a curtsy without breaking her pace and ducked around him in a flash.

Keir frowned. Covering the last few steps to the doorway of his chamber, he stared inside. The shutters were wide open to allow the new spring air inside. A hint of new plants was in the air but all he felt was a tightening between his shoulder blades.

"What goes on here, Gwen?"

His mistress was standing near the bed. She tensed, the hand resting on the bedpost tightening. He heard her sigh before she turned to face him.

"It is time, Keir."

"Is it now?" He swept the room with his gaze. All of her personal belongings were missing. "Except that I dinnae recall when we decided that ye should leave."

"We didna decide because ye avoid the topic every time I bring it up. I decided." She sounded resigned but at the same time there was a core of strength in her that he admired.

"Ye got yer monthly courses, didn't ye?" He stepped closer, reaching for her, but Gwen moved away from his touch. A soft shaft of pain went through him. "Things have changed. Stop taking that concoction of yers and we'll marry now that my father isna here to tell us no."

"You canna marry me, Keir." Gwen offered him a genuine smile. "Dinnae talk that way."

"Ye love me, Gwen, and I will wed with ye. I'm laird now and I dinnae answer to my father any longer. I only refused ye a babe because my father would have seen it born a bastard."

"But you do not love me." Her eyes glittered and she drew a deep breath. "You are correct, my monthly courses have come and it's time for me to go. Before I lose the strength to do what I know in my heart is right."

"I didna say any such thing."

Gwen lifted a small hand up to silence his words. Hard resignation drew her face tight. "You will not say it because you know I love ye and ye're a good man. So it falls to me to speak the words we both know need saying."

"Gwen . . ."

She interrupted him. "You are the laird now. Just like your sister, it falls to you to marry for the benefit of every McQuade. I bring ye nothing."

"Ye're a fine woman, Gwen, and ye'd make a good mistress of Red Castle."

She smiled, soaking up the praise, but her resolve never faltered. "Thank you. But it remains that you do not love me."

Keir hissed but couldn't deny the truth of her words. Lying about such a thing would cause so much more pain when he was found out. "I wish it were otherwise, Gwen. Truly I do."

She moved toward him, reaching up to cup his jaw in her small hands. Her eyes shimmered with unshed tears and his throat tightened.

"I know that, dear one, but you cannot change what fate has

decided. You have treated me so kindly and I was nae pure
when I came to you." Her hands shook and she backed away
before allowing him to comfort her. "I'm nae sorry for that, either. I enjoy life and will nae lie about it. I follow my heart for
better or worse.

"My sisters have married and my mother will be happy to
have me under her roof again." Gwen moved toward the door.
"If ye're going to marry a lass that ye dinnae love, Keir, find
one that brings good things to the McQuades."

"I think ye will bring plenty of good things to this clan as my
wife."

Gwen paused in the doorway. "Nae, Keir. I have never been
a coward. Ye would have become bored with me in a fortnight
if that were so. I do love you and even though it hurts to part
with ye, love is sweet enough to send me looking for it. When
I swell up with my first child, I want to see love in the eyes of
the father and nae just the tenderness that ye give me. But I
thank ye for it and love ye enough to set ye free to try and find
a lass that yer heart softens for. Love is nae something to miss
in this life, if ye can help it."

She stepped back, into the doorway. "Remember that, Keir.
Remember that I only want the best for us both. I have to leave
ye because ye're too kind a man to set me out and I'll nae be
the mistress that ye leave a noble bride for. She'll have little
choice in the matter of who she weds. No one should be unkind to her. When ye bring a bride here, this room should be
waiting for her."

She was right. Keir hated it, but she was correct. He'd never
hurt her by putting her aside.

"All right, Gwen. Ye have always had a way of pushing me
when I need it." He followed her, noticing the shiver that
crossed her fair skin. Reaching out, he stroked her cheek. She

leaned her face into his hand, a soft smile turning up her lips. "But ye'll take a pair of horses with ye. . . ."

"I will not." Her voice was hard as stone now.

"Ye will." She narrowed her eyes but he grinned at her. Her spirit was something he had always been drawn to. "And ye'll take a few other things, including some silver."

"I am nae a whore."

"I didna say ye were. I told ye I'd wed with ye, today if ye like." She glared at him. Gwen never let his size intimidate her—another trait that he liked about her. She shook her head, refusing him.

"Ye'll take the horses and some sheep, since ye're set on this course of leaving me to find love. I'm going to make very sure that ye dinnae end up marrying because ye're wondering how to keep food on the table."

He rubbed her cheek one last time. "Promise me, Gwen, that ye'll come to me if ye need something?"

She reached up and hugged him tightly, her body shaking just a tiny bit. "I will, Keir. I promise."

She ducked out the door, her steps fading down the hallway. Keir clenched his hands into fists, forcing himself to turn around. The chamber was suddenly empty, more devoid of life than he'd ever thought it might be.

Oh aye, being laird was a burden, to be sure.

But it was also a duty, and Gwen was correct. He needed to marry for the clan—find himself a wife who came with powerful relatives and maybe even a good dowry. Love was for common men, most of them never realizing how rich they truly were to have the power of free choice. Being laird came with power but responsibility so heavy a man could feel his own knees buckle at times.

He would shoulder it. Looking out the window, he watched

the McQuade retainers in the yard. Once more the clan colors might be respected. He would make the McQuades a clan to be admired instead of scorned for nighttime raids.

And he would begin by finding a bride who would bridge the gap between him and his neighbors.

The English queen was dead. James Stuart had inherited the English crown from the monarch who had signed his own mother's execution order. The English nobles awaited their new king as spring drove away winter's chill. The English court lowered themselves before the new king and queen.

Helena Knyvett moved through the court, taking care with her steps. She had learned at a young age to control her every action. Each of her hands was resting perfectly on the front of her skirts to display her long fingers. Her chin was level and her expression smooth, no hint of disagreement. It was necessary to stop often in order to give deference to the nobles she passed. No matter, there was no place that she needed to be; in truth, her purpose was to represent her family among the other nobles of England. Her purpose was to mingle among them while being poised, educated, and well bred. Greeting them and making a favorable impression was the entire point of the costly silk damask gown she wore. The corset was stiff and the sleeves tight as fashion dictated, but all of that was something she was expected to shoulder without a single frown to mar her makeup. She needed to present the correct image so that a powerful man might offer for her. Her poise and ability to conduct herself well among other powerful people was what she would bring to a husband. Marriage was about a union between those of blue blood and those who understood how to gain the eye of other nobles.

At least that was what she had been told since childhood. It had been instilled in her every moment of her youth. Her purpose was to further her family. She was to represent her father, always considering what her actions might do for him.

In truth she was quite tired of the games played at court—the whispered schemes and plotting that didn't match the endless respect and greeting done in the middle of the great halls. But in the dark corners, nobles talked about one another in anything but kind terms.

"It took you long enough."

Edmund Knyvett enjoyed court. Helena curtsied to her brother. He rolled his eyes and his lip lifted into a sneer that didn't look good against his velvet doublet and silk sleeves. The only son and heir to the earldom of Kenton, Edmund was lavishly attired and he stood poised on one foot with the other barely touching the ground. It was a courtly pose, one that was considered sophisticated.

"Enough, Helena; if I want polished manners I don't need to spend time with you to see them."

She bored her brother. Her sibling preferred his friends and consorts to family. He often used her as an alibi for his lustful meetings. She would not lie for him but no one ever asked her. Edmund was her father's heir. One day he would be an earl. The court surrounding them dare not risk making an enemy of him. As long as there was a believable story, they chose not to question it. Besides, as his sister, if he suffered the ill will of the powerful men around them, so would she.

Such was court. Full of rumors and intrigue. She had no friends here—only the fear of performing poorly enough to earn the scorn of her brother. Edmund did not suffer silently. Her brother ensured that she understood everything she did that did not meet his standards.

"I came as soon as I received word that you summoned me."

"Yes, yes. That doesn't matter." Edmund began walking. Nobles made way for him quickly and with a slight lowering of their heads. They reached the end of the great hall and passed through to the inner rooms of the palace. Once they left the larger receiving hall there was privacy if you spoke in low tones.

"It is time to place you closer to the throne." Edmund paused, looking through an arched opening in the wall. Queen Anne was in the private garden with two of her children. The new queen was still enchanted by the palace, excitement sparkling in her eyes.

"Have I been offered a place?" She hoped not. Gaining any position among the new queen's ladies would trap her at court while her family interrogated her for every detail she overheard.

"No, but I plan to change that." Edmund looked across the garden toward one of the queen's maids of honor. "That one with the golden red hair. Raelin McKorey. Rumor has it half of Scotland thinks she's a witch due to some nasty business with a laird getting impaled on a royal pike over her. Getting her dismissed should prove simple enough. All I need do is give the queen a suitable reason to dispense with her. I'll tussle her tits and rumple her maidenly skirts in the hallway. That should suffice to disgrace her enough to be dismissed, leaving an opening for you."

Helena's eyes rounded. Her brother had little compassion in him. She knew it from personal experience. The girl in question was dressed in the queen's colors of gold and cream. A scar marred her creamy skin on one side of her face, but she smiled at the young prince and princess. The young princess took her hands and began swinging around in a circle. Raelin's eyes shimmered with happiness and she swung the child higher until both their skirts billowed out like flags on a jousting field. They didn't stop to worry about what others thought of them. Raelin simply kept turning in a circle with the princess holding onto her hands and her feet flying through the morning air.

It was a pure delight to see. To simply play. Now there was something she missed. It seemed so very long ago that she was permitted to indulge in such moments. Such was the burden of noble birth. Image was more important than childhood.

"Get out there and charm those royal brats. Before I disgrace Raelin, the queen must know your face. Or she'll pick some other girl to be her maid."

Helena ached for the Scots girl but she didn't dare voice an argument. Edmund could often turn cruel toward her, doing the very thing she begged him not to just to smother her in his authority. Instead she secretly hoped that Raelin McKorey was wiser than Edmund gave her credit for.

That was entirely possible.

Her brother was like many men, in that he didn't believe women might be clever. She walked silently, gliding around the edges of the garden. The sound of laughter was infectious because it was honest for a change. Not the theatrics often heard at court. The new queen was still getting settled into her new home and often didn't post guards around herself. A pair of burly Scots eyed her when she came closer. Helena lowered herself gracefully and deeply, remaining there.

"Yes? What do you want?" Queen Anne sounded mildly annoyed to have her time with her children interrupted.

"Forgive me, Your Majesty. The sound of the children drew me forward. I but longed for the view of innocence."

The queen smiled, her mother's joy evident.

"Who are you?"

"Helena Knyvett, Your Majesty."

The queen's maids all watched her, but the guards dismissed her and returned to watching the archways for possible trouble.

"I feel we should all learn from children how to truly enjoy a spring morning." Anne of Denmark cast a loving look at her children. She looked up, surprising Helena because she hadn't expected the queen to desire a response from her. Court was full of powerful people who wanted to have their opinion heard and nothing else.

"That is very true, your majesty. . . ."

The queen smiled. Helena found herself caught between two emotions. The children were a delight for her senses. They didn't know how to be calculating yet, hadn't learned about the sharper side of life. But she cringed as well because her brother was no doubt pleased with her now. Wherever he was hiding, she'd bet his mouth was curved up into a sneer. It was an expression she knew too well. That certainly made things much simpler for her, but she detested his schemes.

Still, the afternoon was nice and she had also learned to enjoy the moments that she might. All too soon her family would issue another demand. Such was the life of a nobleman's daughter. In truth, it was the fate of all children, even dictated by Scripture. Many said that even to think against your place was to question the will of God.

Helena didn't believe that. Fine, that made her a poor Christian, but it did not mean her dimwitted. She had a mind and didn't let it grow dusty. There was one thing that court had that she adored; a library to rival any in the entire country. Even more, there were learned men who longed for an interested ear and didn't care if that ear belonged to a woman. She spent hours in the library; the rows of books and instruments of science had become her haven. Even better was the laboratory that Dr. John Dee had begun during the old queen's reign. His students continued his work and sometimes she was allowed to watch silently.

"Helena, come join us in my chambers."

"Yes, Your Majesty."

Queen Anne picked up her son, the young prince clutching her strand of pearls and popping them into his mouth. The princess Elizabeth skipped happily alongside Raelin McKorey, their hands clasped.

Helena followed the queen along with a party of maids of honor, ladies-in-waiting, senior maids, and royal guards. She didn't seem to notice them at all, flowing gracefully in her silk gown while her son chewed on a string of pearls worth a fortune. Anne had been born a princess of Denmark, and she was completely at ease being the center of so much scurry and scrutiny.

Helena had learned to live amidst it as well. She followed her queen into the royal chambers. Everything was lavish but not overly so. The former queen had enjoyed good craftsmanship, too, and many of the carvings in the woodwork were from the days when Elizabeth had hungered for art and commissioned some of the most talented men in the world to bring their craft to England. Theater, painting, and even glass blowing had become English arts under her rein, promoting the growth of the middle class.

Musicians began to play, hidden somewhere behind a tapestry. The walls were inset with carvings that were gilded and painted beautiful colors. Water flowed in one of the outside foundations, the open windows allowing the soothing sound inside.

"Do you enjoy music, Lady Helena?"

Raelin McKorey asked the question, while holding the young princess happily playing atop a wooden rocking horse. It was fashioned with a sidesaddle and a silken mane.

"Yes."

The maid of honor came closer. "Do you play any instruments?"

"Yes, my father had me tutored in mandolin and the virginals." Her father had considered music a necessary skill in a lady of the court.

Raelin smiled. "My father did as well, but I am atrocious." A slight Gaelic accent clung to her words, making the girl sound unique.

"I doubt that."

"Do not, I swear it is true." Raelin laughed. "But dinna ye mind, no one is skilled at everything."

The girl's Scottish brogue was charming. Helena found herself enjoying it. Court had more Scots now that James Stuart was king, but to date she had only heard male voices speaking in the brogue. One of the other maids was listening in. She was a golden blonde with blue eyes that shimmered. She leaned in so that her words would not carry.

"Just make sure you dinnae play cards with Raelin unless you enjoy losing. Her brother taught her how to play like a privateer. She pillages everyone at the table."

Raelin shrugged, a very odd gesture coupled with her formal, gold, maid of honor gown. "This is Catriona McAlister and she thinks that my brother Alarik taught me to play cards. I would hate to correct her; it might destroy her confidence."

Catriona snorted softly. She cast a look about to make sure their conversation was not being listened to. "He did and didna tell me he didna. Yer brother is more privateer than not."

"My maids seem to have taken a liking to you, Lady Helena." The queen's voice silenced Raelin and Catriona instantly. She turned to look at them with a knowing eye. "Perhaps you would entertain us with your knowledge of the virginals."

Queen Anne pointed toward a lavishly painted instrument. A maid instantly folded back the wood cover to expose the white and black keys.

"I would be honored, Your Majesty."

A somewhat surprised look crossed the queen's face but it was replaced by a pleased expression. Helena swept her skirts forward and the maid pushed the small bench seat beneath her. It was all done in a graceful motion that would have made her mother proud. The hours of practicing court manners she'd dictated for her daughter were paying off.

Helena took a moment to remove her gloves. Every ear was poised and waiting on her first few notes. It was a test of her honesty more than a true desire to hear her play. The hidden musicians had stopped to allow her to become the center of attention. But it was a challenge Helena was prepared for. Setting her gloves aside, she placed her fingertips lightly on top of the mother-of-pearl-covered keys. She began the first passages of "Greensleeves" and felt the tension in the room dissipate. Her confidence grew as the song progressed. Her music was not something her brother might use; it was a thing that lived inside her heart. She was never so happy as she was when bringing a sprightly song to life in the air. Her mood only turned somber when she struck the last notes and the virginals quieted.

Soft applause came from the queen and her maids. Even the princess Elizabeth clapped but stopped quickly to grab onto the top of her horse, which was rocking back and forth.

"Delightful, Helena. I am pleasantly impressed."

Helena rose and curtsied low.

"None of that here in my private rooms. Sit and play. Something happy." The queen herself sat in a wide, brocade-covered chair. Two of her maids brought her sewing basket to her. Raelin carried over a length of cream linen that was half sewn into a man's shirt. Helena was slightly stunned.

The queen smiled at her. "Yes, I make my husband's shirts just like any other wife."

Helena cast her eyes away, her cheeks coloring for having been caught gaping like an unpolished girl. To make a man's shirts was considered a sign of affection.

Deep affection.

"How long have you been at court, Helena?"

The queen's question startled her. Helena raised her attention back to her monarch. "A year, Your Majesty."

"And yet you still blush. I find that promising."

Helena turned and sat back on the bench. Her hands began moving on the keys before she really considered what she was going to play. Her memory offered up a soft melody.

Oh, she understood what the queen was hinting at. . . .

But at the same time she was annoyed. There was so much dishonesty around her. Arriving at court had been the completion of years of practice and preparation. As far back as she might recall, all of her energy had been directed toward the moment when she would begin her days among the nobles and ambassadors of England's court.

Disillusionment hurt. It was the cruelest sort of pain—one that dug into her like a dull knife. Each day she found it harder to scrape together enough hope to face the ritual of dressing. It took over an hour and that was considered quite modest. But sitting for her face paint and hair styling nearly drove her insane. What was wrong with the color of her skin?

She didn't understand why it needed so many powders and colors applied. Her own mother wouldn't recognize her. Such makeup hadn't been a part of her training.

Her fingers finished the song but she paused for a moment. Her gaze settled on Raelin McKorey and the fact that the girl wasn't wearing the heavy face paint that the rest of the court clung to. The Scottish girl noticed her stare, raising an eyebrow in curiosity. The queen was working her needle but chatting with two of her older ladies-in-waiting.

"Forgive me for staring."

Fingering the keys, Helena tried to force her mind back to the music. Raelin moved closer, her skirts rustling.

"Were ye staring at my scar? If so, simply ask." There was a hint of unhappiness in the girl's tone. "I deplore the way everyone stares at it and then pretends it isna there."

"Oh . . . no. Not at all. I was noticing how little face powder you use." Helena's fingers went still on the keys. She looked at the scar now. "Honestly, it's not that big of a scar. Which was why I was noticing how little paint you wear. This makeup would cover it up completely if you wished to conceal it."

Raelin studied her for a long moment. The musicians began playing now that Helena had paused.

"Why do you wear it?" Raelin studied her face. "It sounds like you dinnae care for it."

Helena sighed. It was a tiny sound that slipped past the years of training. Raelin's face looked like freedom. She simply couldn't help looking at it.

"My family expects me to conduct myself according to court dictates."

Raelin winkled her nose. "It doesna suit ye to paint yer face like the old queen did." She suddenly smiled. "I know, we shall redo it. Catriona is very good with face powders."

Raelin reached for Helena's hand and tugged her up. The maid scurried in and pulled the little bench out from beneath her skirts.

"What are you two about?" The queen looked over her sewing at them.

Raelin curtsied. "Helena wants to try wearing less face paint. I thought I might help her."

The rest of the ladies and maids of honor waited to see what the queen would say. Her face was smooth for a long moment before she smiled approvingly.

"I think that's an excellent idea. I don't understand these English families painting up their daughters to look like an old queen. You are a girl and should look more like one."

The other maids of honor all smiled. They skipped to the edges of the chamber, returning with several items. Helena didn't know where to look first. Raelin sat her down on a wide padded bench. Another girl shook out a wide piece of sheeting and draped it over Helena's shoulders to protect her expensive court dress.

"Let's clean this off first." Raelin sounded so enthusiastic, as if she were about to begin some work of art, her fellow maids of honor all joining in the moment. Helena suppressed a tiny lament. This was what friends felt like. She felt their hands on her, wiping her face clean. Her skin tingled, enjoying the freedom.

Catriona opened a wooden box that had little trays that lifted out. Carefully sorted in the trays were powders and expensive horse-hair brushes. Two other maids of honor surveyed what was on hand. Their eyes sparkled with enjoyment but they pushed their lips into thin lines while they concentrated.

"You have such lovely eyes." Raelin finished removing the

last of the white powder from her face. "I don't believe I've ever seen a dark-haired girl with green eyes."

"My grandmother was half French."

The girls all leaned in to listen, one of them pulling on her hair to release the high rolls it was formed into. As big as her fist, padded rolls were pinned beneath her hair. The girls removed them and replaced them with much smaller ones.

Raelin selected a brush and fluttered it against a cake of powder. She smiled and applied the first stroke to Helena's cheek. The afternoon seemed to fly by because Helena was enjoying it so much. When Raelin was at last satisfied with her makeup, she carefully replaced all of the brushes and powders before allowing Helena to see her reflection.

"I hope ye approve."

The girl's brogue intensified when she was nervous. Helena didn't wait to really absorb what she looked like; she smiled brightly at Raelin the moment she got a glimpse of her face. It didn't matter if she liked the new style or not. Edmund would make her wear it to endear herself to the maids of honor among whom he hoped to place her.

At Raelin McKorey's expense.

Helena swallowed her distaste. There was little point in regretting one of Edmund's schemes. Her brother had scores of them. Far better to hope that he might lose interest or be satisfied that she had found some favor with the queen without his assistance.

"Dinnae placate me, Helena." Raelin placed one delicate hand on her hip. Helena stared at the informal pose, amusement tickling her nose.

Raelin pointed at the mirror. "Ye havena even taken a good look yet."

"But I already like the way my face feels so much better."

Raelin's eyes shimmered with emotion. "I didna think of that. But I suppose it was uncomfortable wearing all that thick powder."

She sat down and angled the mirror up so that it showed Helena a clear reflection of herself. Having the use of a mirror was quite unexpected because they were such costly things. She held it carefully, making sure to maintain a good grip on it, but just to be sure, she allowed it to rest in her lap. The polished surface showed her a very pleasing sight. You could see the color of her skin once more, only a little powder used to smooth her complexion. Her lips were painted, but with a lighter coral shade instead of the blood red favored by the late queen Elizabeth. Raelin had outlined her eyes in a thin brown that made them look a little larger, and there was a touch of rose on her cheeks. Her hair no longer rose so high above her forehead. Neat rolls parted in the center but they were no more than an inch thick.

A little sigh crossed her lips in relief.

"Now that's much better." Raelin clapped her hands together, her face shining with her accomplishment. "You and I shall be friends. I will help style you and you will play the music. Her Majesty adores the virginals."

"That is very kind of you."

And it was. Raelin McKorey was a maid to the queen, so she didn't have any time of her own. Besides, her family had placed her there in the hopes that she would accomplish all of the things that Edmund wanted of her. Helena smiled at her, seeing so much of herself in the Scots girl, both of them trying to find their way in a world controlled by men and money.

Helena returned to the virginals, setting her fingers onto the keys with a happy heart. Her spirit felt lighter than it had in weeks. It was for certain that her face was lighter. The queen was nodding her head in time with the music while she worked her needle. It was so beautiful, Helena felt privileged to be a part of it.

Edmund could choke on his schemes.

Chapter Two

"**D**id the queen invite you back?"

Helena jumped, her mind foggy from slumber. Fear shot through her for a brief moment until she forced her eyes to focus on the yellow glow illuminating the doorframe of her tiny room. Edmund stood there, a sneer of impatience on his lips.

"Did she?"

"Yes."

There was little point in berating him for waking her so rudely. Her brother might take that as a compliment to his ability to ruffle her feathers. His gaze wondered over her, lingering on her face for a long moment before moving down her body. Her fingers curled around the top of the blanket, clutching it closer. Disgust raked across her.

Edmund snickered at her revulsion. "Don't flatter yourself, sister dear. I am merely trying to gauge just what manner of body you've managed to grow. You're certainly not pretty enough to have the marriage offers piling up on my secretary's desk."

Helena pulled the blanket up anyway, his words giving her little reassurance. It bothered her to have him in her chamber during the night. Her skin itched with distaste.

"I've done what you asked, Edmund. Go on and let me rest."

His face changed, his lips thinning into something quite ugly. She was accustomed to his schemes but this was deeper somehow. Greed shimmered in his eyes.

"I haven't even begun to tell you what I want you to do. But I'm not surprised that you can't understand what needs to be done for our family to succeed." His eyes traveled down her length once more, his lips curling back in disgust. "You're just a female, nothing but a bitch that can speak. It falls to me to give you direction."

He left her doorway, the light of the candle fading down the hallway. It left her in darkness because her shutters were closed. Rolling over and reaching up, Helena found the inch-wide metal rod that secured them. She did it easily from hundreds of repetitions. Pulling it loose, she allowed it to hang by its chain, and propped herself up on one shoulder so that she might open the shutter.

Edmund would have a fit if he knew she opened the shutters at all. Her room wasn't really a room but an attic. He'd had a set of steep stairs built when her parents sent her to join him in the London town house. Residences near the palace were costly and in great demand but she slept in the attic for another reason.

Edmund was selfish.

She smothered a giggle and pulled one shutter open. The night sky was magical. Well, only if one admitted to believing in magic. That wasn't very wise. James didn't seem to have the same zeal for witch hunting as some did, but there were men on his privy council who did.

She pulled the blanket up to her nose to hide any reflections of the moonlight off her plain nightshift. Keeping absolutely still, she could look out over the rooftops of London. She only did it when the moonlight wasn't pointing toward her window. The night was beautiful. Searching the heavens, she located constellations she had first seen in books. Peace settled over her. This was the time that was solely hers. She treasured it.

The corners of her mouth twitched up just thinking about what Edmund might do if he knew how much she adored the tiny attic room.

She hoped nothing. He was her brother, after all. It was sad to think they would never like each other. She still held out hope that they might find some topics that they agreed upon, possibly even enjoy conversing on.

To date it had not happened. The moment she arrived in London, Edmund had begun telling her what he planned for her to do. What use he had for her. It was disheartening, to say the least. They were blood but honestly they were little more than strangers. Edmund had left their family estate at the age of six and she had been barely out of swaddling at the time. He returned from time to time but never for long. Her memory held brief recollections of him at different ages, but it was likely that she held those memories due to the paintings her parents commissioned of their only son. They were huge oil canvases, ones that hung proudly in the dining hall of their estate. She hadn't really known what to expect upon her arrival. What she'd found was a man who was a stranger to her.

Edmund wore lace and ribbons set with gold tips. Pearls adorned his doublet and his slops were full and round. His boots were always polished and freshly blacked. Lace edged the ruffles of his shirt. The thing that looked the most out of place on him was the sword he had strapped to his hip. The hilt was gilded and polished. Edmund had a habit of resting one hand on it, almost lovingly. He was every inch the courtier. His life revolved around the gossip. The first few days she had attended with him, she had stared in wonder while he made his rounds. He wasn't alone in that. Hundreds of people were crowded into court. They competed for appointments with the king. Bribes were frequent and high. Seating at banquets cost you a good amount of silver if you wanted to be seated next to the person of your choice. Edmund dictated every move she made. No one danced with her without his permission. She did not go where he did not bid her to go.

Just like today with the queen . . .

Raelin and the other girls who served as maids of honor came to mind. Even their dresses were uniform. In spite of having known her so short a time, Helena found herself liking the Scots girl. A desire to return to the queen's private chambers was growing stronger, but not due to any direction from her brother.

Poor Edmund. How would he deal with such devastating news?

She laughed at her own jest. It wasn't too terrible to tease her brother in her thoughts. Well, the church would argue about that. Still she didn't feel guilt chewing on her conscience. After all, Edmund made no attempt at all to be pleasant. A few ill thoughts were the least of his due. But she would not linger on them. The only person who would be upset was herself.

Reaching up, she closed the shutter. Dawn would arrive promptly, so best to rest while she might. Edmund would likely have her dressed and in the carriage at daybreak. But she didn't mind, for it meant she might see Raelin again, and the idea of having a friend sent her off to slumber with happy thoughts.

* * *

"Welcome back, Mistress Knyvett." One of the queen's ladies-in-waiting waved the guards out of the doorway. Helena lowered herself before entering.

"Her Majesty is unwell this morning."

"I am sorry to hear such news."

The lady offered a small smile that confused Helena. The queen's illness was no reason for smiles, she would think.

" 'Tis the babe making her ill. It will pass in a few more weeks."

Helena's face reflected her surprise. She had heard no rumors of the queen being with child.

"And you shall keep that knowledge to yourself, madam. Her Majesty does not need to be bothered with the endless congratulations and chattering of every soul who wants to advance themselves by wiggling into her good graces. Now is the time for quiet so that her body may adjust."

"Of course. I understand."

The lady waved her off, toward the circle of maids of honor. They smiled at her, Raelin patting a bench next to her.

"I'm so glad ye came."

Raelin kept her voice a whisper. "Dinnae ye worry, things will be right as rain by noon. Until then, we will have to behave."

There was a soft round of laughter from all the girls that they covered up quickly, and lowered their heads to peer at their sewing. Helena felt her eyes widen when she beheld what was sitting on the table in the center of their group. A small chest, banded with iron to make it secure, was there with its top open. Pearls in more colors than she had ever seen sat nestled inside it—cream, white, pink, gold, and even blue ones. They were sorted into different sizes and held in small silk bags that were all carefully untied so that you might see into each bag.

"Can you stitch?"

"Of course."

Raelin shook her head. "There is no 'of course' about it. The pearls are counted and recounted when removed. Make sure your stitches and knots are secure."

Raelin handed her a silk sleeve that was edged in velvet. Tiny chalk marks showed the design where the pearls were intended to sit. She also handed her a golden needle.

Helena marveled at the little needle. It was so smooth, no rough burrs to catch on the fabric. She rolled it between her fingers, simply enjoying holding such a fine item. The sleeve itself was beautiful and working on it was a pure delight for the senses. The girls whispered all the time they attached pearls. Helena felt Raelin watching her first few stitches but she did not become flustered. Her skills were very good and she knotted the thread with a practiced hand.

The queen finally emerged from her sleeping chamber, her face pale. Her ladies fluttered around her but she waved them away.

"A bit of fresh air. That is all I need."

She was wearing only a dressing gown and that was untied, allowing her chemise to be seen. Her hair was braided into one thick length that trailed down her back. But she still looked so regal. It was in the way she moved, commanding everyone around her.

"Helena, play something sweet."

"Yes, Your Majesty."

Carefully setting her work aside, Helena rose and curtsied to her queen before sitting at the virginals. The queen looked out over the garden but her face lost some of its pinched look when Helena began to play.

"I heard ye were feeling poorly again."

Helena missed a note as the king strode into the chamber.

The queen turned and lowered herself. But the king reached for her hand, raising her.

"I am very well."

James Stuart didn't appear to believe her. His face was darkened with concern. Anne laughed at him.

"This is not our first babe. I will be strong and well."

The king kissed her hand, lingering over it. He suddenly noticed Helena, looking straight at her.

"A new maid of honor, my dear?"

The queen smiled. "This is Helena Knyvett. I enjoy her command of the virginals quite a bit."

"Then I am in her debt."

Helena felt a smile brightening her face. There was no way to ignore the rise of satisfaction inside her. But it wasn't due to some sense of family duty. The king might command the best musicians in the country to play for him. Pleasing his ear was an accomplishment, to be sure. She inclined her head to acknowledge his words, not wanting to lose the melody.

Servants entered with large serving platters that had silver domes over them. They set a table right in the middle of the chamber. The scent of fresh bread and newly cut cheese drifted to her nose when they lifted the domes. The king and queen began dining. Helena watched them from beneath her lowered lashes. It was a fascinating sight because, in spite of their positions, they appeared quite normal.

Not that she might ever dare to call them normal. Many still believed in the divine right of the monarchy. But it was almost an intimate setting, so far removed from the other times she had viewed the royal couple. At banquets, there were horns that announced the couple every time they entered the room. Each tempting and lavish tray was presented to them before anyone else. Earls and countesses served them, doing even the most basic of table chores, such as holding a bowl of wash water for the queen to rinse her hands in before she supped. The ladies of the chamber served the royal couple but it lacked the abundance of lowering and curtsies that was displayed by these very same women in the great hall. There was no lack of respect, simply a lack of pretense.

Helena was suddenly more content than she had been since leaving home. Behind all the polished manners and expected duties, there were people here. She enjoyed that.

Even Edmund and his schemes couldn't tarnish her joy.

London . . .

Keir McQuade looked down on the town with a frown. He'd honestly never thought to travel so far into England. He liked Scotland and was quite content to run his estates.

There was yet another thing that had changed with his father's recent behavior. James might just leave him standing in the outer chamber for months, considering the last McQuade he'd had in his presence had needed running through by the royal guard. The only thing his monarch might be interested in seeing him about was the inheritance taxes due the crown. But the secretary of the privy council could collect that.

Yet it was his duty to wait for his king's attention.

Every new laird swore an oath to his monarch. It was a tradition that needed to be observed even more because of the way his father had disgraced the name of McQuade. Keir looked down on London and tightened his resolve. He wasna afraid of anything that would befall his own person. He was more worried about nae being able to restore his clan to good standing with his king. Being the McQuade laird, that was now his burden. Every soul wearing McQuade colors looked to him to maintain their honor. The men riding with him all wanted to be proud of the name they'd been born with, to wear their kilts with chins held high. His father had made that difficult with raids that cast a shadow over the honor of the entire clan.

He tightened his hand around the reins.

He'd make sure their sons could be proud of being Mc-Quades.

"You're more clever than I thought."

Edmund was drunk, although her brother handled it expertly. There was only a slight slurring to his words and a pinch at the corner of his eyes that she had learned to recognize.

"Don't plan on getting married. I need you."

She bit her lip to retain the harsh words that bubbled up in response. What an arrogant fool her brother was. He mocked himself with his own words. One day he was ready to get rid of her, and the next he was warning her against thinking of marrying. The only thing his warning did was illuminate how little say she had over her own fate. Such knowledge was beginning to chafe, and being told that it was a woman's position to accept it, very old.

Her brother's hunting hounds appeared to have more choice than she.

"Lure Raelin McKorey out tonight."

"That isn't necessary. I am making my own place with the queen." She knew better but just couldn't stand idle while her brother threatened Raelin. The Scots girl was her only friend.

And she was a kindhearted soul as well. She deserved better than to be lured to her ruin. Especially by someone that she had been kind to. Maybe many at court considered that acceptable in the game of getting ahead, but it stuck in Helena's throat, refusing to be swallowed.

Edmund's eyes narrowed. He was an expert at concealing his true feelings, but she had learned some of his expressions, mostly the ones that promised her the harsh side of his temper.

"A position of your own?" He snickered softly at her. "Any player with a bit of skill can do what you have done, sister."

Edmund moved toward her, his gait as refined as ever, and stopped within reach of her.

"I will not repeat my instructions. Do it—once the king retires and his nobles have a chance to leave for the night."

Or suffer his displeasure. She heard that clearly enough. But she refused to aid him in this scheme. Or any others, for that matter. For all his fine clothing, she suddenly noticed just how pathetic he was. Her parents might have spent endless hours drilling her duty into her but they had also taught her honor.

Edmund didn't even seem to know such a trait existed.

"I will not assist you, Edmund. Raelin is not dishonorable."

His hand struck her quick and sharply, her head turning with the blow. When she returned her gaze to his face, she clearly saw the flush discoloring his skin. Her temper itched to retaliate, but acting on such impulses had never turned out well for her in the past. She clasped her hands together to keep them from returning the blow.

"You shall do exactly what I tell you to do."

Greed shone from his eyes, sickening her.

"I will not do anything to hurt Raelin. Or dishonor her."

Edmund suddenly laughed. It wasn't a pleasant sound, but one filled with mockery.

"Do you somehow believe she is sincere? A true friend of the heart, perhaps?" He pressed his lips closed but she could still hear him chuckling. "She's like everyone else. Don't think for a moment that her family didn't send her here with the very same expectations that you have been given."

He backed away from her, raking her with cold eyes. "You will do it or I will have to find a means of influencing you."

Helena didn't answer. A chill shot down her spine, warning her to let Edmund believe her bent to his will. She didn't want to see the cruelty in his eyes, but it sat there glimmering with hot intensity. It sickened her. Sickened her even more to think they shared the same blood. Her throat felt as if there was a noose around it, tightening every day. But she refused to do what was necessary to be free. The only thing she had was her honor. It was the sole item she counted as her possession alone. Even her body would one day be bartered and used at the whim of Edmund. She could not betray the only kind person she had met. But she wasn't sure how to keep her brother from hurting Raelin in spite of her refusals to assist him.

Being born female was a curse.

"A pleasure doing business with you, my lord."

Keir folded his arms across his chest. The fop in front of him scooted back a step, his eyes watching the way Keir's biceps bulged.

"I'll be leaving you to your accommodations then."

The man fled in a swish of his overpuffed pants. Keir snarled softly.

"Och now, that's sure to get us tossed out in the gutter." Farrell McQuade clicked his tongue along with the reprimand.

"After that amount of gold he just stole from me for this wretched place?"

"It's a step up from the gutter."

"For a child's legs, maybe." Keir looked around the tiny town home. It was ancient. The wood around the doorframes was splintering because it was so dry. Considering the rain pouring down off the edge of the roof, that was an amazing thing. "Personally, I was hoping for a wee bit bigger step. Tell the men I'll keep looking for something more hospitable." His retainers wouldn't complain, but they had the right. The dozen McQuade clansmen who followed him would be crammed into three rooms and that was only because he planned to share the upper room with Farrell and his captain. But no laird went anywhere without retainers. It was foolish to travel alone, a death wish. The road had plenty of danger for the unprepared man.

"Why doesn't Jamie move the English court to Edinburgh?"

Keir shook his head at Farrell. "He'd no wear that crown long if he tried that one."

England's noblemen were powerful and a king that was not in sight could very easily be undermined, which left Scotland's nobles paying inflated prices for lodging in London. Most noble families maintained residences near the palace. The McQuades had one in Edinburgh for the times they were summoned to court. But now that James was king of both countries, the Edinburgh house stood empty while Keir was putting out coin for a hovel in London. The house pickings were slim, with ambassadors flooding into the city with the news of Elizabeth Tudor's death making its way across Europe.

"Let's hope Jamie doesna keep us waiting too long." Farrell tried to sound hopeful but Keir shot him a glance. The burly McQuade retainer shrugged.

"Och well, it was a thought."

"Aye. I suppose we'd best get our doublets out. It looks like we're to court, you and I."

Keir's voice lacked enthusiasm but not determination. Better to begin; that way they'd finish their business all the sooner. He did not have much to unpack, as he'd not even bothered with a trunk. He would not know what to do with one. His best doublet was a sturdy wool one. He was a Scottish laird and did not have any plans to join the flock of young men wearing lace and silk. He'd wear his kilt proudly. After all, that was the reason he was here. To restore honor to that kilt. Let the court stare at him and know that he was different. He was Scots and here to do his duty.

He was not going home until he'd accomplished it.

"I've never seen such women in me life." Farrell frowned at the court. Keir elbowed him and shot him a reprimanding look.

"Stop scowling at them, Farrell. We've nae the best reputation."

"Good. Maybe that will keep these females from flirting with us."

Farrell shuddered. Keir fought his own battle to hide his surprise, or horror, as it were. Never in his life had he ever thought that he'd find boys more pleasing to his eye than women. But the ladies of the court looked so far removed from anything he'd ever seen, he couldn't help but look at the men for a bit of relief.

The women's dresses plunged down in the front with naught but scraps of fabric holding their titties in. The points of the stomachers extended a full forearm's length below their waists. The dresses came out at the hips, straight out for over a foot. It gave them the shape of a cylinder. There was not a feminine curve in sight. The view only got worse when he look up to their faces. Most of them were white with red spots over their cheeks. Their hair stood up several inches above their heads and it was stiff, not one single, flowing bounce in sight.

What confounded him were the extremes in the court.

Plenty of women in London wore smaller versions of both hair and dress styles while maintaining a bit of feminine allure. Of course, there was also the need to be able to move that accounted for those abbreviations, but Keir admitted that he liked a more practical-looking woman, as opposed to the ones he was looking at.

Keir suddenly froze, his eyes settling on a woman that he'd not noticed before. It might have been due to her lack of garish face paint or just due to the overwhelming horror he found himself facing.

But she was charming.

He'd never been a man to chase a woman because she had a pretty face. He always needed something more to snare his interest. The stark contrast in her dress drew his attention. The garment did not look like it was a cage laced around her. Instead the skirt flowed simply from her waist over a modest set of underpinnings. The men she walked past did not give her any attention. In fact, a few of them looked down their powdered noses at her modest neckline. Only the very tops of her breasts peeked over the top of her bodice. Among so many bulging mounds it was quite captivating. But what kept his eyes on her was her height. She was slender and too thin for his taste, but her head rose high enough to look several of the men in the eye.

He'd be able to kiss her without bending over.

The sides of his mouth twitched up. Och now, he was being a rakehell with that idea. He did not even know the lass's name and here he was imagining what her lips tasted like. His smile grew broader. At least it was a far better thing to be thinking about than how much he detested the current fashion of court ladies. A fair bit better indeed. Whoever she was, she became blocked from his sight, leaving only her memory.

He did not care for waiting.

His face returned to its pensive expression. He'd never been an idle man. Running Red Stone took all of his time but it was a labor he enjoyed. Awaiting Jamie's pleasure was something that tore at his gut.

He was staring at her.

Helena looked through her lowered eyelashes at him. He was a Scot and no mistake about it. Held in place around his waist was a great kilt. Folded into pleats that fell longer in the back, his plaid was made up in heather, tan and green. She knew little of the different clans and their tartans but she could see how proud he was. The nobles she passed among scoffed at him but she didn't think he would even cringe if he were to hear their mutters. She didn't think the gossip would make an impact. He looked impenetrable. Strength radiated from him. There was nothing pompous about him, only pure brawn.

Her attention was captivated by him. She had seen other Scots wearing their kilts but there was something more about him. A warm ripple moved across her skin. His doublet had sleeves that were closed, making him look formal, in truth more formal than the brocade-clad men standing near her brother. There wasn't a single gold or silver bead sewn to that doublet, but he looked ready to meet his king. It was the slant of his chin, the way he stood.

"You appear to have an admirer, Helena."

Edmund sounded conceited and his friends chuckled. Her brother's words surfaced in her mind and she shifted her gaze to the men standing near her brother. They were poised in perfect poses that showed off their new clothing. One even had a lace-edged handkerchief dangling from one hand.

She suddenly noticed how much of a fiction it was. Ed-

mund didn't believe them to be his friends but he stood jest-
ing with them. Each one of them would sell the other out for
the right amount. It was so very sad—like a sickness you knew
would claim their lives but could do nothing about.

"A Scot, no less."

Edmund eyed her. She stared back, unwilling to allow him
to see into her thoughts. Annoyance flickered in his eyes when
she remained calm. He waved his hands, dismissing her.

She turned quickly before he heard the soft sound of a
gasp. She hadn't realized she was holding her breath. It was
such a curious reaction. Peeking back across the hall, she
found the man responsible for invading her thoughts completely. He had a rugged look to him, his cheekbones high and
defined. No paint decorated his face. His skin was a healthy
tone she hadn't realized she missed so much. He was clean-
shaven, in contrast to the rumors she'd heard of Scotland's
men. Of course, many Englishmen wore beards. But his hair
was longer, touching his shoulders and full of curl. It was dark
as midnight and she found it quite rakish.

He caught her staring at him. She froze, her heartbeat accel-
erating. His dark eyes seemed alive even from across the
room. His lips twitched up, flashing her a glimpse of strong
teeth. He reached up to tug lightly on the corner of his knitted
bonnet. She felt connected to him, her body strangely aware
of his—even from so great a distance. Sensations rippled
down her spine and into her belly. She sank into a tiny curtsy
without thought or consideration. It was a response, pure and
simple. Her heart was thumping against her chest and she felt
every beat as if time had slowed down.

A woman crossed between them, interrupting her staring. It
was enough time for her mind to begin questioning what she
was doing. Fluttering her eyelashes, she lowered her gaze,

forcing herself to move through the court with slow steps. She ordered herself not to look back. She was warm, warmer than the day warranted. The reaction fascinated her but it also struck a warning bell inside her mind. She should not look back.

But a part of her didn't care for that. It clamored for her to turn and find him again. His eyes were as dark as his hair but lit with some manner of flame. She wanted to know if he was still watching her, wanted to know if she glimpsed the same flames in his eyes that she felt in her cheeks.

Ah yes, but fire burns . . .

Helena smiled. She enjoyed the way she felt, a silly little sort of enjoyment that made her want to giggle. The reason was actually quite simple. The way he looked at her made her feel pretty. Court was full of poetry and lavish compliments, but none of it had touched her. His eyes did. The flicker of appreciation was genuine.

She had never felt such before.

"Good day to ye."

She froze. The man must be half specter to move so quickly. But she wasn't afraid of him. Quite the opposite. Her gaze sought his, curious to see if his eyes continued to fascinate her up close.

She was not disappointed. Her breath froze in her lungs, excitement twisting her belly. His gaze roamed over her face and a pleased expression entered his eyes. In fact, it looked a bit like relief.

She was suddenly grateful to Raelin all over again for having freed her of the heavy makeup. The way he looked at her made her feel pretty for the first time in her life.

"Good evening."

He offered his hand to her and more excitement raced

through her. She lifted her hand to place it in his but Edmund gripped her wrist before she touched the Scot. Her brother's grip was cold and harsh. He didn't have a care for his strength, crushing the smaller bones of her wrists. She didn't feel the pain because lament burned through her for the contact she was being denied.

"My sister is on her way to play for the queen."

She didn't want to see the Scot bend in front of her brother's arrogance. That idea flashed through her mind and she did not tear her attention from his face, watching to see if he allowed Edmund's name to impress him. For some odd reason, she needed to know. She actually wanted him to stand tall, even if that was unwise. But it would be gallant and noble.

Whoever he was, Edmund did not impress him. One dark eyebrow rose mockingly. Helena felt warmth spread through her heart. It was not that she enjoyed seeing her brother disrespected, but it was endearing to watch a man refuse to swallow Edmund's arrogance.

"And she has no time for dawdling." Edmund glared at her. "Go on with you, Helena."

She couldn't disobey a direct order, not in public. The scandal would taint the entire Knyvett family.

Oh, but she wanted to.

Her gaze returned to the Scot. His eyes were dark as ink and just as solid as the written word. His lips curved slightly for her. The soft skin of her own tingled in response. Her cheeks burned hotter but a grumble from her brother sent her feet to moving.

Damn Edmund and his ambition. . . .

Edmund waited until his sister complied before scoffing at Keir once more. It was almost too amusing to hold inside. But the way the man spoke to his sister was not entertaining. It reminded him of the way his own sister had lived under his father's rule.

"My sister is a noblewoman of blue blood. Our family is one of the oldest in England, sir. You will keep your hands away from her."

Keir grinned. It was a full curving of his lips that flashed his teeth at the whelp trying to impress him. He took one long step toward the man and was rewarded with a whitening of his pallor.

"Strange thing is, I do believe ye might have just been discussing a hunting bitch instead of yer own sister. It sounded that cold-blooded. If she's the lady you proclaim her to be, why are ye talking to her like a dockside hussy?"

"How dare you . . . Scot! Do you know who I am?"

"Nay, but so far I'm nae impressed with the way ye treat yer sister. Titles are nothing but old words without honor."

Keir turned and left. He did not need one of England's nobles wrought with him, but he could not stomach the man without speaking his mind, either. He was drunk on his own power, exactly like his older brothers had been when his father was still laird of the McQuades. They did whatever pleased them and the suffering caused by that selfishness bothered them naught at all.

But that was not what he wanted to think about. He scanned the court, searching for her. Something in her eyes had drawn a response that baffled him. The moment that her hand had been moving toward his own was etched into his memory. It was as tantalizing as it was frustrating. The only thing he felt certain of was the fact that he wanted to see her again.

Without her scheming brother. He was not the first pompous man who had tried to step on him, but Keir was not planning on letting the man interfere with discovering if the lass could snare more of his attention.

"There's nae a great deal of affection between yer brother and ye."

Helena froze only halfway around the corner. For a moment she thought she imagined the Scottish brogue. It was the truth that she was dwelling on the man. But he stood in the hallway as large and real as might be.

"Do you often appear in front of ladies?"

He shrugged, drawing her eyes to his shoulders. For some unknown reason his body fascinated her. She simply enjoyed looking at him, tracing the bulges that pushed on his doublet, running her gaze along his arms and wondering what his skin looked like beneath the sleeves of his doublet. She had never been so interested in a man before, which made her curious.

"'Twas the best way to get back to the conversation yer brother interrupted."

"I see." She didn't care for how soft her voice was. Lifting her chin, she stared straight at his face. Indeed, the man was large, but that was no reason to simper. "There was no need. My brother was truthful; I am expected by the queen. Yet I apologize for how rude he was."

There was no disguising the lament in her tone.

"I'll be the judge of whether or no I needed to find a way to place that kiss on the back of yer hand."

He was a proud man; she heard it in his voice. But his words irritated her. He was quite sure of himself indeed.

"Nay sir, I shall be the keeper of my own hand."

She wasn't sure why she spoke so heatedly to him. Her heart was beating faster, making it hard to remain poised and in place. It was almost as if she needed to prove that she would not surrender to his will without due consideration.

"Good day, sir. I must be on my way now."

She brushed by him, her knees feeling wobbly. Her eyes widened but he couldn't see her face.

"Och well, I'll be happy to meet yer challenge, lass."

Helena spun around in spite of knowing that it wasn't the wisest thing to do. Allowing anyone to view her emotions would only lead to misfortune on her part. Even this man who fascinated her so. There could be no good end to it.

"I did not issue you a challenge. You really shouldn't believe that I have."

He was very close behind her and she gasped when she realized that they were only one step from each other. Her feet stepped back before she thought. But the cumbersome court dress was not made for such motions, and her heel landed on her hem. The weight of her body pulled on the skirts that were trapped beneath her long corset. She tipped backward, off balance, knowing that she was falling and helpless to do anything about it.

She gasped but the sound didn't have time to completely cross her lips before she was sucking in a very ungentle-sounding breath. The Scot caught her forearms, controlling her weight as if she were a child. She felt every finger in spite of her clothing.

"You shouldn't."

That dark eyebrow rose once more. "Shouldna keep ye from falling?"

He set her back on her feet, as though she were a figurine. Behind her stays, her heart was truly racing now and her breathing accelerated to keep pace. The increase in her respiration drew his scent into her senses. Her thoughts ceased for a time, her mind settling on that scent and how much she liked it. She wanted to hum with satisfaction. That idea startled her with just how intense it was. This was more than curiosity. At least more intense than she was comfortable with.

"You shouldn't touch me."

He released her forearms but trailed one hand down the length of her arm. A shiver shook her, racing down her back. Her gaze fell to his fingers. He gently clasped her wrist and lifted her hand toward his lips.

But he didn't kiss the back of her gloved hand. He pressed a soft kiss against the inside of her wrist. The delicate skin reacted to the touch of his lips like fire. It burned up her arm and into her body. Time remained still, suspending her between heartbeats. She noticed so many details in that moment. The way his lips curved, it was far more than a grin. He looked hungry and her belly twisted in response to that knowledge.

"Ah, but the look in yer eyes says otherwise, lass." His voice turned husky but he stepped back and reached for the corner of his bonnet. He tugged on it, the simple gesture conveying more respect than any reverence she had ever seen. The reason was simple: it was genuine.

"And I'll be happy to take up that challenge in spite of that brother of yers."

"You are an arrogant man, sir."

He flashed a grin at her. "Aye, well some call it confidence."

Frustration sent her teeth into her lower lip while she tried to force herself to think. "What do you mean by that?"

His eyes flashed with determination. "I believe that I mean to court ye. There is something between us that needs a wee bit of investigation."

Helena was suspended between the need to laugh and the urge to gasp. "My brother will never allow it."

The Scot shrugged. "Then I suppose 'tis a good thing I wasnae planning on courting him." His lips became a mocking curve that showed her even white teeth.

Helena pressed her lips together. The man was toying with her. But what vexed her so was the fact that she was jumping at his bait like a fish. So many years of polish and practice should not be undermined so easily. Court was filled with men who would cheerfully make prey of her if she could not hold up to their flirting. She was failing at all of the things that she was expected to be.

"Good day."

She turned and left, covering the distance to the queen's chambers with quick strides. Her fingers twisted in the fabric of her skirts as she drew closer to the guards at the doors because she was not entirely certain that she would be admitted. Edmund was correct—the queen had many musicians to choose from.

But she needed the pikes to remain uncrossed to allow her to enter. The man behind her was disturbing her with his ability to unsettle her usual calm so easily. She needed sanctuary and time to sort out her feelings. Tension drew the muscles across her shoulders taut when the guards looked at her. Holding her chin level, she stared at them, forcing herself to appear confident of her position with the queen. They considered her for a moment before lifting their pikes to clear the doorway. Two uniformed servants drew the doors open.

Her knees felt weak, but what alarmed her the most was the lament that crossed her heart when she heard the soft click of the doors closing behind her.

"Now you can tell me. We're friends, aren't we?"

Raelin fluttered her eyelashes in an attempt to cajole her into doing what she wanted. Helena shook her head.

"It was nothing."

The Scots girl narrowed her eyes. "Oh aye, so much a nothing that ye were blushing bright as a summer sunset." Raelin sighed. "I have never blushed like that. No' even once."

"That's not fair."

Raelin lifted her eyebrows. "What is no fair?"

A faint flicker of victory lit her friend's eyes, but it was too charming to really become annoyed with. Helena rolled her eyes.

"Pouting like that. I do consider you a friend." So much so that she would challenge Edmund over her. Many would condemn her for such. Blood was considered thicker than anything else.

Mischief glittered in Raelin's eyes. She leaned close, so that their words wouldn't carry.

"So tell me what sort of man put so bright a blush on yer cheeks. Don't make me beg. Canna ye see how jealous I am?"

"You have no need of envying me. Truthfully, I am jealous of you." Helena had never spoken such a truth. Her inability to control herself in relationship to the Scot was unnerving.

Raelin sighed and slumped as far as her corset would allow. "No man has ever made me blush. My brothers would be happy about that but you should have seen yer face when you arrived this morning." Her lips curved into a smile. "'Twas a sight. You looked all aflutter and all of the things I hear about but have nae felt. Just looking at ye made me feel like there is some grand part of life that I am missing because I have no looked into the right pair of eyes."

"Really?" Had it been so obvious? Helena looked down at the broach she was polishing. It was slightly frightening to know her friend had read her fascination right off her face.

"Now dinnae look like that." Raelin didn't even look at the

piece of jewelry she was polishing. Her hands moved on it
while she looked into Helena's eyes. There was a hint of
pleading in her eyes that had nothing to do with idle curiosity.
She actually sought something by asking, as though she were
trying to understand something important.

"I simply encountered a man that . . . um . . . held my attention."

"Why did he captivate you?"

Helena shifted, heat touching her cheeks just from talking
about him. It was somehow exposing to hear Raelin using a
word such as *captivate*. The girl didn't know how correct she
was.

"It wasn't that intense."

"Aye, it was. You didna see yer own face. I did." Raelin eyed
her suspiciously. "Why are you squirming if it wasn't that intense? We cannae be true friends if you want to be deceptive
in private."

Helena sighed. "You are very persistent."

Her friend smiled in triumph but there was a flicker of compassion in her eyes. "I'm not toying with you, truly. It is just
that there are so many who pretend friendship to sit here near
the queen. You seem different. I am hoping that ye are. Serving the queen can be very lonely."

"I understand what you mean. Ever since I have arrived at
court there have been many who wanted to be near me in
order to flirt with my brother. They covet his impending inheritance and seem to have no qualms about pretending
friendship to me to try their charms on him. It does indeed become very lonely."

Raelin nodded her head. "You do understand. I'm glad. So
very glad." Her voice trailed off as though she was afraid to
allow her emotions to be exposed. There was a camaraderie in

the moment, one that Helena was hungry for, too. Raelin filled an empty space in her soul and she was grateful.

Raelin reached out and slapped her arm lightly. "So tell me about him. Were ye unable to look away like the poets say?"

"I couldn't seem to stop looking at him. My eyes were drawn to him, like the only candle in a pitch-dark room. Honestly, it's as if I didn't have any control over what I was thinking. His face keeps pushing its way to the front of my thoughts. I can't seem to banish it."

"What drew ye to him?"

Raelin sat poised, waiting to hear the answer.

What indeed . . .

"Something in his eyes . . . I don't really understand it myself." She wished she did. It would make it far easier to block his face from her mind. Too many times today he'd appeared in her thoughts, stealing her attention away from whatever she was doing. Such a fascination was bound to lead her toward despair.

Raelin sighed.

"It's nothing to be envious of. My brother was quite angry."

"Your brother noticed?"

Helena looked down at the broach. Raelin covered it with her polishing cloth.

"You cannae stop now. Tell me the rest."

Lifting her face, she stared at her friend. "He tried to kiss my hand but Edmund sent me off to join you. My brother was quite rude."

"And what did the man do?"

What did he do, indeed? What sounded so innocent held her over a flame that licked her body. . . .

Helena felt the heat from her blush spread. It flowed down into her body, across the sensitive skin of her breasts and all the way to the tips of her nipples. Raelin slapped her hand, jerking her out of the moment.

"He followed me. Into the hallway. To place the kiss on my hand that Edmund refused him. My brother's position didn't appear to worry him at all. He claimed that I challenged him." Helena let out a slow breath. "Are all Scotsmen that persistent?"

"He was Scots?"

Helena nodded. "He wore a kilt and bonnet. No lace or high fashion at all. Only a doublet and a large sword strapped to his back."

"Och now, if he said ye challenged him, ye'd best prepare to deal with him again. My countrymen are never timid when it comes to a lass who has captured their interest."

"My brother will be quite angry with me over it if he notices me daydreaming. That is nothing to be envious of."

Her friend shrugged once again. "I quite disagree. Never once have I met a man that did that to me. I can ignore them all at my pleasure and they can do the same to me." Raelin spread her hands out wide. "Which leaves me lonely and begging to hear about yer good fortune. I am truly a pathetic creature."

Helena frowned. "You shouldn't say things like that. I should have better discipline." She shivered, the topic shooting a chill down her spine again. "I need to stop thinking about him. That is why I didn't want to tell you. I can't continue to dwell on him."

"But it's wonderful to find a man who does that to you. Maybe ye'll fall in love with him."

Helena recoiled from the look of bright hope in Raelin's eyes. "That will gain me naught but a broken heart."

"Or a spring wedding to a man ye're eager to share yer bed with."

Helena laughed. The sound was too loud, drawing looks from the queen's ladies. Raised eyebrows that critiqued them from where they sat at the other end of the chamber. Her fingers began moving over the broach once more.

"All it will get me is a broken heart. Affection is no reason to marry. I'll cry on my wedding night because of who my family weds me to. Edmund would never allow a match with him." She'd been taught to think that way, but today for the first time she questioned it. She had never believed that a look could make her blush. Never even considered that such a thing truly happened.

Or that one kiss, against so innocent a place, might be so moving. Yet it had happened. She could still feel the pulse of excitement lingering in her blood. It was far more potent than any wine. The delicate skin on her inner wrist tingled with renewed longing for another touch from those warm lips.

"That is a shame. Ye should be happy on your wedding night." Raelin replaced the earring she'd been cleaning and took up the matching one.

"You sound as though you have some say in who you wed." That was ridiculous, but there was something in Raelin's tone that implied it. "Is that allowed in Scotland? A lady having say in who she marries? Even if that choice is not a man with a title?"

"My brother would listen to me, if I told him someone had taken my fancy."

"Now I am jealous." And it sounded too good to be true. But they were in England. That harsh truth sliced through her excitement. Even if things were different in Scotland, she had been born English.

Raelin smiled. "Will you show him to me?"

"I don't even know the man's name. Much less where to begin looking for him."

"If he's here, he's waiting to see the king. We'll begin in the great hall."

Raelin took the broach from her hands and set it back inside the open chest of the queen's jewels. They were all clean anyway. But the ladies-in-waiting often dictated chores to the maids of honor and there was no arguing permitted.

Raelin grasped her hand and took a look across the chamber before pulling Helena off her bench. The queen was in her bedchamber and her ladies with her. She tired easily now and was retiring for the night. But the queen was also particular. She'd felt pressed upon and wanted only her ladies near. Chores had been handed out to the maids to take them away from the bedchamber. No one was left in the outer chamber except the pair of them.

"If I see his kilt, I can tell you what clan he's from. Maybe even if he holds a title. We have nobles in Scotland, too, ye know." Her friend offered her a bright smile. "No one will miss us. Not now that the queen has begun to retire."

"You are a conspirator." But she was tempted. She wanted to know his name.

Raelin hurried them past the royal guards outside the door before giggling.

"'Tis so, but it's fun." Excitement laced her voice. "Besides, we are together. A walk isn't so bad since there are two of us. I get out so little, I never get to meet men that might make me blush. Perhaps I'll want to steal his interest from ye."

Her friend's excitement was infectious. Helena smiled and clasped the hand Raelin closed around her own. They hurried down the wide hallways like curious children on a feast day. Now that the queen had retired for the night, many nobles had begun the process of returning to their town homes. Everyone attending court wanted to be noticed, so they did their best to be present any time the king might step into the great hall. Or send a summons for them. The chamberlain kept a list of those men waiting for an audience with His Majesty. Just getting your name on that list took a great deal of influence and often a bribe. If you failed to make a good enough bribe, your name might be very low on the list and the chamberlain might forget to mention to the king that you were waiting for a very long time.

But once the queen retired, the king often took to his private chambers with his friends. That ended the day, giving weary nobles the chance to retire until they rose at dawn to begin the entire process once again. Helena had been keeping such hours since arriving. It was becoming difficult to remain awake during services.

Tonight she didn't care. Excitement flowed through her. They circled the private garden used by the queen and crept out into the hallways that led toward the great hall. Long shadows darkened the hallway. Lamps were lit but their light became lost in the vaulted ceilings.

"Maybe the poets are reading."

"You mean 'wenching,' " Raelin declared boldly.

Helena smothered a laugh. "You say the most outlandish things."

" 'Tis the only way I survive serving the queen. Her ladies are quite prudish and I refuse to forget that I am young enough to think about men."

"Raelin . . ."

Her friend shrugged. "I only said think about men. What's wrong with listening to a little posy? We'll both marry soon enough and find ourselves shipped off to country estates to produce heirs. I, for one, would like to take a few memories along."

"I agree."

The young men of the court liked to practice their poems on the maids after the hall was emptied for the night. Edmund had warned her to keep well away of such gatherings. Ladies that were seen by the flicker of the candles were considered light-skirts. That didn't stop some of the bolder noble daughters from going. One or two had snared herself a titled husband by ignoring the possible gossip and invading the male-dominated activity. But doing so was a very risky gamble. Many had not fared so well.

"We'll stay in the eves. Ladies do it all the time. No one shall see us."

"That's wickedly naughty." And she had never thought about it. The great hall was surrounded by hallways that had arched openings. At night, a dozen people might be standing there. If you were near the candles, the darkness beyond would be impossible to see into. It was so clever and so tempting.

Raelin laughed. "I know. My brother would have a fit if he knew. But I often wonder if that's because I might see him attending. And enjoying himself."

Helena laughed; she couldn't help it. Edmund would be enraged if she caught him doing anything that he'd rather she didn't know about. Which only made her laugh harder. Her belly ached with it. She stopped to catch her breath and Raelin swirled around in a circle, her golden skirts flaring up. She laughed softly, her head pointing at the ceiling like a little girl on a spring morning.

"Perfect."

Raelin screamed, the sound erupting from her as Edmund emerged from the darkness like a serpent striking at prey. He grabbed at Raelin, ripping her bodice with one harsh motion of his hand. She snarled and tried to fend off the hands pulling and clawing at her clothing. Lace tore and her strand of pearls broke. But she did not make it simple for him. The Scots girl fought Edmund, hitting him and yanking on his fine velvet doublet, raking her nails down one side of his face. Edmund raised his hand and struck her in retaliation.

"Stop it, Edmund! Let her go!"

Her brother cursed at her and sent her tumbling with another blow from his hand. Raelin stopped trying to free herself and launched a fresh attack on him when he tried to follow up with a kick. Edmund took full advantage of her change in direction, hooking his hands into her bodice and tearing the golden silk so that her corset showed.

"Hold there!"

Guards charged down the hallway, their boots echoing. Light suddenly surrounded them all, illuminating a tousled-looking Raelin with Edmund standing nearby.

"What goes on here?"

Her brother arrogantly raised one eyebrow. More footsteps announced the arrival of witnesses. Raelin stood in shock, her hands trying to cover up one breast that was too exposed. Helena struggled to her feet, fighting with her dress while she struggled to get her feet on the floor and not on the damask that made up her skirts. Faces emerged from the shadows to stare at them. Edmund smirked in victory.

Whispers erupted among the spectators. Each hushed voice sliced as deeply as sharpened steel. Panic appeared on Raelin's face. The change from Raelin's normally smiling face was so sharp it horrified Helena, choking her with the ugliness of the condemning people around her.

"I'll tell ye what goes on—that bastard needs some manners beaten into him."

The man emerged from the darkness.

Helena stared at the face that had occupied her mind since

seeing him that morning. There was nothing kind in his expression now. Rage flickered in his eyes and it drew his features tight. His breathing was rapid, betraying the fact that he had been running.

"If I hadna been all the way across the hall, I'd have snapped the whelp's neck by now. He put rough hands on her." He pointed a thick finger at Edmund.

Raelin's eyes rounded when she saw him. But the Scot didn't look at her. His attention was focused on Edmund, whose face didn't betray even a hint of remorse. Instead he looked at the guards with a small smirk on his lips. They broke under the weight of his stare, one clearing his throat.

"He is the heir to the Earl of Kenton, a peer of this realm." One Royal Guard member spoke quietly, his tone thick with warning. The Scot didn't even blink. His face remained in its disapproving expression. Edmund's blood didn't buy him any tolerance from this man.

"What he is, is an undisciplined whelp who doesna know how to treat a woman with respect. Look at her, man! He ripped her dress down her body, and you English dare to call us Scots barbarians? I'd lay one of me own clansmen low for doing the same."

The whispers began again. They rose in volume until it felt like they were pounding against the inside of her head. The horror was too much to bear. Helena reached for her friend and felt the Scots girl clasp her hands in a crushing grip. Raelin held her chin steady but it must have cost her greatly.

"Make way for the king!"

The crowd gawking around them split apart, backing up to the walls. James Stuart didn't look amused. Everyone lowered themselves before him. But he only had eyes for Raelin. She tried to lower herself but wobbled on unsteady feet. Silent tears fell down her cheeks as she hugged her ruined bodice over her exposed breast. The king's face flushed, rage flickering in his eyes.

"Get up. All of you! What is this nonsense?"

The king's gaze settled on Raelin. A frown marred his forehead. His expression quickly changed to one of anger when he turned to look at Helena and the Scot.

"My chambers! Bring them all."

Raelin's hand shook. She was holding Helena's hand so tightly, the tips of her fingers were beginning to lose feeling. But you wouldn't have known such from the way her friend held her face—smooth and composed. All traces of panic evaporated as though she was sitting down polishing jewelry in the queen's chambers. No more tears fell from her eyes; she stood sure and steady with her eyes on the king.

The king sat in an ornately carved X-chair that was placed on a raised section at the back of the room. A costly Persian carpet ran beneath it and velvet curtains covered the wall behind him. It was a lavish display with only one purpose—to ensure that everyone entering understood that they were in the presence of the king.

More X-chairs were neatly lined up against the far wall facing the king's, but no one sat in them without permission. Such was an honor, and James was in no mood to grant that tonight. Everyone lowered themselves and remained with bent knees while their monarch surveyed them. James Stuart took his time, his displeasure clear.

"Enough. Rise."

The room was so silent, Helena heard the servants moving behind them to light the candles. Large iron candelabra stood in all four corners of the room. They each held five candles in an X formation. The room brightened as the servants touched the wicks with flame.

"What's yer reason for leaving one of my queen's maids of honor looking like that, Edmund Knyvett?"

Her brother shrugged. His lips curved into a satisfied smile that shocked her in spite of how many times she had seen him behave selfishly. No hint of remorse or pity entered his eyes. Quite the opposite, her brother looked very pleased.

"Passion isn't very often soft. Some like it rougher than others." He cast a look down the length of his nose at Raelin.

Raelin tightened her grip but made no other sign of her distress. Helena felt her own stomach twisting with nausea. Her brother had all but called Raelin a whore. James wasn't amused. His hand curled around one of the ornately carved arms of the chair.

"I heard a scream that didna sound like passion."

Edmund flicked his fingers toward her. "My sister is easily shocked. My parents sheltered her to preserve her virtue. Helena doesn't understand the games that the other ladies at court like to play."

"Ye're a liar." The Scot was furious but his voice was so controlled it made him seem deadly. The king held up his hand, but the man didn't instantly back down. He sent another look at Edmund that clearly said he wasn't afraid of his position. Helena bit her lip to keep from gasping. Never once had she witnessed anyone, save her father, standing up to Edmund. This man only controlled himself for the king, but he shook with anger, clenching his hands into fists.

"Lady Helena."

"Yes, Your Majesty?" She snapped her gaze back to the king, heat brushing her cheeks. She had to break this habit of staring at the Scot. Immediately.

"Was it passion and your naiveté, or something else?"

Tension gripped her so tightly, time froze. She became

aware of each heartbeat and the time between them. Edmund looked down his nose at her, so supremely confident of her obedience to his will. She hated him for that. For the first time in her life she became aware of what it felt like to actually hate. She hated the callousness she saw on his face. It was ugly and horrible in a way that threatened to make her sick. The Scot watched her, his eyes burning once more, but this time he seemed to be hoping that she would not disappoint him by lying. She actually felt the weight of his opinion and she discovered that it mattered to her what he thought of her.

"It was not passion and I was shocked by my brother's behavior. It was none of Raelin's doing."

The king leaned forward. "Ye were together?"

"Yes, Your Majesty."

Edmund's eyes bulged. Promise of retribution burned in them, but Helena did not lower her head. She stared at him, proud of herself. She had spoken the truth. The shame was her brother's to bear.

The king sat back, his expression pensive.

"It was much more than that, Yer Majesty! He struck her." The Scot was still enraged. The tone of his voice sent a shiver down Helena's back. She was suddenly very grateful that she had spoken truthfully. This was not a man to cross.

"Ridiculous. I am a gentleman. A descendant of one of the oldest noble houses." Edmund sneered at the Scot.

"Is that a fact? I noticed ye didna simply say ye didna strike her. If ye're innocent, speak it plainly."

"Enough!" James Stuart's voice cracked like a whip. He pointed at the Scot. "I'll question you when I'm ready. Hold yer silence." He pointed at the captain of his guard.

"Captain, ye will escort my queen's maid of honor back to the queen's chamber. And I mean every step of the way."

There was a click of polished boot heels against each other, and a moment later Raelin was being ushered toward the doors. She didn't release Helena's hand but tried to pull her along.

"Lady Knyvett will remain."

The king's guard didn't allow them any time to question the will of the king. Raelin was taken away without another word. The king glared at her brother.

"Edmund Knyvett, ye may be the only son of the Earl of Kenton but I'll no have ye placing rough hands on maidens." The king never raised his voice but there was no mistaking the authority in his tone. "Ye shall be in the great hall when I summon ye and yer sister will be in my queen's chambers on the morrow. Dinnae make my chamberlain call yer name twice."

"Your Majesty . . ."

"Begone." James Stuart's voice cracked like a whip. The guards standing next to him were lowering their pikes. Helena curtsied and backed toward the door. Her brother hesitated, earning him a scowl from the king.

"Do not test me, sir. Your name protects you thus far but ye dinnae have any more grace to impose upon. Best ye get out of me sight afore I recall some frozen country that needs an ambassador."

Edmund offered the briefest of reverences before quitting the room. Helena followed him. His strides were long and fueled by a hot temper. There was no missing the fuming glance he raked her with when he passed her.

Oddly enough, she wasn't frightened. A strange manner of contentment settled over her. She'd spoken truly even though so many around her used deception to maintain their family position. Deep in her heart, she realized that true friendship was a gift Raelin would not be granting to anyone who didn't treat her with respect in return.

Her cheeks heated, and it had nothing to do with the pace she was forced to keep. Her conscience pricked her because defending her friend had not been her only motivation. Simply put, she hadn't been willing to disappoint the Scot. He was a man of honor. He didn't care for her brother's impending inheritance or the political advantage that might have been his had he looked the other way. He was the first man that she had met at court who held his honor above his hunger for power and position.

James Stuart fingered his chin. Keir didn't move. He'd expected his meeting with the king to be a tense one. But he was distracted by the knowledge of who his mystery lady was. He'd spent too many hours attempting to discover her identity. Not being able to reach her in time to beat her brother off her and Raelin McKorey had his temper white-hot. But his interest was even hotter, because she had stood up to her brother and spoken the truth. Now that was a woman he wanted to get to know better. The kind he might bring home to Red Stone and truthfully hear her called mistress by his clansmen. She was worthy of it.

But he would have to do what he came to London to do first: swear his fealty and restore his clan to good standing. He could nay offer for her before his name was worthy of her. Keir aimed his attention at the king. James Stuart studied him long and hard.

"Ye're McQuade's youngest son?"

"Aye, Yer Majesty, I am."

The guards standing on either side of the king moved slightly closer, their fingers tightening on their short pikes. His father had been run through with one of the weapons when he tried to drive a dagger through Raelin McKorey during a fight with Brodick McJames. His two older brothers had launched an attack on the royal guard in defense of their father and ended up dead along with his sire. All of it had been done within inches of the king and queen. The name Mc-Quade had been tarnished ever since. He kept very still, with his hands at his sides. It wouldn't take much to see the guards using their deadly pikes on him. He could see the distrust in their eyes.

"How long have ye been at court?"

"A few days."

The king lowered his hand and gripped the arm of his chair. "Why have ye come, McQuade? I didna send for ye."

Keir felt his jaw tighten. He did not care for the tone of the king's voice, but he'd expected nothing less. Still, the disdain was hard to listen to.

"To swear my fealty to you. As tradition dictates."

The king sat up straighter, his face drawing into an expression of consideration.

"Is that a fact?"

"It is, sire, and my duty."

The king nodded. "Aye, so it is, but I'm a bit surprised to see ye attending to the matter so promptly."

Keir shot the king's hard gaze right back at him. "Honor is no' something ye put off to another time. It's time the Mc-Quades had a laird who set a correct example. That is why I'm in London."

"Well now, I'll not be arguing with that." The king waved his hand. "And what of this business with Raelin McKorey?"

Keir felt tension tighten across his body. "That whelp needs a good lesson. He tore her gown like a rabid animal. Ye saw the trails of her nails on his cheek. 'Twas the result of a desperate attempt to free herself. I couldna get across the hall fast enough."

"My guards are very diligent." James stroked his chin again. "Edmund Knyvett is a powerful man and will soon become even more so. I dinnae think many men would have interfered."

"Ye have my sympathies on the condition of yer court."

The king chuckled. He covered it quickly, looking surprised by his own response. "Ye're no' very much like yer father, or ye're doing a grand job of disguising yer nature."

"My father liked to tell me how much like my mother I was. He had no tender feelings toward me beyond the fact that I was born a son instead of a daughter."

The king nodded absently. "Aye, yer father held no affection toward yer sister Bronwyn."

"I do."

"And what of Raelin McKorey? Yer father put that scar on her face."

Keir did not answer. He stared at the king, allowing his actions to speak for him. He'd never been a man of prattling conversations and he was not going to begin now.

The king grunted. "I suppose that was nae a necessary question, considering ye just threatened one of my English nobles on her account."

"He grabbed her like a drunken sailor on the waterfront." Keir spoke through clenched teeth. "Ye should have let me give him a few lessons in manners."

Telling the king what to do might not have been the wisest thing, but his temper was still hot. It was taking a great deal of effort to remain in place while the English whelp left with his sister in tow. It was a sure thing that she would not be having an easy time of it now that she'd refused to lie for her kin. It was something he understood, and that was for certain. His father had always detested him for his resolve to retain his honor. "What of his sister? She's a good lass."

James stiffened. "Ye're a keen one, all right. Things will nae go well for her tonight. 'Tis a curse, but I must handle these English nobles carefully. The lass impressed me with her courage."

"Aye. She's nae a coward."

The king lifted one eyebrow. "I dinnae think her brother will be taking very kindly to yer tone, considering ye just threatened to beat him."

Keir smiled. He couldn't help it. "I'm here to swear my oath to ye, nae dabble in schemes that involve ripping the dresses off maidens." Disgust edged his words, but he didn't care.

"Most men wouldna let me hear that tone. They would not dare use such in the presence of their king."

"I've just traveled to London to kneel before ye when I know a few of my neighbors havena made the effort and wear their lairdship proudly. I am nae a dishonest man. My father often berated me for it. But if what ye prefer is men that coddle yer ego, best we get on with my duty so that I can ride out of yer sight."

The king chuckled. It was an honest sound that drew surprised glances from his normally frozen guards. The men recovered quickly but their eyes strayed to him, surveying him. James laughed harder until the room was full of the sound.

"Coddle my ego?" He slapped the arm of his throne. "I believe I may like ye, Keir McQuade. A rather pleasant surprise. Join my court for a few weeks. I've a mind to get to know ye a bit better afore I hear yer oath."

Keir lowered himself. James raised an eyebrow.

"What? Nae objection to remaining among the English?"

Keir straightened. "There're one or two things that draw my interest here. The idea of making sure the name McQuade is restored to a standing of honor is a good enough reason to remain. Ye may have more objections from your English lords to me than I have to them."

James sobered. "Being king does have advantages. Ye're here at my invitation. They will keep their grumbles low. Stay." Something crossed James Stuart's face. "Stay and court the girl. I believe it will be interesting to see what her brother makes of that."

He should have been satisfied, but he was not. Keir ground his teeth all the way back to his hovel of a residence. He'd done what he set out to do, or at least he'd made a good beginning of it.

But he was itching to find her.

Helena.

He had a name to go with her face, but he was more frustrated than before. He sighed. Laying his kilt aside, he propped his sword next to his bed. The thing was too short and narrow for his frame. At least thinking about Helena gave his mind something to dwell on besides how much he longed for Red Stone and his own bed.

Court the girl . . .

Well now, it appeared that he had something to accomplish before he rode back to Scotland. Helena's face came to mind. She had courage, all right—maybe too much—because it was soliciting a response from him that was rather out of line, considering she was a maiden. He grinned and pinched out the candle beside his bed. His cock was hard and he could hear the carousing from the inn on the corner: music and women laughing while they sold their favors.

It did not interest him.

Instead, frustration kept him awake for several hours. He could not help her and that twisted his gut.

But tomorrow would be different. He had the king's permission to court her.

He would be happy to obey.

Chapter Three

"**B**itch!"

Edmund hit her across the face. Her body spun around with the force he used. She tasted blood, but only stumbled, managing to keep her balance. She turned to see her brother's face contorted with rage.

"Traitor. Stupid bitch." He aimed another blow at her face, this one popping loudly. Pain spiked through her head, turning her vision blurry for a moment. She sucked in a deep breath to steady herself. The maids standing near the door flinched but they dared not abandon their post. They remained stiffly at attention while the master of the house raged.

"You've ruined me!" He stomped across the floor to a large X-chair and flung himself into it. He pounded the wide arm of it with a fist.

"Ruined! Do you hear me, you idiotic bitch? Why didn't you keep your mouth shut? It was a perfect plan. . . ."

He hit the chair's arm again and looked around for the staff. "Wine!" he bellowed at the maids. They tripped over their own feet trying to serve him. But both made sure to duck their chins and keep as far as possible from his hands.

Helena couldn't blame them. She stood where she was, rather grateful that Edmund had retired to his chair. It was his favorite spot to rail at her from. There was a familiarity about it that gave her strength. Edmund gulped at his tankard, his eyes peering over the rim at her.

"I'm going to find you a husband." He hit the arm of the chair with the base of the goblet. Dark red wine sloshed over the rim, staining the white cuff of his fine shirt, but he didn't even look down to investigate the damage his negligence had done.

"Someone willing to take half your dowry, because I intend to keep the rest of it. Maybe more." He snarled at her and drank some more.

"Get out of my sight! More wine! And get someone comely to serve me."

The older maid sent the younger one through the doorway with a quick flick of her fingers while Edmund was still glaring at her. The younger girl fled without a sound on the wooden floor, a grim testament to how many times they had heard their master order that very thing from them.

Helena began to lower herself, simply out of habit, but stopped, the throbbing in her cheek freezing her before she finished lowering her head. She heard her brother growl but turned her back on him. There was no point in staying.

Nor was there any point in worrying about his threats.

She drew a deep breath once her door was closed. It really was only an illusion of security, but for the moment she would indulge herself in enjoying it. Edmund was master of the house. He would invade her privacy any time he chose, but she slid the small bolt across the metal brackets anyway.

She sighed, the tension leaving her shoulders. Or at least a portion of it. Things were not as settled as she might wish for. Edmund never forgave and he never forgot. But she knew that. Had understood it very well. She straightened her back and began disrobing.

A soft knock on the door sent her teeth into her lower lip. She scolded herself for jumping. Edmund wouldn't be knocking softly. Not in his current rage. She slid the bolt to allow the door to open.

"Ma'am." The younger maid curtsied before coming into the room far enough that the door might close. She held a basin of fresh water in her hands, and a length of clean toweling was draped over her arm.

There was no conversation. The pair of them were together in their need to escape the notice of the master of the house. Neither might help the other; the only thing they could do was take comfort in each other's company. In spite of blood and station they were both women, struggling in a world controlled by men, leaving them with the task of outthinking the man who believed himself master of the house.

But the water was welcome. Helena drew the toweling over her face, enjoying the feeling of her skin being clean. The endless requirements of court pressed in on her. Just like the tiny room, she felt as though there was so little of herself in anything she did. It was a helpless sensation, one that threatened to sink her into a lake of despair.

She stiffened her resolve. Pity was a poor thing on which to spend her energy. Tomorrow she would think of something to do that would lift her spirits.

Without warning, Keir McQuade's face invaded her thoughts. Her cheeks heated up and the sensation traveled down her body. It seemed to ripple all across her skin, awaking it in a manner that she had never experienced. She was suddenly aware of the way her breasts felt without her long stays pressing them up into position. Lying in her narrow bunk, she could feel her nipples drawing into points. The darkness seemed to grant her permission to focus on the reaction of her body. She was fascinated by the idea that just the thought of him might draw such a response from her hours later.

What would his kiss do to her? A true kiss, that is. One placed right on her mouth. . . .

Helena shivered and drew the bedding up to her chin. She was toying with dangerous ideas. Ones that might see her heartsick. Keir McQuade would never have permission to court her, much less wed her. Not after tonight. Lingering in the sensations that he caused would only make her unhappy when she faced the man Edmund gave her to.

She would never know his touch unless she wanted to join the other noblewomen who sought satisfaction outside their wedding vows. She didn't want to think of him that way. A bitter taste filled her mouth because she wanted to think of him as noble and above breaking commandments.

Like a knight of the round table. Faithful to his honor above all earthly temptations. . . .

She sighed and closed her eyes. Childhood was behind her. Her blushes were not the innocent sort that young girls had. No, the way her nipples drew into hard buttons was proof of that. It was time to be practical and banish Keir McQuade from her mind. Along with dreams of men with honor and noble character. They only lived on the pages of books.

However logical her thoughts might be, they left her cold and unhappy. Compared to the warmth Keir McQuade kindled inside her, it was a bleak night that promised to become frigid.

"Put it down."

Edmund's voice startled her. Helena turned from where she

sat in front of a mirror, preparing for the day ahead. The young maid backed up until her shoulders were flat against the wall. The older maid placed a wooden trencher on the side table. It was covered with a cloth.

Edmund looked at the younger girl. "Begone."

She dropped him a clumsy curtsy and fled.

"You will not be going to court today."

Dread gripped her with icy fingers. She recognized the tone of Edmund's voice. Her brother was feeling cruel.

"The king ordered me to."

Edmund snickered at her. "The king isn't ruled by the whims of women, not even a royal one. The queen is meant to be bred. Since her belly is full, the king will have little interest in her."

"I didn't tell you the queen was with child. . . ." Her words trailed off, horror clogging her throat. Edmund glared at her.

"No you didn't, dear Sister. But rest assured that you are not my only means of gathering information." His lips thinned. "However, since you have proven your unwillingness to perform as you are directed, I have no further need of you. Nor do I intend to allow you any freedom to further disgrace me."

"You dishonored yourself." Perhaps it was unwise to voice her thoughts, but they refused to remain inside her.

"Honor is for girls and soldiers serving in the infantry. It is a pretty tale that keeps them doing what they're told even when the ground is soaked with blood."

Helena stared at her brother. "I do not even know who you are."

His eyebrows rose. "How very interesting, Helena. I feel the same way about you. Are our parents really so soft with age that they allowed you to remain a whimsical child?"

Her temper rose. "They taught me not to lie, Edmund. That is not soft. It is in the Scriptures."

He scoffed at her. "No one at court is honest. Do you think that Scot is anything but another man looking to further his interests? Don't be such a fool." Her brother raked her with a chilling stare. "His interest in you is pathetically transparent. He wants to fuck you."

"Edmund!"

His words were so blunt. Never had she heard that word spoken.

"Stop it, Helena. I saw you blushing and simpering at him. Where do you think all that leads?" Her brother leaned toward her. "It concludes with your thighs wrapped around his hips."

"You needn't be so coarse."

"And you shouldn't be such a lackwit. Your virginity is valuable. That blue blood filling your veins is the item to be bargained. Knyvett is among the oldest names in England. I have no intention of allowing you to squander it on some Scot because you haven't the intelligence to see beyond your lust."

He shut the door abruptly. There was the scrape of metal and the grind of the chain. Helena flew across the cramped space, only to hear a key turning. The sound was so cold she felt sure it pierced her heart.

"Edmund?"

All she heard was her brother's amusement drifting through the door. The sound began fading and she heard his footfalls becoming fainter and fainter. Pushing on the door, all she heard was the sound of the chain rattling. Hurrying to the window she opened a shutter and peered down. A groom stood with her brother's horse. He inclined his head and her brother came into view. Edmund never looked up. He mounted his horse and took the reins from the groom. With a kick of his heels, his horse joined the busy flow of traffic on the street. With the sun rising, wagons and pushcarts were beginning to make their way along the road.

She was locked in.

Helena sat back on the bed, trying to decide what she thought of it. Fear crept around her composure. There was no way to ignore the icy dread filling her.

Her father was ill. She had shied away from dwelling upon it, thinking instead of what possibilities court might present her with, but the truth was as hard as the chain on her door.

Edmund was not delusional. He ran the family now. The only task left unfinished was the passing of the signet ring that her father still wore. She was truly at his mercy and her brother knew it. His ambition would see no boundaries set by her father.

She reached for the wooden tray and uncovered it. The offering was meager: a round of bread, some slices of carrot, an apple, and a slice of cold lamb from the day before. The cook had clearly rummaged among her leftovers for what the trencher held.

Who knew how long it would have to last her. Edmund held the key, she had no doubt. Reaching for the carrot slices, she chewed on one slowly. The day suddenly stretched out before her endlessly, the possibilities for disaster too numerous to endure considering.

But she had little else to distract her from it. Naught save Keir McQuade, that was. Helena willingly let her mind shift to the Scot. She had never found a man she considered handsome before. His body amazed her. Of course, that was to be expected. He was a large man, far greater in height than most of the men he walked among. His shoulders were wide and he had a habit of crossing his arms across his chest that made him look even broader. Certainly it was all those differences that drew her attention.

It is not, and you know it. . . .

That tingle returned to her nape. Reaching up, she stroked the skin and shivered. Her skin was alive and pulsing with a level of sensation she had never experienced. Was that lust? To avoid being coarse, she might call it attraction, but there were so many who would declare it sinful nonetheless.

Whatever it was, her blood seemed to carry it through her body like fine wine. She felt her heartbeat everywhere, from her toes on up to her belly. The rhyming couplets so often recited at court suddenly made more sense. She could understand their passionate words now because this level of sensation was insanity: haunting, intoxicating, and luring her away from pure thoughts. She was not interested in sinking to her knees in order to use prayer to banish the growing feelings. She wanted to savor them, all the while hoping they increased in intensity.

Well, it was not all that bad. She suddenly smiled. There was no lasting harm in her daydreams because Keir McQuade would never know of them. That was the saving grace. She looked at the locked door and sighed. Cold dread resumed its hold on her. Fate was not going to be kind to her. It was best to embrace it now; that way, it would hurt less when Edmund turned the key and pronounced his sentence on her. Just as any convict, she would pay the price for having transgressed against his rule.

She would never set eyes upon Keir McQuade, save in her dreams. She felt that in her heart and it hurt.

Many would call her mad.

Raelin McKorey watched Keir McQuade from beneath her eyelashes. It was a skill she'd perfected after five years at court.

His father had tried to murder her. The scar on her cheek itched. She fought the urge to scratch it. The itch was only in her mind—after all, the cut had fully healed now, but anytime she thought about that moment when the old Laird McQuade had sent his dagger plunging toward her, the scar itched. His elder sons had called her a witch. It was a rumor that clung to her. No man had offered for her hand since. She rarely had dance partners who were unmarried and she knew the reason why.

Her temper heated up. Oh aye, she knew. Young men came to court and flirted with her and then they rejoined their relations and never again approached her.

Witch . . .

That was the legacy Keir McQuade hailed from.

But he did not look the same. She understood Helena's fascination with the man. He was the image of strength, no doubt about it. Uncertainty held her in its grip but she had no other option. Fortune favored the bold, after all.

Besides, she could not shake the memory of him rushing to her aid. He had not known it was her but he had been enraged even after seeing her face. For a moment her heart had frozen when she'd spied the colors of his kilt. She had seen that heather, tan and green wool in her nightmares—dark visions full of terror and the scent of blood.

Yet today she was seeking out a McQuade. Fate was as intricate as bobbin lace. It was impossible to follow the thread through the pattern no matter how hard you tried. In order to weave it, you had to cast the bobbins over one another until every bobbin had interacted with all in use.

So today she would ask a McQuade to help her friend.

With a whispered prayer she moved forward and felt the man's eyes on her. Raising her chin, she looked straight at him, issuing her invitation with a quick motion of her gaze cutting toward the doorway. Men understood such things and women learned them when they came to court. She walked on by, looking for all the world as if she had never intended to stop.

The hallways that led away from the great hall were full of turns and arches that offered privacy. She paused in one, fingering the fabric of her skirts.

"I'd have thought the queen would keep ye a little closer today, Mistress McKorey."

His tone implied that he agreed with that notion.

"Be assured that she has ordered it so. I left without permission."

Raelin turned, rather grateful to see that the man was still several paces from her and holding still. But a shiver still crossed her neck because Keir McQuade was plenty large enough to close the distance quickly if he were of a mind to do so. His father had lunged quick enough to slice her cheek open before she moved.

She shook her head and forced her mind onto the world of the living. Dwelling in the past would not aid her friend.

"I owe ye a debt of gratitude for defending my honor in front of the king."

Keir scoffed, his expression turning dark. "No ye don't. No woman should suffer such treatment. Be she lady or common born. 'Tis small enough payment for the wrong my father did ye and the name of my clan. It is I who need to assure ye that the raiding my father inflicted on his neighbors will nae be tolerated on McQuade land while I am laird. I only wish I could undo the rumors my kin attached to yer name."

The scar itched and she reached up before her thoughts forbid her to. Keir's eyes focused on her fingers. She jerked her hand away, humiliated by her own impulses.

"I am stronger than gossip."

He grinned. "Of course. Ye are a Scotswoman, after all. I expect as much."

There was a flicker of admiration in his eyes that touched her. But she felt the bite of guilt for forgetting why she'd sought him out.

"Helena has nae come to court again."

Keir frowned. His lips pressed into a hard line and his eyes narrowed. The expression was dark and foreboding. Raelin watched his eyes, trying to see what manner of man he was.

"Her brother has disobeyed the king. Why didna ye take yer complaint to the queen instead of me?" There was temper edging his words, like he was forcing himself to direct her to someone other than himself. It was a trait that she recognized from her brothers. They were men of action, not prattling discussions. The structure of court, with its necessary steps to doing everything from supping to greeting the king, frustrated them near to death. Hope flared inside her, hope that she may indeed have made a wise choice in seeking out Keir McQuade. But she would have to dispense with polite terms.

"She is the man's sister. He has the right to direct her, and she is no' a maid of honor. I did hope that might change soon, but complaining to the queen will gain Helena nothing. She cannae interfere between a brother and sister without causing a scandal. The king fears his nobles and he would think long before allowing even Edmund Knyvett to be blackened. It is a delicate balance that often claims the sacrifice of a few innocents. Everyone shall be so sorry for her ill fate but that willnae change anything. Her brother can do anything he wants with her."

Keir McQuade stiffened. His hands tightened around his biceps. Raelin watched the rage dance in his eyes for a moment.

"Why do ye tell me?"

"Ye made her blush." His expression changed, and this time she stared at his face and felt envy rise. True jealousy blossomed within her. But it was not a bad thing. She clutched at it, absorbing the sight. It gave her hope that love might someday touch her.

Keir shook his head. "Why do you come to me?"

"Because I think ye are nae like yer father and so ye may understand how different Helena is from her brother."

Keir's face darkened. Raelin stared straight at him. "I dinnae know if ye can help her, but I believe ye are the only man who has enough honor to think on it. Besides, ye are Scots and I have faith in the fact that ye are more a man of action than conversations."

And she was helpless. It hurt, causing an ache in her heart that nearly sent tears down her cheeks.

"I thank ye for telling me. Forgive me, but I've something pressing to attend to."

She offered him a slight lowering of her head, but Keir Mc-Quade was already turning around before she rose. His kilt swung from side to side, betraying how quickly he was moving. A smile brightened her face while she strode back toward the queen's chambers. She did not care if she was discovered. Helena was her friend. A lecture from one of the ladies-in-waiting would be little compared to what her friend must be suffering after she refused to lie for her brother.

He was a snake.

She grumbled through set teeth. There were dangerous men at court, some more trouble than others. Edmund Knyvett was the worst. He used his fine blood to mask a rotten core, his appetite for power having eaten away every bit of decency.

But he was Helena's brother and her guardian. Even the king could not interfere easily. Another noble might. Keir Mc-

Quade was a laird. Many of the English did not respect the title, but James Stuart was a Scot.

It was hope. In whatever small fashion, it was the only thing she could think of, and she muttered a silent prayer before slipping back into her place.

Chapter Four

"What are ye talking about?" Farrell scratched his head. "We do nae even know the lass is in trouble. We're nae her family. Hell, ye have done no more than flirt with her. Or so I thought."

Keir shot his man a deadly look. "Ye're a suspicious man. I like to enjoy my tumbles a wee bit more than that. She's in trouble, that much I'd bet me horse on."

Farrell looked stunned, and with good reason. His horse was a fine animal. One Keir was nae in the mood to lose.

"I think ye're daft. Her brother will likely order us run through."

But his clansman still reached for his bonnet and tugged it down over his forehead. They would follow their laird but he wanted more than his father had from them.

Keir eyed them. "She's in trouble that stems from her speaking up on my behalf. I've a need to be looking into that. The lass went against her own blood for me."

Understanding dawned in Farrell's eyes.

"I suppose we cannae stand idle when the lass was telling the truth. Seems like that brother of hers needs a good thrashing even more than we figured. So what is yer plan? We dinnae even know where the lass is."

"That should be the simple part. Her brother is a powerful

man who likes to make sure people treat him accordingly. Sniffing out his trail shouldn't take very long." What it would require was coin, but he had been managing Red Stone for years. It was the only thing his father had ever praised him for. The estate was profitable, unlike many that failed to change with the times. He'd done it for the clan, for the better life it brought to McQuade families. Today was the first time he was going to enjoy the silver in his purse for purely personal reasons.

He was going to bribe every servant he found until he discovered just what Edmund Knyvett had done with his sister. Maybe he did not have the right to go poking around in the man's affairs, but he did not care.

It was something that was etched into his memory.

"And then what are we going to do? Teach the little lordling a greater respect for womenfolk?"

Keir cut a glare toward Farrell but the man only smiled in return. He deserved the teasing, normally would have welcomed it. Something about Helena Knyvett soured his disposition.

He hadn't needed Raelin to tell him that Helena had blushed for him. He'd known it, seen it with his own eyes and spent too many hours dwelling on it for his own good. Or hers, for that matter. He was a man of action and his mind was spending too much time considering just how much he'd enjoy a little less thinking and more doing in relation to her.

"It's nae completely absurd." Keir looked at his man. "But that wouldnae be the wisest thing I might do."

"And how do you figure that?" Farrell asked.

Keir tilted his head to one side. "She's a fine candidate to take to wife. A bit of negotiating might be in our best interests."

Farrell laughed. "Och now, lad. And here I thought ye were

looking for a wife that came with connections. If ye wanted one that was from a family that detested the very thought of ye, we could have stayed home."

Keir winced. It was a hard truth that his father had made enemies of most of his neighbors. For all that Raelin McKorey had come to him, her family would be furious if he paid her court. His father had raided her family's land for a good decade.

But it was not her that blushed for him. Maybe he wasn't any good at choosing a wife for her worth alone. Gwen's words lingered in his mind, and the way she'd always looked at him, haunting him with something that he'd not ever felt. Gwen loved him but he'd never felt the same emotion for her. It was a fact that he was jealous of that. It was as if she felt deeper and more intensely than he had. He'd have married Gwen but he was relieved when she rejected him. It gave him another chance to find a woman who warmed more than his cock.

"We sound like a pair of old men, flapping our lips when there's work to get done."

Gaining the saddle, Keir wrapped the reins around his fist. His men followed him and they rode into the street without another word. The roads were almost deserted now that the sun was setting. Their horses' hooves echoed off the closed shutters of the shops and homes lining the roads.

For a man with silver in his pocket, no one was hard to find in London. Especially not Edmund Knyvett, heir to the earldom of Kenton.

What sickened Keir was the glee some of the informants took in delivering their information. Edmund seemed to have no fear of those he walked over.

That made him a stupid man, in Keir's opinion. Every man,

woman, and child wearing the McQuade plaid owed him their loyalty from the moment they were born, but he would not be making the mistake of thinking that meant he should abuse them. The clan was only as strong as the effort they all put into the new harvest. A wise laird respected his retainers and earned their respect in return.

Edmund did not seem to share that opinion.

The town home wasn't hard to find, the crest above the iron gate proclaiming it a nobleman's house.

It was the sort of town home that most nobles kept for when they were at court—small, rising three stories. The windows were dark, but the shutters on the very top one were open. Keir stared for a long moment at the dark space within the window. A tingle crossed his neck and something gnawed at his gut. An eerie feeling of foreboding clamped onto him, refusing to be swept aside by logical thinking.

"What are you doing now?"

"I'm going to knock on the door."

Farrell shook his head. "This I have got to witness with my own eyes."

A uniformed housekeeper answered the knock quickly. But she turned suspicious when she got a look at him. The woman had to tip her head back to meet his eyes.

"I've come to see Lady Knyvett."

"As if I'd be letting anyone inside without the master home."

Keir propped a hand on the thick wooden door, refusing to allow her to close it in his face. She looked past him at his retainers, her eyes growing wide.

"But ye are admitting that the mistress is here?"

The woman looked at the ground. "I won't be answering any questions from you. The master wouldn't like it." Her tone was coated in regret and she raised her face to show him an expression of lament. "I might lose my place just for speaking with ye. Go on now. The mistress cannot come out of her room. The master made sure of that, he did."

"Made sure? How did he make sure?"

Keir pushed past the woman because she didn't respond quickly enough to suit his mood. She gasped, scampering after him. She reached for him but he dragged her along easily.

"Point me in the right direction, woman, or I'll poke me head into every room until I find what I want."

His men followed him, cutting the housekeeper off from any curious eyes on the street. Keir did not waste time on the ground floor. He found the stairs that led to the second floor and was up them before the housekeeper found her tongue.

"Where, woman? Ye'll tell me, make no mistake about it. Because I am nae leaving until I see her with my own eyes."

"Oh, the girl is in the attic. It were none of my doing. I swear I tried to force the lock when the master didn't return home last evening. But it held true. I swear it, I tried to open the door."

Keir turned so quickly the woman ran into him. He set her back a pace, disgust rolling through him so thick it threatened to push him into a rage.

"How many days has she been locked in?"

The woman wrung her apron. "Three, and the master hasn't come back. He holds the key. I swear on Christ's sweet mother there is no key here. She's up there."

She pointed a shaking hand past his shoulder. Another set of stairs rose into a dark shadow. The sun was gone and there was no friendly glow of even one candle set on the attic floor.

"Get some light up here."

The housekeeper hurried to comply, but Keir suspected that the woman was simply happy to be given an excuse to run away from him. A flick of his fingers set two of his men on her heels. The woman glanced behind her and began whispering prayers when she realized she had not escaped. Let her ask for divine help, because he had the feeling there was going to be hell to pay when he laid eyes on Helena.

What manner of a man locked a girl up for three days without fresh bread? Even convicts were treated better at the prison.

Even in the dark he made out the heavy iron lock secured to the wide handle that normally would have been used to pull the door open. So close to the roof, the floor was cooler than the rest of the house. Keir didn't bother to think about what he was doing. He'd worry about the rights and wrongs of the situation later.

"Helena?"

She must be going insane. Helena heard her name as clearly as a church bell. The room was dark and it was pressing in on her after three days. But she welcomed the chill of night. Her mouth was dry as dust. A faint glow appeared under the door. She stared at it, mesmerized by the light. It looked like a beacon. She resisted the urge to look at it like salvation. But her belly burned and grumbled, refusing to listen to anything her mind had to say about remaining strong in the face of Edmund's demands. While her will was strong, her body was starving.

There was a grinding of metal and a splintering of wood. It seemed so loud after hours upon hours of only her thoughts.

"Helena?"

She shivered, her mind hearing Keir's voice, which was absurd. She looked around the tiny attic room, her gaze touching on her small bed to force herself to recall where she was.

Allowing her thoughts to dwell on Keir McQuade had clearly been a mistake, for now her wits were addled.

The door burst open, allowing the light to flood in. A small cry of happiness passed her lips; she could not hold it back. But she froze when the light also washed over Keir, as large and imposing as she saw him in her mind. She was afraid to move, lest the moment shatter and she be forced to admit it was all nothing but fantasy brought on by lack of food and water.

"Sweet mercy."

It was her brother's housekeeper who spoke. The woman looked around Keir and covered her mouth with her hand. Horror reflected in her eyes. Helena felt her mind shift back into working order, but it was not fast enough to keep her hand from rising to cover the worst of the bruising on her face. By daylight she had viewed her brother's mark quite often. Half of her face was darkened, the spot on her cheek the deepest purple.

Keir was enraged.

She watched the emotion dance in his eyes, practically felt it leap across the space between them, it was so hot. His attention lingered on her face, studying it for a long moment. Her pride rose, refusing to endure being pitied.

"It is nothing."

"The hell it isna."

Keir looked around the room. His face reflected his displeasure. Helena raised her chin but knew what he was seeing. The room was tiny and cold now. Her dress was rumpled from days of use without pressing. On the bed she had piled her traveling clothing to help fight the chill because she had no hot coals to provide heat.

"What are you doing here, Keir?"

His gaze flew back to her face, something different flickering in his dark eyes. One corner of his mouth twitched before his attention settled on her bruised cheek once more. Rage returned to his eyes but it was tightly controlled, which made it even more formidable.

"I'm going to do what needs doing."

He turned in a flare of kilt. The housekeeper shrank away from him, but that didn't save her from his notice.

"Care for her, or answer to me when I return."

He was already down the stairs when Helena managed to force her body to break through the chill that hunger, thirst, and pain had locked her into. She followed him down to the second floor.

"Keir . . . wait."

Humiliation flooded her when her knees knocked against each other, refusing to hold her weight. She crumpled on the stairs, her hands grabbing at the walls and slipping because there was nothing to hold onto.

Keir turned and caught her, gripping her forearms and lifting her with an ease that astounded her. It also sent a ripple of excitement through her. It was maddening to think she enjoyed the demonstration of how much stronger he was. But she could not lie to herself.

He placed her gently on her feet but maintained his hold on her arms until she proved that standing was not beyond her strength.

"Christ in heaven."

More expletives followed. Keir's men stared at her, their faces reflecting their disapproval. She was honestly surprised by the disgust on their faces. Many men ruled with their fist.

That sobered her. She could see the rise of anger in their eyes. Every one of them wore a kilt, and the doublets they had on were plain, built for protection against the elements, not for fashion. These were men of action, not hollow words.

Like their leader.

"Keir, you must let it be."

He reached out and gently cupped her chin. It was but a whisper of a touch. She was shocked that a man so large and powerful might control his strength so completely. She quivered because it struck her as tender, the sort of touch she dreamed of receiving from a lover. But the two thoughts were in conflict, because a lover was only imaginary for her, but the hand on her chin was very real.

"He is my brother. My legal guardian. Even the church will not intercede."

Keir's face tightened, a muscle on the side of his jaw pulsing. But there was a flicker of something in his eyes that sent a shiver down her spine because it was deeply intimate.

"I enjoy the sound of my name on your lips." His voice dipped into a husky tone that shook her. Excitement raced along her skin, raising gooseflesh. But his expression changed, turning hard and determined.

"But I treat my hunting hounds better."

His voice was cold and hard. Several growls rose from his men. Her pride hated it. Hated the fact that he, that *they*, were right.

"I will be just fine. I assure you that I am strong enough to withstand a temper tantrum from Edmund." She lifted her chin away from his hand, unwilling to allow herself the comfort. Strength was what kept a person going. She mustn't weaken. Edmund would exploit it.

Keir's lips twitched again. But there was nothing nice about the grin that showed his teeth to her.

"I know ye are stronger. But I'll no' be standing by while

that whelp punishes ye for something I accused him of doing. It was nae yer word that colored him guilty."

"But the king didn't trust you—" She stepped back and covered her lips with a hand. "I didn't mean to speak harshly."

"Ye spoke the truth as ye witnessed it. Jamie was nae sure what to think of me. He'd never laid eyes on me and only had my father and older brothers to draw memory of McQuade values from." He shook his head. "Ye spoke in my defense and that is nae something that I'll be allowing to be punished."

"But there is nothing you can do to prevent the way Edmund deals with me. It is best to leave matters."

He reached across the space between them and stroked her uninjured cheek. Sweet pleasure crossed her flesh, driving some of the chill from her body.

"I do enjoy it when ye issue me a challenge, lass." There was a glint in his eyes that was hard and determined. "Be very sure that I intend to meet it head-on."

He turned his attention to the housekeeper. The woman jumped, a startled sound coming out of her mouth when Keir held up a solid silver pound. Her eyes rounded, one hand rising, but she didn't reach for the coin. Shock and disbelief held her frozen.

"Take good care of yer mistress. I will return."

He placed the silver in her palm. The woman lowered herself, but Keir had swept from the room along with his men before she finished. A gust of night air brushed Helena's face as the front door was opened on the lower floor.

"Well now. Indeed, I've never seen the like."

The housekeeper tucked the silver into a pouch that hung from her belt. She patted it before looking at Helena.

"My Christian name is Margery. I'm going to get that young Avis to haul in some water for bathing."

Helena wished the idea of a bath didn't send such joy through her. She wanted to refuse because it was yet another thing that money bought. She was so weary of the bribes and false friendship offered to her brother because of his power and fortune. Oh, she was harsh to think poorly of Margery— that coin was several months' pay for a housekeeper. Pride did nothing to soothe hunger, pain, or the bite of winter.

But this was bought with Keir's coin . . .

And that left her at the mercy of her feelings. She shook her head to dispel them. She did not know him. One encounter ripe with flirting did not tell a person anything about another. It was just the imprisonment that had her wanting to smile as though her gallant knight had just rescued her.

She did smile. There was no stopping her lips from curving. Keir was gallant. No matter what, she would never stop believing in that. If that made her whimsical, so be it.

But her eyes swept the room, and all around her were Edmund's things. His armor and bow. Dress swords that sat gleaming in the firelight. There were ruffs set carefully on stands, the lace starched and pressed in preparation for the master to wear them to court. The entire chamber was used just to display his wardrobe so that he might walk among his things and easily select what he wanted without waiting for things to be brought out of closets.

It was the reason she slept in the attic. Edmund used all the chambers on the second floor for his personal things. He refused to have them placed in trunks. Instead, every suit of clothing was hung from the walls, every pair of shoes displayed so that he might walk in and see every option for dressing each morning. Even his personal saddles were kept on the bed that she should have been sleeping in. Their ornate decoration declared how much her brother valued himself. Everything he owned had to be decorated and of the highest quality. There was not a single pair of sturdy boots in sight. Nothing there was merely made for purpose instead of presentation. Each shirt had lace and embroidery. Every doublet was sewn with gold or silver bangles.

The selfishness sickened her.

"I'll bathe in the kitchen, Margery."

The housekeeper couldn't suppress her smile. It was pure relief because she would be saved the chore of hauling water up a flight of stairs.

"I do not belong here and I've no desire to be the mistress of this place."

But that left her with little. Despair had been stalking her for days and she was becoming familiar with its icy touch. Yet she was still not sorry. No hint of repentance lived in her heart. Edmund might think he was punishing her but the truth was her brother was intent on breaking her spirit. And that was the one thing she would not allow him to touch.

Chapter Five

Keir found the fop gambling at an inn on the south side of London. It reminded Keir of the lodging he was renting. The place smelled like stale ale and unwashed bodies. Prostitutes mingled with the customers, many of them displaying their nude breasts, to the delight of their audience. But they were quick to slap any hand that tried to touch without paying.

"Are you in or not, Ronchford?"

Edmund Knyvett was soaked in wine, as were his companions. They occupied a large table that had silver and gold coins sitting on it. More money than some of the onlookers might see in an entire year was wagered on the turn of a card. But they didn't even notice the hungry eyes of those watching. Keir felt his disgust rise another notch. Edmund Knyvett was so arrogant, so expectant of being given his noble due that the man never entertained the idea of having to fend for himself.

It sickened Keir. His own men surrounded him, but he did not plan to lead them without having the same skills that they all did. The day he was their weakest link was the day that he was dead and buried.

"If you want to lose some more. Fine with me, Edmund."

Ronchford's hair was greasy and his once-fine doublet was a

tattered rag. His men looked like dockside thugs and they were eyeing the growing pile of coins with bright eyes. Edmund was too drunk to recognize the signs of an impending ambush, and his men were busy fondling the prostitutes. A slight motion caught Keir's attention and he watched as one of Ronchford's men pressed a silver penny into a girl's hand. She hid it quickly and then unlaced her bodice, to the delight of the Knyvett retainers.

"That's a sorry excuse for a man." Farrell shook his head.

"Aye, indeed it is."

"He's no' even worth thrashing in that condition. He'd no' feel it until he sobered up."

"Aye."

But there was always more than one way to settle a score. Keir bit back the urge to punch the arrogant bastard in spite of how intoxicated he was. He'd learned under his father's rule to plan his attacks wisely or taste bitter defeat. Sometimes, getting what you wanted meant looking for another route.

"Tell the lads to keep their eyes open and their mouths closed. We'll do our drinking someplace less likely to end us with slit throats."

"Aye, that's for sure." Farrell glanced behind them and shook his head. "What's yer plan?"

"I'm going to join the game."

Farrell raised an eyebrow. "Is that a fact?"

"It is." Keir walked forward and took a chair before the two men bothered to investigate who was invading their space. Edmund slammed his tankard down with a thud, but Keir tossed a full bag of coins onto the table. The sound of money drew more interest from Ronchford than Edmund's displeasure.

"You're not welcome at this table . . . Scot!" Edmund sneered and lifted his tankard to take another huge swallow.

Keir patted his purse. "Is that a fact?" The coins hit one another, giving off a faint tinkling sound. It drew smiles from Ronchford's men and even some of Edmund's. The lordling tried to remain disgruntled but his gaze strayed to the leather bag, greed flickering in his eyes.

"I like him well enough. His money is my kind of friend." Ronchford snapped his fingers and a wench bent over the table to deliver a tankard to Keir. Her breasts almost brushed his nose but the scent of her unwashed skin made it simple to ignore her.

Helena was so much sweeter. . . .

Keir shook off the thought, banishing Helena to a corner of his mind. He needed his attention on the men in front of him.

Edmund growled but his eyes shifted to the money. "Fine. You want to lose your money? I'll be happy to take it."

There might have only been three of them playing, but the game was the center of attention. Keir studied Edmund and Ronchford, but only Ronchford was as intent as he was. Edmund had dismissed him already, believing himself superior. Keir lost the first hand just to encourage that assumption. But it was Ronchford who scraped the money toward himself. Keir almost felt sorry for Edmund Knyvett. The boy wasn't the first noble to run into men like Ronchford: men who made their fortunes by stripping it from noblemen who had never been anywhere that their blue blood didn't pave the way to success for them.

He also wasn't the first to believe that being born into a noble family made him better than those around him.

But Helena's face rose to the front of his thoughts and all mercy died. The cards were dealt out again and Keir tightened his attention to the task at hand. An hour later Ronchford's men were growling at his own. Every McQuade clansman was becoming more eager to give them what their grumbling asked for. Edmund's money had dwindled to a few coins.

"I'm bored." He waved his hand over the table.

"Don't be a sore loser, laddie." Keir patted the pile in front of him. "Mind ye, I'll be happy to give you a round to take it back from me."

Ronchford licked his lower lip. "He's out of coin."

Edmund sniffed. "A Knyvett is never out of coin." He raised a hand and snapped his fingers. A neatly dressed man instantly answered the summons, although there wasn't a look of subservience in his eyes. It was more calculated, more knowledgeable than that. Keir studied the man, picking out the details of fine tailoring in the man's doublet. There wasn't any of the gold beading or lavish lace such as Edmund wore, but there was piping and corded buttons that displayed the same level of tailoring. The only difference was the materials. The man had money, no doubt about it, and his presence in the gaming house told Keir he was a loan merchant. Part of the middle class who made good profit off making loans to the nobles.

A fat purse landed on the table in front of Edmund. He smirked and arched an eyebrow at Ronchford.

"I say we dispense with this toying about." He slid the entire amount into the center of the table. Ronchford matched him, greed brightening his face.

"I'm game." Keir tossed his own gold into the pile and waited for his cards. Part of him was fighting the urge to remain at the table. That was McQuade money and he was still not accustomed to considering it his due as laird. But fortune favored the bold. Besides, he still had plenty of coin left in

front of him, courtesy of Edmund's intoxicated betting. Keir
let his head tilt to one side, his eyes closing to slits. Ronchford
smiled before shifting his attention back to his own cards. Edmund wasn't as candid. The lordling chuckled.

"Do you like the wine, Scot? I hear it's difficult to come by
in Scotland."

"That it is. Must explain why I've enjoyed so much of it."
Keir lift the tankard to his lips and took a swallow. Edmund
watched him, glee dancing in his eyes. He looked back down
at his cards, his emotions showing plainly on his face. Keir put
the tankard down close to the edge of the table. Farrell slipped
it off, replacing it with an empty one, just as he'd done several
times during the night. The serving girl refilled it a few moments later, to Ronchford's delight.

Predators. Keir had never seen men that reminded him
more of a pair of predators. Their only desire was to feed and
please themselves.

Keir held his emotions behind a carefully controlled mask
of drink-induced jovialness. Inside he was disgusted. The pair
of them were little better than thieves or wolves. They tar-
geted the weak.

Edmund turned his cards over with a flourish. Ronchford
smiled and showed his own. The man was already reaching
for the money when Keir tapped the tabletop. It was a soft
sound, but everyone was focused on the high-stakes game.

"It looks like luck favors me this round." Keir slurred his
words just a small amount.

Ronchford cursed. His fist hit the table, making the coins
bounce. He stared at the cards and cursed once more.

A second later he pushed back from his spot, his chair legs
skidding on the floor. He scraped his remaining coins back
into a purse. "I'm done with playing with Scots."

"Oh, such a shame." Keir pulled his winnings toward him

and took another swallow of wine. Edmund was silent, his attention on the pile of money in front of him. Keir fondled it, sliding his hand into the coins and allowing them to slip through his fingers.

"Nothing sounds quite like that, now does it, laddie." Keir announced.

Edmund looked across the room, but the loan merchant shook his head. Anger turned his face red and his gaze returned to the pile of gold and silver coins in front of Keir.

"What are ye going to do with that much coin? Buy sheep?" Edmund demanded

It was a common slur, one that Keir had heard before. The English nobility considered Scotland a barbaric place, devoid of modern homes and comforts. It was an attitude most of his fellow lairds enjoyed allowing to flourish. It kept the English out of their ancestral lands.

"Well now . . . I do enjoy knowing we've got sheep aplenty." Keir rolled his head and lifted the wine tankard to his lips. Edmund leaned forward.

"You should set your sights on English land."

Keir opened his eyes wide. "Now, where would I find a man willing to sell me land? Ye English nobles enjoy keeping that in the family."

Keir allowed a thick brogue to settle over his words. Edmund reached into his doublet.

"My sister has a dowry that includes a rich parcel of land."

"I thought ye didna care for me, laddie." The lordling winced when he called him laddie once again. "Why would ye offer me the chance to marry into the family?"

"I like your money."

"Och now. That's the sort of thing I can be appreciating." Keir took another swig of wine. "Let me see it."

Edmund tightened his fingers around the parchment. "Do we have an agreement?"

"Nae afore I've looked at it, we don't."

Edmund hesitated. The parchment crinkled but he extended it. Keir had to control the urge to snatch it out of his hand. He made his movements slow and uncoordinated.

"Well now. Isna that a sweet document. 'Course, it wouldna mean anything unless it were signed and sealed."

"My father's seal is on it."

"Och now, are ye saying that yer daddy is the one I need to be negotiating with, laddie?"

Edmund's face turned red. He reached for a candle. "My father is no longer running his estate. Everything is mine to direct. And I want everything in front of you for the land. You get Helena for your wife but not a shilling more. Only the land that is her dowry."

"Sounds better than sheep. Doesn't it, lads?"

His men didn't disappoint him. They slapped their thighs and chuckled, making a few heated jests along with it. Edmund saw exactly what he wanted to see—a bunch of ignorant Scots who were easily duped. That was something his fellow Scots had been using against the English for centuries—their own arrogance. Edmund smirked, his confidence in his superiority restored.

"Well then, sign it and we have a deal."

Cold-blooded whelp . . .

The only sympathy Keir had was for the mother who had once rejoiced at Edmund's birth. It was a shame that his father had failed to mold him into a man. He poured melted wax from the candle onto the parchment and pressed his own signet ring into it. Keir suppressed a shudder for the callous way he signed over his sister.

But he did nothing to stop the burning flow of satisfaction that filled him when the parchment was handed back to him.

His . . .

Such a powerful idea. Beneath his kilt his cock hardened.

"Och, well I think it's time for ye to be heading home, laird." Farrell patted him on the shoulder, a couple of other men helping.

"Is it now?" Keir played his part, smiling at his men while Edmund was absorbed with the pile of coins gleaming in the candlelight.

"So it is." He tucked the parchment into his doublet while his men pushed him through the door. They laughed and staggered until they stepped onto the street. The second they did, every man straightened. Their pace increased tenfold on the way to the stable where they'd left their horses.

Keir swung onto his horse, his men only a breath behind him. "Let's clear away from here, lads." Before Edmund set some of the low-life scum hiding in the dark corners of the tavern after the document that would allow him to claim Helena.

By the time Edmund's men gave chase, there wasn't a Mc-Quade kilt in sight, the night masking them and the drink the English had partaken of dulling their wits. They shrugged and looped their arms over the prostitutes, giving them their attention.

Scots. They were only Scots. . . .

Edmund Knyvett smiled. He was pleased. Only a mild amount of annoyance interfered with his happiness when his men failed to return with the parchment. He was not concerned. The parchment meant little. Why, it might take years for him to decide that Helena was ready to take her marriage vows. Her dowry and its rents remained his until she knelt at the altar.

Gullible Scot. He needed to play cards with the man again.

"That bastard sold ye his sister?" Farrell asked the question for the third time.

Keir merely shrugged. "If I say anything, it's bound to be something profane which would be a wee bit misplaced, considering I'm happy with the bargain."

"Ah, but will the lassie be happy with it? Now there's the question. What are ye going to do with an English noblewoman on McQuade land?"

Keir rubbed his chin. Tension knotted his shoulders. Helena Knyvett was everything he'd hoped to bring back in a wife. Even if her brother detested him, her family relations wouldn't risk offending him. They'd all consider that Edmund didn't have a son of his own and that fate might deliver the title he was set to inherit into Helena's children's hands.

Aye, that was what he'd set out to accomplish. But the tension tightened. He'd never been unkind to a woman before. Locking Helena into a marriage that might not please her left a bitter taste in his mouth. But his responsibilities as laird saw him riding toward court at first light. 'Twas a laird's duty to bring home a wife whose dowry would add to his clan's estate. He was locked into it as surely as Helena, whose own family would see her wedding for position. The only comfort was in knowing that she'd never feel his fist against her cheek.

For the moment, it would have to be enough.

"Keir McQuade."

The royal chamberlain called out his name before noon. Keir wasn't surprised. The gossips began feasting on the topic of his newly acquired bride the moment he arrived and his men spilled the information exactly as instructed. Edmund Knyvett scowled at him before the lordling even made it halfway across the great hall, his noble friends hurrying to whisper in his ear.

"Edmund Knyvett."

The chamberlain sent his white staff into the stone floor with a single bang. It echoed through the abnormally quiet great hall. The king sat on his chair looking regal and angry. The royal guards on either side of him stared straight ahead but their eyes betrayed how much they were listening to everything that happened in the presence of the king.

"The pair of you have had a busy night." Thick annoyance coated the king's voice. He looked at Edmund. "Tell me ye didna settle a game of cards with yer sister's dowry."

"I hardly think that a game of cards is anything for Your Majesty to waste your valuable time on. The Scot and I simply found something we have in common."

"Careful, Knyvett, I'm a Scot myself. Keep saying the word like a curse and I might take insult."

Edmund narrowed his eyes. "Your mother was an English princess."

"And my father was a Scotsman. Which is why I am yer king and McQuade's as well. Now enough stalling. Half my nobles are fearing that their daughters might become the winnings of drunken no-goods while the other half are considering putting their own daughters up in exchange for debts that need settling. It's a damned mess the pair of you started."

Edmund chuckled. He didn't seem to have any more self-discipline in the presence of his monarch than he did elsewhere. Keir was not so foolish. James kept them both standing to drive home their position compared to his.

Keir simply reached into his doublet and pulled out the parchment. James Stuart slapped the arm of his chair.

"And you want to swear yer fealty to me? What sort of man are ye to be accepting something like that?"

"I tracked down the bastard to beat him senseless. I settled for winning a fortune from him."

"You have nothing but a parchment until I decide that my sister is ready to marry. I am her guardian."

James rose, his guards instantly stepping a half step forward. "Why did you want to fight with him, McQuade?"

"Because he beat his sister for telling you the truth, and locked her in an attic for nae being willing to watch another girl's reputation become stained. He left her there for days without food while he went gaming. He is nae a fit guardian. I say ye should give yer blessing to our union so that I can treat her appropriately."

"I say you shall not have anything to do with my sister." Edmund's voice rose. "Even my king cannot order a peer to marry. Helena is a peer and you are beneath her! I'll see her an old woman before kneeling at the altar beside you."

Keir's fist connected with Edmund's jaw. He staggered backward, a look of stunned shock on his face. The royal guards lowered their pikes and Keir stared at the deadly ends of the weapons.

"Give me that parchment, McQuade."

The king waved his guards away and took the document. He scanned it with a critical eye.

"Both yer and yer father's seal's are on this, Knyvett. McQuade can take ye to court and win."

Edmund tossed his head. Hatred blazed from his eyes. "But that will still not get him a wife."

"Ye would do that to yer own sister? Drag her through years

of legal bickering while her chance to bear children is passed over by time?"

Edmund resumed his poised appearance, one foot placed in front of the other, while his face appeared bored. "Women are meant to be used to further their family connections. Helena is no different."

The king considered his comment for a long moment. He lifted one thick finger. "Peers are meant to serve their king. I can think of several posts in Scotland that need an ambassador."

"That is—"

"Is what, sir?" James Stuart gripped the arms of his chair but remained sitting while Edmund sputtered. "It is the will of yer king."

"McQuade is nothing! My sister is pure nobility."

"Ye're the one who bartered her like a common whore," Keir snarled through his teeth.

"You broke into my home. I don't have to discuss anything with a thief."

"But you do have to serve yer king."

Edmund sniffed, disdain clear on his face. He shot a look full of seething hatred toward Keir.

The king raised his hand and pointed at Edmund.

"Ye'll be my man on McQuade land, since the last laird was run through by my guards. Laird McQuade will give you accommodations and you shall remain there until I summon ye and yer sister back to court. My own royal guard shall escort ye north."

Keir sent his fist into his opposite hand. The loud popping sound bounced off the walls of the receiving chamber. Edmund paled, fear showing on his face.

"Unless the man were to marry," James continued, his voice as smooth as honey. "New couples need their privacy."

"But he is . . . common!"

"Common? He is a laird, which is a title as old as yer own, Knyvett." James Stuart rose. "The man came to court to kneel before his king while ye are here to further yer own schemes. I've had enough of this. Open the doors!"

Royal servants obeyed, pulling the doors wide to allow them to be viewed by everyone in the great hall. A hush instantly fell over the courtiers as they lowered their heads. Keir's men stood right outside the door and took instant advantage of the chance to join their laird.

The king turned to face him and extended his hand. "I will hear yer vow of loyalty, McQuade. 'Tis clear to me that ye're a man who will tell me the truth even when I don't want to hear it."

Keir knelt, every one of his men following. His heart was suddenly beating faster. He was almost grateful to Edmund for giving him the chance to prove himself to the king. But that wouldn't keep him from giving the boy the beating he had coming once they reached McQuade land.

"My word, my strength, and my blood forever!"

He took the king's hand and kissed it in a tradition that went back farther than the Roman Empire.

"Ye will rise and be acknowledged as Baron Hurst. I confer yer father's third wife's title onto ye. Yer sister Bronwyn doesna need it since her husband has his own title."

"Sire . . ." Enraged, Edmund protested.

"Yer father petitioned me for it several times. Rise, Baron Hurst, Laird McQuade."

Keir pushed to his feet, certain that his father was screaming in hell. The man had gone to great lengths to get what his third wife held in her name alone. He'd tried to soil his own daughter's name just to keep the land and title that he'd never known was willed to her female offspring, and not her husband. Applause filled the great hall while Edmund stifled his objections.

Keir stared back at the man, the open door providing the perfect opportunity to press him.

"When is my wedding?"

Edmund pressed his lips into a tight line but the silence in the hall rippled with whispers. He ground his teeth, his lips turning white all the while the whispers grew in volume.

"Tomorrow."

Chapter Six

Edmund slammed into the town house again. Helena simply shook her head. If her brother ever appeared happy, she was afraid she might faint dead away at his polished boot tips.

"You think yourself so cleaver."

"What vexes you now, brother?" Helena refused to shirk in the face of his temper. Edmund could simply deal with the fact that she was restricted to the town home instead of the attic.

"You and your dim little view of the world. Unable to grasp the fact that I was doing you a favor by trying to disgrace that McKorey witch." Edmund surprised her by looking down the hallway. She was used to him bellowing for wine the moment he arrived. Instead he shut the door.

"Well, you will be the one to suffer. Unless I help you. I shouldn't."

Dread crept down her neck. Edmund was sober, making his words harder to ignore.

"The king has decreed that I am not a fit guardian for you anymore."

"Am I going home?" It would be too good a turn of fate, but she couldn't help but hope.

Her brother smiled. It was a cold curving of his lips that sent ice through her heart.

"You're getting married."

Expecting such news didn't make it easier to absorb. Helena felt the announcement hit her as solidly as Edmund's fist had connected with her face. He watched her face, enjoyment lighting his eyes.

"Your little defiance in front of the king has netted you a change of authority by royal command."

"Who?"

"Sir Ronchford."

Helena gagged. She could not hold it back. Philip Ronchford might have been born into a good name, but the man was rotten. He was also old enough to be her father and some to spare. Keir's face surfaced in her mind, just as she told Raelin it would, and tears stung her eyes.

"Tomorrow night you will be his wife." Edmund leaned closer, sneering in her ear. "After all, the man really doesn't have any time to squander. He wants an heir and needs to get to deflowering you quickly. I understand he has quite a bit of stamina in spite of his age."

"Don't be horrible, Edmund!"

"Me, dear sister? The king has ordered you wed. I have done nothing save try to better your lot!"

And the details did not matter. . . .

Helena turned and paced across the room. Her simple traveling dress was much easier to walk in, the wool skirts flipping away from her rapid steps. Which was good because her heart was pounding. Sweat popped out on her forehead and she could not keep her thoughts from racing. The image of Ronchford looking into her bed, leering at her with a mouth full of blackened teeth made her gag. She hugged herself, trying to fend off the idea of him reaching in to pull the bedding back and bare her for his possession.

"I don't know why I'm even bothering to suggest helping you escape. . . ."

Helena froze. Distrust shot through her, but the idea of avoiding marriage to Ronchford was too tantalizing to ignore, even if she suspected that her brother was scheming yet again.

"How?"

Edmund smirked at her, enjoying the fact that she was waiting on his whim. Her temper rose. She was suddenly so horrified she wanted to throw something at his mocking face. He had brought her to this terrible fate. She snarled at him, shaking with the need to exact vengeance. His eyes went wide but he whispered the words she was desperate to hear.

"Run away."

He leaned in closer. "I cannot be suspected of assisting you, so you cannot be seen leaving."

She swallowed, trying to gain a hand on her panic.

Edmund's voice was suddenly so welcome because it offered her a solution that did not include spreading her thighs for Ronchford in less than one day. She wouldn't be the first young bride that found herself at the mercy of an old man once the church blessing was given. She'd be Ronchford's for the taking, and he would take. Ronchford was every bit as selfish as her brother.

"I am going out as I normally do. My driver is trustworthy. He will wait for you by the market and take you to Bride Dale."

Bride Dale . . . their aunt Celia's home. The woman was in her elderly years and never had anyone to visit. It would be a quiet place to remain out of the notice of nobles. Hope glittered in front of her like water to the parched. All she needed to do was reach for it.

Hope took hold of her, sweeping aside thoughts of thieves in the night. The market was only three short blocks away.

Even if Edmund was serving his own interests in assisting her out of London, what did it matter if it was also what she desired? What matter if it took her beyond Ronchford's reach?

"I'll tell the king that you ran away, leaving a note about a convent. You can return next year, properly repentant of your maidenly fears."

Helena didn't think. She was still held in the grip of panic. Edmund promised her deliverance and she didn't care about his motivations.

"I will get my cloak."

Edmund smiled at her. A tingle went down her neck but she refused to hesitate. All of her options were grim but there was something about taking matters into her own hands that felt good. Remaining in the town home would see her pacing throughout the night, dreading the dawn.

She would take her chances.

The streets were far from quiet. But the level of noise was much less than during the day. Helena noticed every sound more—the dripping of water onto the cobblestone street or the faint sound of a horse's hooves pulling her brother's carriage down the next block.

Her own steps echoed and she tried to place her feet softly. Light twinkled through closed shutters; only a few front doors were lit with welcoming candles. She left the block where their town house was, turning the corner onto a street that was lined with merchant shops. They were all closed tight against the night. It was darker here; the moonlight guided her.

"Well, now. Look what we have here."

She gasped, but no sound made it past the hand that clamped over her mouth. It was hard and brutal, pulling her back against a chest. She struggled, kicking and twisting to break free.

"Stop your spitting, it won't make no difference."

A sharp blow struck her across her cheek, sending a bright sparkling of stars across her vision. She turned halfway around but didn't stop her struggle. With space between her and her assailant, she thrust her hand out and smashed her palm into his nose.

"Bloody hell!"

Triumph spread through her, but it was short-lived. Another set of arms gripped her from behind, pulling her arms behind her.

"I'll teach you some respect." Another slap hit her face. Pain threatened her vision with darkness. Pulling in a deep breath, she resisted the pull, fighting to remain awake. Leather bit into her wrist as her hands were bound tightly behind her back.

"Sure she's the right one?" The man behind her asked the question. He reached up and gripped her hair to angle her face toward the moonlight.

"Who else would be scampering down this road right now? Knyvett kept his word, all right." He stepped up close, breathing his foul breath into her face. The silver moonlight washed over Ronchford's features, drawing a snarl from her lips. Her panic evaporated, leaving only rage burning inside her. She would not yield to his possession.

"Release me!"

He laughed at her instead. His grubby fingers gripped her chin before boldly stroking down her neck and onto her breasts. Revulsion threatened to choke her.

"I've paid a pretty amount to have your brother turn his back. I plan to enjoy what I've bought, madam."

Betrayal burned through her rage. Edmund's revenge showed in the gloating eyes of the man fondling her. She should have suspected, shouldn't have leaped at the hope her brother dangled in front of her nose. The king would never have ordered her wed to Ronchford as a means of giving her a proper guardian. Not Ronchford. The man was worse than Edmund. She should have considered the facts, but had been too caught up in the whirl of emotions to think before leaving the town home. Now she was at the mercy of the night and the men that crept through its shadows.

Ronchford looked quite at ease.

"I'm going to enjoy these tits." He yanked on the buttoned-up doublet she wore, the sturdy wool resisting his efforts to bare her cleavage. Her flesh crawled, revulsion twisting her stomach. She renewed her struggles, franticly twisting and bucking to escape the two men.

They cursed, both men howling with outrage. Surprise flashed through her, her mind finding it hard to believe that she had hurt them with her bucking. But she was suddenly free and didn't waste time trying to understand how it had happened. With her hands bound behind her, she couldn't run without stepping on her skirt. She hurried as fast as possible but came up short as another man blocked her path. He was huge. She lifted her face, tilting her chin up to find his face.

"Ye have a habit of finding rough men, Helena. I believe I'll have to break ye of yer need to wander."

Relief flooded her, making her knees weak. Her lungs burned, demanding deep gasping breaths.

"Thank heaven."

"Nay, thank the fact that I am nay a trusting man, lass."

Hard suspicion edged his voice. Soft steps crunched on the cobblestones behind her. The shapes of Keir's men materialized from the darkness, the moonlight glittering off the blade of a knife.

"Nay, leave her tied."

"What? You can't mean that."

Keir stepped up closer. She caught a hint of his scent and noticed instantly how clean he smelled compared to Ronchford.

"Oh, I do. It will be all the better for hauling ye off."

He bent his knees and lowered one shoulder until it was even with her waist. A moment later she was tossed over it like a sack of grain. Her head hung down his back, the blood rushing to it.

"Keir—"

A solid whack landed on her upturned bottom. She sputtered, but had to clamp her lips closed when he started walking and her head swung back and forth across his back. Her face burned with her temper when she heard the faint sound of his men chuckling.

Men—they were impossible to stomach!

"What are you doing, Keir McQuade?" Helena had struggled to see the man. He'd placed her right in the center of a bed. It was a fine bed, the blankets soft and rising up around her weight. But she didn't have time to be distracted by such things.

"Claiming what is mine." He stood across the room. Two candles burned on the table near him, their light bathing him in gold. A huge sword was strapped to his back, the handle of it rising above his left shoulder. She stared rather stupidly at the thick leather of the scabbard because it had kept her from being cut while she lay over his shoulder. He reached up and untied it. Twisting around, he pulled it from where it was latched to his wide leather belt and set the weapon aside.

"What are you talking about?" Her thoughts were racing and she honestly didn't believe that she could absorb any more. Especially something like thinking that Keir McQuade considered her his. Part of her leaped at the idea, but her temper was far past being willing to listen to anyone tell her that she was their property. She sat up and pushed herself off the bed. Even with her hands still bound behind her, being on her feet felt less helpless.

He turned to study her. His eyes darkened, his face set into a hard expression. It was a stark contrast to the teasing look she'd seen from him before.

"I didna want to think you'd be so foolish as to try a stunt like running down a dark street." His expression darkened. "But 'tis a good thing that I set me men to watching the house. 'Tis the truth, I expected yer brother to try to smuggle ye out of the city."

Confusion swept through her. Helena clamped her lips closed against the next question that wanted to sail past her lips.

Who to trust . . .

There were too many men telling her that she belonged to them. Her earlier fascination with Keir had blinded her to the fact that the man was every bit as dangerous as Ronchford or her brother. All of them wanted control of her for their own agendas.

"And I was foolish enough to think that ye would nae be so opposed to wedding with me that ye would flee." Hurt edged his voice but it was the reprimanding note that gained her full attention. She was sick unto death of being corrected.

"I was on my way to a convent."

Edmund would have taken exception to her tone. Keir tilted his head and crossed his arms across his chest. The pose made him look larger and more imposing. Her gaze wanted to shift to where the muscles of his arms bulged. There was only the thick fabric of his shirting covering it, the sleeves of his doublet unbuttoned and secured behind his back. In the cool night he should have been cold, but he didn't look like even the temperature affected him. The strength practically radiated off him. She shook her head, refusing to become mesmerized by him.

"A convent?"

"Aye, a place where men wouldn't rule me."

One corner of his mouth twitched, curving slightly upward. His arms uncrossed, sending a shiver down her spine. It was such a foolish response, one she detested. There was no reason she should be so attuned to his movements. It made quarreling with the man near impossible.

"Well now . . ." He closed the distance between them, watching her while he did it. She suddenly understood exactly how a doe must feel when the hunters closed in for the kill.

"If ye were to become a nun, wouldn't ye be expected to obey the pope without question?"

He touched her. It was a simple brushing of his fingers across the lower curve of her jaw. But she shuddered. Sensation flooded her, rippling across her skin as quick as lightning.

"At least he would be a celibate man."

Challenge flared up in his dark eyes. Her memory offered up the way he'd looked the first time she'd encountered him. This was not a man who ever gave up on what he considered a challenge.

"I dinnae think ye are made for the life of sleeping in a cold bed, forever a virgin." His gaze lowered to her lips and her mouth suddenly went dry.

What would his kiss taste like. . . .

She shook her head to banish the idea. Keir's fingers cupped her chin to still her.

" 'Tis the truth that ye are far too responsive to my touch to devote yerself to such a life." He brushed a fingertip over her lower lip, drawing a soft gasp from her. Her heart accelerated and her breathing deepened. His scent filled her senses once again. It was full of dark mystery that touched off heat deep in her belly.

She slipped to the side, away from his disturbing touch. The fact that they were alone suddenly filled her thoughts. Her confidence deserted her in the face of that knowledge. The heat growing in her belly frightened her with the fact that she could not seem to control it.

"I do assure you I have the will to devote myself completely to what I choose. A convent will be devoid of temptations, making it much easier."

"Well, I agree that ye are a temptation."

His mouth touched hers. The kiss wasn't timid but it lacked the hardness that she expected from so large a man. She jerked away from him but he followed her, one arm slipping around her waist to keep her close.

A small whimper passed her lips. She couldn't hold the sound back. There was too much sensation to keep it inside. No amount of practice or self-discipline could help. She was overwhelmed. It swept over her, drowning her will to deny what she craved.

His lips toyed with hers, playing across their tender surface, slipping and toying with her until she moved hers. Another hand cupped the back of her head, tilting her face up so that his mouth could cover hers more completely. His kiss deepened, demanding more from her. He pressed her lips open, the tip of his tongue invading her mouth. He was suddenly too close, his body too hard and overwhelming. Need pulsed along with her blood and fear rose along with the heat—fear of her own response to him.

She struggled to regain her freedom but her hands were still bound. The leather biting into her wrists provided the leverage to regain her wits. She felt her skin tearing with her fight, the scent of blood rising up to mask the smell of his skin.

"No . . . release me!"

He muttered in Gaelic. She didn't need to understand the language to recognize a curse. His tone drove the meaning home.

"Aye, that needs doing. Here, sit up."

He didn't remove his hands from her. He shifted his grip until his hand was holding her upper arm. "Hold still, lass. I don't want to cut ye."

He was correct, of course, but her body wouldn't listen to her brain. Standing, she quivered and fought the urge to move away from his disturbing form. He ended up following her, turning in a small circle when she retreated even more.

She clenched her teeth and forced her feet to stand in place. The cool blade of a knife pressed against her wrist the moment she stilled. The bindings popped and she spun away from him.

"Easy, lass. I'm nae the one that keeps laying me hand across yer face when I'm cross with ye."

No, what he did was far worse because she could not shut it out. . . .

"I should have run that bastard Ronchford through. Yer wrists are bloody."

"It is nothing."

With a frown, Keir slid his dagger back into the sheath that was attached to his belt. "It appears that we are back to disagreeing."

His gaze settled on her wrists for a moment, anger flickering in his eyes. There were only a few cuts that actually bled. Helena forced herself to stop rubbing at the bruises and lowered her hands to her sides.

"I don't believe we ever began agreeing on anything."

He grinned, flashing his teeth at her. "Well now, come back here and I'll be more than happy to remind ye how much we both enjoyed that kiss."

"No."

He lifted one eyebrow and took a lazy step toward her. "No?"

"You heard me correctly."

"Tell me why not." His voice deepened and took on a thicker brogue. "Ye kissed me back as sure as the sun will rise in the morning."

She moved away from him. "I didn't deny that. It doesn't mean I want to . . . to . . ."

"To kiss me again?"

"Stop toying with me." She snapped at him. She needed him to return to the suspicious man who had watched her from across the room. This teasing Keir was too hard to ignore because she had allowed her dreams to be filled with him. It had been such a foolish mistake to allow her thoughts freedom.

"I do assure ye, Helena Knyvett, I'm nae playing." He raised one hand and offered it to her with the palm facing up. "Come to me."

"I will not." Even if her body was clamoring for her to comply. "It would be wicked."

His eyes flickered with something that sent a ripple of excitement through her.

"Exactly."

He captured her in one long stride, his body closing the distance exactly the way she'd suspected he might be able to do. In a mere breath she was surrounded by his heat once again. The scent of his skin filled her senses and triggered a response that threatened to wipe all thoughts from her mind. There was only his touch and her desire for more of it.

"Please, Keir . . . *I am a virgin.*"

She hated her weakness. Hated the fact that her body quivered in his embrace. Tears stung the corners of her eyes because the hands she'd placed against his chest didn't want to push him away. Her fingertips longed to seek out his skin. But her honor demanded she resist, demanded that she not allow him to treat her as though she was a light-skirt. Even if he had found her in the street at night.

"I know, lass. I never doubted that."

His voice was too tender, too sweet. Tears eased from her eyes because she longed to just melt against him. She was so tired of standing firmly in control, as she was expected to do.

He cursed again in Gaelic. But he didn't release her. One hand cupped her chin, raising it up so that he could view her shame. She shuddered, biting into her lower lip to contain the tiny moan that wanted to escape.

"Ye didna cry when that bastard hit ye." His voice was husky and full of some emotion she could not name. But it pierced her heart. Two more tears eased down her cheeks.

"Edmund hits harder."

His gaze lowered to the side of her face that was still black and blue several days later.

"But ye shed tears for me." He leaned down and kissed one. She shuddered, that single kiss burning hotter than a coal. A moment later she was free. She felt the chill of the night air, her body lamenting the loss of his hard body against it.

"I do nae understand ye, Helena, but best ye understand that I'll no' be allowing ye to come to harm. My men will not allow ye outside. Dinnae make a fuss about it."

"But . . . why are you intent on keeping me?"

Keir paused with one hand on the door. Creases appeared on his forehead.

"I'm nay a fool, Helena. Dinnae think I'll be easy to bend because yer tears gained ye what ye want tonight. I'll be sharing that bed with ye tomorrow night as any groom would expect."

He shut the door firmly behind him. Helena stared at it stupidly. Groom? For all that she knew of the definition of the word, it made no sense to her mind.

Edmund had told her she was to wed Ronchford, but the man had tried to abduct her.

And Keir had rescued her, only to imprison her. . . .

It was a tangle of deception that nauseated her, threatening to make her retch when she reduced every man down to one thing—his desire to possess her. Like a pair of silver candlesticks.

The memory of Ronchford's hands clawing at her breasts made her adjust her thinking. Not like a set of candlesticks. Yet still the same sense of ownership. Always what they wanted. Always a matter of what she was expected to surrender to their whim.

Behind her stays, her nipples beaded, the soft tips becoming more erect until they were hard with longing. There was no banishing the need. It lived deep in her belly, growing hotter when Keir was in the same room with her. She was suddenly repentant of every time she had thought herself superior to women who followed their longings into the arms of lovers. She had been so ignorant. Perhaps it was wicked, but it was also more intense than anything she had ever experienced. Dismissing it was impossible, but more importantly she did not want to part with it.

Oh no. She wanted to unbutton her doublet and let the air brush across her skin. The garment was stifling, her skin was begging for freedom. More than her skin. Her body clamored for release from the bonds of her childhood learning. Maybe it was the darkness, but she longed to see Keir back in the room in spite of her rejection of him.

Her tears had sent him away. She shuddered again because it was so tender, so noble of him. How was she to resist her longing for him when he continued to act so gallant?

Maybe you shouldn't . . .

Temptation was cruel. Her flesh now warred with her pride. She was so alone, she ached with it. Her groom? Who exactly was she expected to marry and when? Sitting down on a small lounge, she laid her head down on its silk surface. Resting in the bed was out of the question; her mind rejected it. She could barely tolerate the sight of it, so she allowed her eyelids to close.

As much as her body longed to lie with Keir, her pride refused. She didn't want to give him her purity because he believed it belonged to him. Ronchford was that sort of man. So was Edmund and a hundred others who had viewed her at court like a mare on display with her bloodlines neatly laid out to increase her value.

She wanted Keir to remain noble—untarnished by the marriage game. She wanted to make love with him, not part her thighs so that her blue blood might be bred into children who would be reared to take their place. She'd always been instructed on what was expected.

Tears eased from her eyes for the fantasy that would dissipate the second she opened her eyes again. But for the moment, she allowed her dreams to take her away from the aches and pains of her flesh. The longings remained, keeping her warm as her lover held her.

"Well ye don't look very pleased with yer victory." Farrell glanced around the kitchen. "I, for one, am rather impressed with the new accommodations. If ye're going to have to pay the inheritance taxes on a title, at least ye got something in return."

Keir had to agree. The Hurst Barony came with little. Most of the land was bound to his sister Bronwyn, but the king had settled a small estate on him along with the title. There were taxes due on the inheritance of such a title, but it had gained him a town home that he was not ashamed to bring his bride to.

There would no doubt be wages due the staff as well.

He looked around the kitchen. Nothing was rundown. The long table used for preparing food showed use but not more than any in the kitchens of Red Stone castle. He decided that he did not need to know why the house was in such good repair if the title had been without a lord for over thirty years. It was his now and that was what mattered.

"I need the men to take shifts tonight. My bride is nae to leave the house or send any letters."

He clenched his teeth, grinding his jaw with the tension that held him. Farrell abandoned his lazy position.

"She doesna want to marry with ye?"

She'd wept. . . .

Keir snarled and poured himself a glass of whisky. Farrell watched him for a moment before standing up and leaving to post the guards Keir had ordered. The whisky failed to burn away the bitter taste in his mouth.

She'd wept. . . .

Why?

The whisky burned but his question burned hotter. He needed to know.

The little drops had stabbed into him deeper than any dirk ever did. It did not make any sense. She'd enjoyed his kiss. He knew the difference between a woman who kissed a man back because she desired him and one who merely wanted to stroke his ego. Being the third son of a laird, he'd experienced plenty of girls trying their hand at deceiving him with false affection in the hope of securing a future by his side.

Helena had trembled against him and offered him innocent little kisses that were enough to burn away any sense of control he had. All he wanted to do was go back into that chamber and kiss her until she shivered again.

The candles had burned low in the bedchamber. Keir opened the door slowly, taking care that the hinges wouldn't squeak. It was a fine chamber, the windows hung with velvet and the bed canopy made of rich brocade. There was a fireplace but it was cold because the staff hadn't realized that they were getting a new master.

The bed was empty.

Keir swept through the room, stopping when he found the cause of his mental dilemma. Small wet spots marked the silk beneath her cheek, but the smile on her lips made his own curve up. Maybe he was a fool to care about a woman at all; there were plenty of men who would tell him that.

But he enjoyed knowing she was in his care.

Aye, the knowledge settled a great deal of his unsettled thoughts. There would be plenty of time to discover what caused her tears. They were not the first couple who married while still mostly strangers. Pulling a blanket from the bed, he covered her with it. She looked too content to move and there was a part of him that wanted to join her in that bed too much to risk carrying her there.

He was not sure he had enough self-discipline to walk away.

"You imbecile." Edmund Knyvett, heir to the Earl of Kenton, felt fear creep into his heart for the first time in a very long time. He was not a man who feared. In fact, he was not a man who worried very often. His place was secured and he had been born to it by divine decision.

"It was such a simple plan. I sent her right into your hands!"

"Well, that Scot took her out of my hands!" Lord Ronchford snarled and reached up to gingerly test the lump on the top of his head. He winced and cursed. "I want my money returned."

"No. I did what I promised. The money is mine. It is not my fault you couldn't conclude the transaction on your end."

"Now see here!"

Edmund hit the table with a fist. His men leaned forward, lending their weight to his side of the argument. "I did what I promised."

"But I didn't get to marry her." Ronchford's eyes glowed with his rage. He lowered his voice and leaned forward to keep his words from carrying across the tavern.

"Don't cross me. You'll regret it. I swear that on my mother's tits."

Edmund looked down his nose at the man. "As I said. I completed my obligation. This business matter is finished."

He stood up and left, never looking back. He was a peer. It was not his responsibility to get Helena to the church. For Christ's sake, he'd managed to get her to run off into London in the dead of night. All in all, his little sibling had managed to deliver a fortune into his keeping. It was a shame that the king wanted her wed in the morning. With a few more months and another parchment bearing his father's seal, he might be able to sell her a few more times.

Well, what mattered was the gain he'd managed to get for the trouble of housing her. Maybe in a few years he might pressure the Scot to do his bidding. All in the interest of Edmund using his position to ensure a good place for his nephews at court. Even the Scot would bend for that. Even the proudest man crumpled when it came to his family. Once Helena was bred, he'd have an entire new bunch of opportunities to exploit.

Chapter Seven

"Mistress?"

Helena frowned. No one ever called her mistress.

"Mistress? Forgive me, but you must rise."

Helena opened her eyes. A young maid stood in front of her. The girl was dressed neatly in a fine wool livery dress, each button on her doublet shiny and untarnished. A crisply ironed apron was pinned neatly over her chest and a linen cap covered her head.

"The queen has sent a carriage for you, mistress. You must rise immediately. The royal guards are waiting."

She must still be dreaming. But her vision showed her the same finely adorned room. Only a hint of light was coming through the open windows, the sun not yet fully risen. The girl fiddled with her apron, clearly agitated.

"Helena."

Keir's voice was too strong to be in her dreams. The only tone she heard in her dreams was his teasing one, not this hard one.

She sat up, jerking her head around toward the door. He was frowning at her, distaste in his eyes, but there was something else that cleared the slumber from her mind, because she wanted to understand what it was.

He hid it behind a stern mask before she figured it out. Keir was already wearing his kilt, but the doublet she'd always seen him in was missing. All that covered his chest was a shirt, and the cuffs were rolled up his forearms, allowing her a look at the clearly defined muscles.

"The queen sent an escort for ye."

"Why would she do such a thing?" Helena stood up, rubbing at her forehead. She was cramped from lying in her long stays and hip roll. The center of her back ached when she moved.

"Because we are to wed in the presence of the king and queen."

"Wed? You were telling me the truth?"

Her question was insulting, but not by design. Keir frowned at her, clearly disliking the slight. The maid looked at the floor and did her best to appear invisible. Keir crossed the distance between them and her belly tightened. Her body instantly responded to his—it was immediate and uncontrollable.

"I have never lied to ye."

And he didn't like having his honor questioned. She heard it in his tone, but she also felt it in her heart. A little bubble of joy appeared to ease the ache she'd fallen asleep with. The tarnish on his gallant image was rubbed off in her mind.

"But Edmund told me . . ." She shook her head. "Of course he lied. Another scheme. . . ." It shouldn't hurt, but it did.

"Yer brother told ye what?"

Keir was still hiding behind an expression devoid of clues to his true mood.

"It doesn't appear to matter."

He stepped closer. "I disagree. I would enjoying hearing what yer brother said that sent ye out into the night if it wasnae that you and I were to wed this morning."

She saw the hurt flicker in his eyes. It was surprising, because she'd never have guessed that anything she did might injure his emotions. He cupped her chin in a warm hand.

"Who did ye run away from, Helena?"

"Edmund said I was to wed Ronchford this morning." Just saying it made her shiver. But Keir had another response. Pleasure lit his eyes, spilling over to cover his face. A firm look of satisfaction entered his eyes.

Jerking away from his hold, she moved several paces across the chamber. The maid took the opportunity to flee the room. A tingle went down her nape when she realized, almost keenly, that she was alone with him once again. She seemed to have no ability to control her wicked thoughts when they were close. "That does not mean I was running to you."

Her pride fueled the comment—that and the need to hold on to some part of herself. She felt crushed beneath the weight of so many hands pushing her toward what they wanted.

"Is that so?"

Keir crossed his arms over his chest, his face returning to that unreadable mask. "Well now, I suppose 'tis a grand thing that I didna trust yer brother to keep his word, else ye would be spread out on Ronchford's bed this morning."

It was a blunt thing to say aloud. Helena lifted her chin in the face of it. But her cheeks colored in spite of her posture. "All that much better for ensuring that I end up in yours."

His eyes darkened with promise. Her belly twisted in response. The desire she'd battled last night rekindled to lick across her skin.

"I'll no' deny it." He stalked her, chasing her across the chamber. She stiffened when she realized that she was retreating and forced her feet to stand still. But he enjoyed the show of courage, approval glimmering in his eyes when he reached her, and all she did was tilt her head up so that their gazes remained fused.

"But ye're nae as unhappy about the prospect of sharing my bed as yer words would like me to believe."

He stroked her cheek and a shudder shot down her back. She felt her face turning hot beneath his fingers.

"I dinnae think I ever noticed a blush so much as I do on ye." His fingers smoothed over her cheek, his dark eyes intent on the patch of bright skin. His face told her that he liked what he saw and she suddenly felt pretty.

"That blush tells me ye're thinking about me, just as I'm thinking about you."

"That does not mean we should wed."

He crossed his arms over his chest again. The posture was a warning that his mind was not going to be changed.

"Nay, the parchment that I won from yer sniveling brother says ye're to be my wife and I dinnae care very much about the means."

"You won me?" She choked out the words.

"Aye, at cards." His voice was as solemn as a mourning bell. But he offered her a kind look when her eyes widened in shock. "It doesna matter, Helena. What's important is that ye will no' return to yer brother's keeping and ye won't have to risk yer safety by running through the night."

"Because I shall be wed to you."

He crossed his arms again. "Scotland is nae as bad as the gossip paints it."

He assumed that her objection was to his country, but Helena was held in the grip of wondering how to keep her heart from becoming his possession. It was one of the only things she had that was hers alone. He was the only man who seemed to stir such deep emotions inside her.

That terrified her.

"Go on, Helena. Dinnae make me put ye in that carriage.

Even if I were opposed to this marriage, I'd have to obey my king. Just as ye do."

"How could you be opposed to something that you have obviously gone to great lengths to ensure?"

She didn't wait for his reply. Part of her hoped that there would be no carriage waiting for her, but that shattered when she entered the entryway of the town home. Royal guards stood there, their livery a mark of their authority. To wear the uniform was a death sentence if you didn't truly serve the royal guard.

She sighed. There was nothing but to go forward. Taking the hand offered, she climbed into the closed carriage. Such a vehicle was very expensive. It was completely closed, even the curtains drawn over the windows.

But the seats were plush and comfortable. She settled against them, stroking a hand over the fine fabric.

The carriage rocked. Helena looked toward the door to see Keir angling his wide frame through the doorway. He cast a frustrated look at the interior ceiling before taking up the entire other side of the carriage with his larger frame.

"You're going to the palace without a doublet?"

He flashed her a grin and nodded to the footman to close the door.

"I'm going to the palace with you, my sweet lass." She shivered, because his voice had become soft and teasing. This was the man she allowed into her dreams, and her body was quite willing to remind her of how much she did dream of him.

"Because I think 'tis a shame that we've no' had the chance to circle one another."

Excitement rippled through her. She pushed it aside, trying to ignore it, but the promise lurking in his eyes made it nearly impossible.

"I don't know what you mean."

The carriage jerked and began moving. Keir reached across the space between them and easily captured her upper arms. A soft squeal passed her lips as the man lifted her right off the seat and onto his reclining body.

"Och now, I know ye don't. Which is exactly why I need to spend a wee bit of time introducing ye to the delights of anticipation."

"Anticipation of what?"

His mouth sealed out everything, this kiss more demanding than the ones he'd teased her with last night. Her hands were flat against his chest and the shirt he wore did little to mask the heat coming from his skin. She'd never noticed that a man might smell nice. Keir did. The scent invaded her senses, clouding her thinking.

But it was his kiss that destroyed her last bit of sanity, his mouth taking hers in a kiss that was demanding, but sweetly so. She twisted, unsure of how to deal with the delight. He didn't capture the back of her head but followed her, tilting his head to fit his mouth against hers. Her heart raced, making it difficult to draw in enough breath. She lifted her chin to escape from his mouth.

"Keir . . ."

He trailed his kisses down her neck. Pleasure shot down her body from the touch. His lips were so hot against her skin, and why had she never noticed how sensitive her neck was?

"I want to take ye home to Red Stone where I can steal ye away into the tall grass for a bit of play. The sort of games that lovers enjoy when the spring is warm and the grass sweet enough for rolling in."

His hand cupped the back of her neck, holding her still. He placed two delicate bites on the skin and she shuddered. A soft growl rumbled from his chest, drawing her eyes back to his. Passion burned there. It was hot and needy, just like the tension pooling in her belly. She had never been so aware of her breasts or the way that they were flattened by her stays. The mounds felt trapped behind clothing that was suddenly uncomfortable. Every inch of her skin begged to be free.

Begged to be bare for his hands to glide across . . .

"Keir . . . You shouldn't . . ."

"Shouldn't touch ye? Why not, Helena? 'Tis what we both longed for within the first few moments that our eyes met."

He cradled her body with a firm arm beneath her knees. He laid her back so that her bottom touched the seat beside him but he kept her legs across his lap.

" 'Tis nae common, this sort of attraction."

"Which is why it should not be given too much attention. Passion leads to sin."

He undid the first few buttons on her doublet. "Och now, that's nonsense, seeing as how we are going to be wed in a few hours."

"You believe what I think is nonsense?"

He spread the open edges of her doublet apart. The morning air swept over her skin, drawing a sigh from her. She wanted to sink back into the flood of sensation and leave the talking behind. The pleasure called to her, tempting her with its rich intoxication.

"Nay, but I do think ye spend too much time fighting yer own nature. Ye want me to touch ye. I see it in yer eyes. And I am no' a blackguard set on spoiling ye. I'll wed ye gladly."

His fingers trailed over the tops of her breasts. She jerked and fisted her hands in her skirts as sensation shot through her. A little gasp passed her lips and she heard him chuckle in response.

"That is no nonsense, lass. It is pure passion. I'm going to enjoy showing ye its way."

He leaned down and pressed a kiss against the swell of one breast. It was too much. She arched upward, unable to contain all the pleasure. It tore through her and she danced over the flame. His lips were so hot, they burned over the swell of one breast until he reached the valley of her cleavage. The tip of his tongue traced the seam where her breasts met, slowly licking deeper. Between her thighs her passage suddenly felt empty. It was bluntly carnal but she couldn't shy away from it, either. Hidden somewhere beneath the fold of his kilt was the hard flesh that would ease that emptiness.

"Tonight I am going to discover what shade yer nipples are."

"Keir! You can't say things like that."

He lifted his head, his lips curved into a roguish grin. "And why not? I'm intent on gaining the church's blessing on our union aren't I?"

"Yes, but talk such as that is wicked."

He chuckled, the sound deep and male. She seemed to notice so much about him that was different from her own female gender, as though they were fashioned to fit against one another.

"Did yer father raise ye to be one of these puritans? Intent on no' enjoying anything life has to offer?"

She laughed. "Obviously you do not understand puritans. They shun face paint and silk dresses, among other things that they consider vanities."

He touched her face, tenderly trailing his fingers over her jawline. "I may need to convert. I cannae wait to see ye bare of all this court fashion." He reached up, poking softly at one of the pads her hair was still rolled over. "The thought of seeing ye with yer hair flowing down over yer shoulders haunts me."

Something in his tone sounded needy. But the look on his

face humbled her. She felt so beautiful just witnessing the way he looked at her. She reached up, drawn to him. Her hand hesitantly stroked over his jaw, absorbing the texture of his skin. His eyes closed to slits, enjoyment shining in them.

"Touch me." His voice was husky and so tempting. It was liberating, too, granting her the chance to choose what she wanted.

"I'm not sure how. . . ."

But she longed to do it. Her hands smoothed over his chin and onto his neck, her fingertips slipping over the warm male skin until she reached the collar of his shirt. She froze when he rubbed a hand over her thigh. Even through the fabric of her skirts the touch set off another round of need from her passage. This time she felt a pulsing need from the folds of her sex. One, small point pressed between the delicate tissues, swelling and demanding the touch of his hand.

"I am going to enjoy allowing ye to learn, Helena."

"You want me to . . . to be a bold wife?" Wicked and tempting, the idea caught fire inside her.

"Aye."

His mouth took hers with a hunger that stole her breath. All teasing was missing from the kiss. He took her mouth and thrust his tongue in deeply, invading and stroking along hers until she mimicked his motions with her own. His hand cupped the back of her head, holding her prisoner while the kiss continued. Heat rose between them until she hated her dress, hated the shirt keeping her fingers from making contact with his skin. She clawed at his shoulders, a faint tearing sound startling her.

It drew a chuckle from Keir. He lifted his head, grinning at her. His expression was too full of arrogance.

She slapped him on the broad chest that fascinated her too much.

"You are toying with me."

"Not so. But it's the truth that I'm hoping I've heated ye up enough to share my frustration with ye."

He pulled her up onto his lap once more; the way he moved her so effortlessly, she shivered.

He smoothed a hand down her back in response. "Are ye truly frightened of sharing my bed?"

She longed for it. . . .

Helena bit her lip, shocked yet excited by her thoughts. He snarled softly, frustrated by her silence. He buried his head against her neck, nuzzling the sensitive skin and placing soft kisses against her throat.

The carriage stopped and she heard him mutter in Gaelic.

"I suppose ye'll be leaving me to wonder why ye shuddered and no' answered."

"Does it matter? This carriage confirms that I must wed you."

He sat her on the opposite seat, his face set back into a blank expression.

"It matters to me, and I will know why ye wept last night. I swear it."

The door opened and pain pierced her heart for disappointing him. That was the one thing she dare not risk telling him. It was the only fear she had because it was the only thing that she could count as her own. She did not enjoying seeing him unhappy with her silence. He frowned, reading her refusal from her face. But his eyes glittered with renewed challenge.

"All right then, Helena. Do yer best to push me away, but I'm giving ye fair warning that I will not budge. Ye belong to me."

The queen's chambers . . .

"Well now. Ye are wedding the man who made ye blush after all." Raelin McKorey was forcing a smile onto her lips. Helena knew it because she recognized the strain in her eyes. Raelin dabbed another brush into a face powder but Helena raised her hand to keep the girl from lifting it.

"Unless you plan to paint me like the first day you met me, put that brush away."

Raelin nodded, her eyes settling on the purple bruises her efforts had failed to mask. "Yer brother is a horrible man."

She didn't lower her voice, nor was there any misgiving in her voice. Catriona McAlister nodded in agreement. "I dinnae care if the man will inherit an earldom. I'll nae even dance with him ever again."

Catriona reached for the cloth draped around Helena's shoulders. "Come now. We need to dress ye for yer wedding."

It was an event that Helena had heard so much about throughout her childhood. It felt rather surreal to be preparing for her wedding, because the steps were so normal. The girls pulled her simple doublet and wool skirt from her. A blue silk gown was brought forward for her to wear. It wasn't overdone with lace and pleats. The simplicity of it was what charmed her but she would have worn it in spite of detesting the reason it was given to her. It was a gift from the queen, one of Her Majesty's own dresses.

"You do not need anything else, Helena. A bride should be simple and sweet with her own charms. You are quite beautiful."

"Thank you, Your Majesty."

Anne of Denmark, queen of Scotland and England, smiled at her. She reached for a silver brush and carried it over to Helena herself in spite of her ladies trying to intercede.

"You must wear your hair down."

"Oh, yes." Raelin pulled the pins out eagerly. The queen began to pull the brush through her hair, gently untangling it. So many hands touched her, tending her. Time flew past and there was no more time to think or ponder.

Not that it would have mattered. Her life was moving forward in its habit of taking her along no matter what she wanted.

But there was part of her that looked forward to seeing Keir at the altar. That part of her that had felt Ronchford's rough hands on her breasts rejoiced at knowing Keir would never allow another to touch her.

No, the arrogant man considered her his.

She saw it shining in his eyes when he saw her enter the private chapel used only by the royal family. His gaze touched hers, sending a bolt of awareness through her just as he had done the first time she looked into his eyes.

Only this time she knew what she craved.

At least she had picked a fine man to want. He was a sight to behold in black doublet and kilt. There was not a man in brocade or silk damask that she considered his equal. It was the nobility, the pure intensity of his spirit that made him so.

Edmund stood near the altar, his expression carefully smooth. The small chapel was filled to near bursting with Keir's men and her brother's men all watched over by the king's royal guard. Tension filled the air, tightening as she approached the altar. The bishop, dressed in his black robe and white smock, glanced nervously around before a quick motion from the king's hand made the man begin the ceremony. He mumbled through the first set of prayers and rushed on to the vows faster than she had ever witnessed. In a remarkably short amount of time, she was wed.

* * *

Helena sighed. She drew a deep breath, savoring the moment of privacy. Sneaking away from her own reception proved simpler than she'd thought. The court was only using her wedding as another excuse to flirt and observe one another. It might have been a feast day or birthday celebration. All that seemed to matter was that there was music, food, and the royal couple in attendance. She crept away into the hallways for a few moments alone.

"Nothing good will come of this marriage."

Edmund emerged from an archway. He moved silently, placing every step artfully.

"Enough, Edmund. It is done."

He shook his head, snickering at her. For all that she had heard the sound many, many times before, it agitated her.

"I said enough, Edmund. Your schemes must end now or move on to someone else. I am a wife now."

"Nothing is done until the union is consummated." He tsked at her. "Sweet little ignorant sister of mine." His amusement suddenly died. "Unless that Scot plowed you last night."

Her face burned. "It would serve you right if he did. Ronchford is a horrible man, Edmund. How could you send me to him?"

She shouldn't care, but couldn't seem to keep the hurt from her tone. She had tried so hard to be agreeable with her brother. It was difficult to absorb how little he cared for their blood connection.

"He is a rich man with many more powerful men owing him money and favors." Edmund sneered at her, uncaring of the torment his words inflicted. "Marriage is about power, not whether or not you like the man."

"Did you sell me to him? As you gambled me away to Keir?" She wanted to hear him say it, so that she might never again think of him kindly. Blood or no blood.

"Of course. I'm rather pleasantly surprised that I was able to arrange two transactions for the same sister. Much less disappointing than I first imagined it would be when you were delivered onto my doorstep."

"You are a monster, Edmund. I swear I will never think of you as my brother again."

"But I am your brother, little sister, and it would be in your best interests to obey me." He cast a glance about, making sure they were still alone. "Think about your children. When they come to this court, they will need their titled uncle to pave the way for them."

She choked on her horror because she could not say it did not matter. Family connections were what made it possible to succeed. It was not fair, but neither was life.

"Excellent. You have finally realized that listening to me is the best course of action." He leaned closer. "Refuse to consummate your union."

"What are you talking about? The man is my husband by royal command."

"And a little-known titled Scot who only wants to better himself through breeding you. Refuse him so that I have grounds to annul your marriage. The king is a businessman; he will come around in time. This will not be the first marriage he has annulled. I need your virginity to stand up to a midwife's inspection."

Anticipation showed in Edmund's eyes. It was ugly and greedy, sickening her.

"I am done being your property, Edmund." She lifted her chin. "You sold me. Twice."

He shook his head. "Don't let that itch between your thighs make you do something you will live to regret, Helena. You are a peer. I can wed you to a far more powerful man. Think of your children. Don't let that Scot dilute your blue blood with his common stock."

The cold-bloodedness of her brother's word froze her. She was naught but a possession to him.

"I am wed, Edmund, and I want nothing to do with you."

He reached for her, his hand curling around her upper arm. She barely had time to feel the compression of his grasp before he was stumbling across the stone floor.

"My wife spoke plainly enough. Dinnae touch her. Nae ever again."

Keir's voice was deadly. She turned her attention to stare at him. She thought his body strong, felt that strength but never really understood how deadly he might be. She was witnessing it now, the side of men that women only heard about in hushed tones, as he stood in front of her. This was the part of him that could kill for what he believed in.

"Do you really think I am afraid of you, Scot? I am the earl of Kenton!"

"Nae yet, ye aren't, and if fate has any sense of justice, ye never will be. I swear I hope that becomes so. Ye have no honor."

A startled gasp from the shadows invaded their conversation. Catriona McAlister stood there with a hand covering her open mouth, clearly hearing Keir's words. Taken alone, they were harsh indeed.

"You have some nerve to threaten me, Scot. There are laws here in England. Don't think to get my title through marriage to my sister."

A royal guard stood next to Catriona, frowning. The horror of seeing suspicion on his face sent her belly to cramping. Edmund held too much power.

Too much.

* * *

Keir didn't ride in the carriage with her on the way back to his town home. But he was so close, she could actually feel him watching the carriage. A peek out the curtains showed her his men, all riding in formation around the carriage. Under different circumstances, she might have felt honored by their escort. Tonight, all she felt was guarded.

Not that she should be surprised. Most noble weddings were about the business transactions between the families. The bride, and many times the groom, had little concern over their personal feelings for one another. Edmund was nauseatingly correct about that.

It also wasn't uncommon for the bride to be guarded like a chest of jewels. Helena snorted. There was no one about to hear the ungentle sound and she indulged herself in the chance to simply be grumpy.

You don't completely dislike the situation. . . .

She growled at her own thoughts. Behind her stays her nipples tingled, little feathers of sensation drawing slowly over the sensitive skin. If that was lust, she lusted for Keir. Her nipples drew into hard buttons, craving freedom from her clothing. She fingered a lock of her hair. It lay over her shoulder in a long, untied and unbraided length. It was amazing how free it felt to be without pins and rolls. Somehow, she felt more feminine than ever before.

The carriage stopped, rocking slowly back and forth before coming to a rest. The footman opened the door, but it was her new husband who offered her a hand to use for balance.

She remembered that hand being offered to her . . .

But they were not alone. She took his hand, conscious of his men watching her. They lined the walkway to the town home, and where they ended, the staff had appeared to take up positions honoring her arrival as the mistress. Each one of his men stood proudly. They inclined their heads when she passed.

Well . . . she did not disappoint her family when she walked down their length. It was all the years of practice keeping her chin level and her back straight. But sweat trickled down her back. Tension clawed at her but she kept it hidden behind a serene expression.

But her thoughts were settling on the man holding her hand. Somehow, in spite of all the terrible reasons why he was the one escorting her into his home, she was pleased with who it was. It was a confusing idea—one that made her sneak a peek at him while she struggled to understand just how she should feel about being won in a game of cards.

He was pleased.

There was no other way to describe the expression on his face and it went deeper, into his dark eyes. Something flickered there, a flare of heat that sent more sweat down her back. Determination shone from his eyes, and her belly tightened.

"Mistress."

"This is Terri. She won't be showing ye to an attic."

He spoke proudly. But her cheeks colored. It was Edmund's shame, but she still felt the weight of it anyway.

"This way, mistress. We've a bath ready for ye."

Keir didn't release her hand immediately. His fingers tightened, drawing her attention to his face. Promise flickered in his eyes as hard and overwhelming as his body. She pulled on her hand, craving distance from yet more demands.

She dropped him a curtsy before keeping her eyes on the ground and following the housekeeper. If that was cowardly, so be it. She was too tired to be anything else. But it wasn't a fatigue brought on by a longing for sleep. Even knowing that her wedding day would be the end of negotiation and family bartering, she was still slightly nauseated by the process.

It would be very easy to begin thinking like a piece of property instead of a person. But she refused to give up that single thing that was still hers. Even if it might be far simpler to drift along with the currents that were dragging her.

Chapter Eight

"I've spent a fair amount of time thinking about you looking just like that."

A man's voice shouldn't be able to send such excitement through a body. At least it would be much better if Helena didn't find Keir's tone so delicious, so husky and steely strong. She was tempted to allow it to help hold her up.

He had bathed as well, the firelight that danced off the water making his hair shiny. He moved forward, his steps silent. Only the fire crackled and a faint howl of wind came through the closed shutters. It was a luxurious room, to be sure, but all she seemed to notice was the man intent on sharing it with her.

His gaze moved over her hair. It was dry and she'd brushed it into a fluffy mass of silk lying over one shoulder. She had never considered her hair anything unique. Blond and red hair gained attention. Hers had always been too dark. But Keir liked it. His face reflected his pleasure. He reached out and fingered a lock.

"I hope ye never put those things back in it. Ye're a fair bonnie sight now that all that powder and paint is nae on yer skin to hide the beauty beneath. I am drawn to ye as ye are, no' some ideal made up by men who spend too much time judging the people around them."

It was by far the most tender compliment she had ever received. No rhyming couplet or comparisons to Greek goddesses. It was simple, and for the first time she believed it.

"I suppose it is a good thing you like who you have married."

He frowned but didn't answer quickly. Instead he walked toward the bed and leaned his sword up against the wall, leaving the brass handle within easy reach of the bed. He'd taken the side nearest the door, and she noticed it. Another ripple of emotion went through her. No one had ever placed themselves in front of her unless they were paid by her father to do so.

Keir did it because of who he was.

He'd shrugged into his shirt while still wet. Patches of the linen stuck to his torso, giving her a glimpse at the hard ridges of muscles beneath the garment. Heat licked over her skin and it had nothing to do with the fire burning near her feet.

He turned and caught her looking at him. Her fingers fumbled the brush handle and she set it aside before she embarrassed herself further by dropping it.

The man's ego didn't need that much stroking.

"I suppose I cannae blame ye for nae trusting me, even if I wish otherwise."

"Trust?" Her voice was a whisper, but full of emotion. It would be so easy to believe in him, but that would only set her up for misery when he left her for a mistress. She didn't doubt that it would happen. The man had won her playing at cards and her worth was in parchment and what she brought him. Once she was breeding, he'd be finished with her. It was normal and expected, but it hurt her to see Keir standing near the bed she would lose her chastity in. She had wanted to keep him in her heart as her gallant knight. Reality would shatter that dream tonight.

"Aye, trust me, lass."

He reached for her but she struck his hand away before contact was made. His eyes flickered with his displeasure and her temper gave her the strength to banish her longings.

"I do not *have* to trust." She hugged her arms over her chest, covering her nipples. The conflict between the longings of her flesh and the irritation in her mind was becoming so loud, she wouldn't be surprised if she woke up insane once the night had passed. "Trust is the only thing that is mine to give. Everyone is so intent on telling me what I must do, what I shall do and what is expected of me. But trust is not something that is given, *husband.*"

She drew a stiff breath, banishing the stinging tears that were threatening to fall down her cheeks again. "Even when your men and my king ensure that I am yours for the taking, my trust is the thing that shall be locked away from you all."

She forced her arms to unclasp. Reaching down, she grasped her chemise and drew it up and over her head. She felt the brush of the night air against her skin from head to toe, and the heat from the fire behind her. "But the maid who dallies with the stable boy is far richer than she ever imagined, for I envy her wealth of choices."

His face tightened. A muscle on the corner of his jaw twitched. She held her chin level. She wasn't afraid of him, only sick of conforming to everyone's dictates. His gaze touched on her face and the resignation there. He didn't care for it; she witnessed it in his eyes. He wanted something more from her.

"Well now, that is where we disagree again, because trust is something that is given. 'Tis a sweet gift."

"You are speaking of surrender."

His gaze left her face. He tried to fight the urge to look at her nude body but lost. It fascinated her to see him so beaten by his own urges. Somehow it hinted at a power she hadn't thought she held. Some small form of controlling influence by which he was weakened.

"Aye, lass, I am talking about surrender, but nae a cold one. I didna go searching for yer brother to win ye. I went looking for him to smash my fist into his face for hitting ye. But I am no' going to quibble over how I gained what we've both been dancing about since looking at each other. I witnessed the desire burning just as hot in yer eyes as I felt in my own blood."

After all the subterfuge and deceit of court, the simple honesty of Keir's words sparked an undeniable need for him, and she regretted her harsh words. She wanted him and it was allowed now. Letting the details interfere would only hurt her and Keir. He watched her, his dark eyes stormy and unhappy with her. She felt it keenly.

"I'm . . . not cold . . . toward you, Keir."

The muscle on the side of his jaw flexed. She stared at the little throbbing point, her hands moving up to cover her bare breasts. She felt exposed now that she'd admitted she wanted him.

He captured one hand, gripping it in his larger one.

"Nay, I'm the one who's doing things badly. I'm acting like a lad instead of showing ye the way to proceed."

He carried her hand to his lips. Turning her hand over, he pressed a kiss against the tender skin of her inner wrist. A moment later he grazed that delicate skin with his teeth. She gasped, a startled sound passing her lips. She jerked her arm, but not out of any true desire to be free. It was simply a reaction, her body moving without any thought behind the motion.

A deep chuckle rumbled from his chest. "Aye, you are nae cold to me." His thumb rubbed over her inner wrist, smoothing through the tiny wet patch of skin.

"A bit uneasy, to be sure, but that's my duty to soothe. A pure delight, because it tells me that ye are pure. 'Tis a gift that I am humbled by, lass. Never doubt that."

He meant it. His tone was tender but determined. She let herself get swept up in that tone. It was the one her gallant knight used in her dreams.

"I promise to spend more time courting ye, Helena."

He swung her off her feet, drawing another gasp from her. "Why do you pick me up? I'm not trying to avoid my duties."

"I enjoy carrying ye." He placed her in the center of the bed, satisfaction flickering in his eyes. "But the idea of chasing ye is interesting, too. I do believe I'd enjoy following ye a great deal."

He sounded like a boy—a naughty, mischievous one, at that. "I run fast."

"So do I, but I confess that I just might slow up enough to trail behind ye for a good long while if ye're planning to run as ye are." His gaze swept down her bare length. "Nude."

"Stop your playing." She reached for the turned-down covers. But her husband taunted her by lying down across them. She suddenly felt on display, and drew her knees up to conceal her breasts.

"Dinnae do that. Ye are stunning, Helena."

He sat back up and hooked his fingers into his shirt. The collar was already open, allowing him to pull the garment over his head with one smooth motion. The unveiling of his skin captured her attention, drawing her thoughts away from her own modesty. He was covered in muscle—hard ridges of it ran over his chest. Dark hair coated the wide expanse, trailing down to where his kilt covered him. His belt was undone but still lying around his waist. Her cheeks colored when she realized that he'd unbuckled it while she was lost in admiring his chest. But he'd left his kilt in place to avoid spooking her.

The fact that he felt she needed coddling annoyed her. She realized that she didn't want to lie back and be taken. Ideas swirled through her mind, touching off demands from her body. Keir watched her, his dark eyes focused on her. But his hand was gripping the covers beneath his hand.

"Go on." Her voice had turned husky.

He raised one dark eyebrow. Helena sat up, facing him. She kept her arms down, so that her breasts were fully visible.

"I'm not a coward."

"I didna think ye were." His expression turned hard. "But there is no reason to rush."

"If you are so relaxed, why are you twisting the bedding?"

His fingers tightened even more. "Because I'm trying not to pounce on ye."

Helena laughed. Keir looked perplexed by her amusement, but he was not annoyed. Confusion covered his face and she shrugged.

"Men do not pounce."

"Maybe nae in England. But be very sure that I am a Scot, lassie."

His voice had deepened, along with his brogue. It was the only warning she received. A mountain of muscle surged toward her, the bed swaying beneath her back as he pinned her down.

"We Scots tend to be a wee bit more physical."

"I . . . see . . . that."

She turned her head from side to side, completely overwhelmed by the contact of skin on skin. His chest pressed against her torso, covering her. But he caught most of his weight on his elbows, leaving just enough to send need coursing through her.

"I was hoping to be able to prove it to ye. One touch at a time." His lips grazed the side of her throat. She quivered, never having suspected that one kiss might cause such a riot of feeling.

"But I'm a selfish man. Impatient it seems, too."

"What?" His words confused her. Speaking annoyed her. She turned her head to lock stares with him.

"I want yer hands on me. I swear I'll wait all night if that's what it takes for ye to relax enough to touch me like ye were in the carriage."

Her hands moved up his arms instantly. She didn't think about it—she didn't need to. His eyes narrowed with enjoyment, and as she stroked up to his shoulders, she watched the way his face reflected his delight.

"I did that after you kissed me."

"Och well, if I'd done that again, waiting would be out of the question." His voice was playful but she saw a contradiction in his eyes. Passion burned there and it touched off an answering hunger deep in her belly.

"I agree." Her lower lip was dry. She licked it and froze when his eyes moved to follow the tip of her tongue.

"Do that again." His voice sounded strained, as if his control was being tested. "On second thought, allow me."

He leaned down, closing the distance between them. She suddenly felt as if she had waited forever for his kiss—had, in fact, been anticipating it since the moment the carriage arrived at the palace.

It was worth the wait.

His mouth teased hers, the tip of his tongue sweeping across her lower lip. Sweet delight rippled down her body, igniting the hunger he'd left her with earlier. There was no question about it. Passion rose hot and thick to claim her back into its grasp. The hair on his chest felt good against her skin. She noticed how hard he was compared to her softness. Her breasts gently compressed beneath the body of her lover. It felt so good that she wiggled, gently rubbing herself against him.

A low growl shook his chest and his kiss changed. It deepened, his tongue thrusting into her mouth to slide around her own. A shiver shook her, sending a soft moan past their joined lips.

Heat radiated from him and from her as well. Even with the fire far across the room, she didn't feel the chill of the night. The wool of his kilt was tangled between them. Her skin was alive with a magnitude of sensations, all of them heightened to far above normal. The fabric felt coarse and she lifted one leg to escape it. Keir reached down to grip her knee and bring it farther up. It spread her thighs, giving his hips a space to settle into. Her other knee bent, making room for his larger frame.

He didn't rush to penetrate her. His fingers smoothed over the skin of her thigh, rubbing in a slow motion that sent pleasure racing toward the open folds of her sex. At the top of her sex a point began to pulse. It throbbed with longing, begging for Keir's hand to move toward it.

"Yer breasts are beautiful, lass." He moved down her body, placing soft kisses on her neck and then on her collarbone. "I swear it's a good thing we're wed because I've spent too much time thinking about sucking these sweet nipples."

His breath teased her nipple and it drew even harder. He cupped it, gently closing his hand around the soft mound. When his lips closed around it, she moaned. His mouth was so hot it burned, but she arched upward, offering her nipple to him.

Keir took complete advantage of her invitation, closing his mouth around her nipple. He sucked hard on it, the drawing motion increasing the heat. Desire pooled in her belly, making her aware of how empty her passage was. She was achy with the need to be filled. The fabric of his kilt frustrated her because it separated her from what she craved. She writhed beneath him, seeking to slip between the fabric and his warm skin. Reaching down, she grasped at the wool, tugging on it with fingers curled into talons.

"When we agree, 'tis a glorious thing, lassie."

His voice was dark and full of promise. He rose up above her and yanked his kilt aside with a long sweep of his hand. He didn't give her a chance to view his length. He covered her again, settling between her spread thighs. She reached for him, running her hands up his arms, her fingertips exploring the hard ridges her eyes had enjoyed so much. Feeling them was tenfold more enjoyable. Everything about the moment was a feast for the senses. Thought disappeared while touch, scent, and emotion took command. Lifting her head, she kissed his neck, pressing her lips against the skin that felt so warm and smelled so very male.

His chest rumbled with a growl and it made her bolder. Straining up against the weight of his body, she kissed his chin. The need to kiss him drove her. She didn't want to lie back and receive, she wanted to press her lips against his and initiate the pleasure.

Keir waited for her, remaining still while she angled her face so that their lips could meet. He didn't take command of the kiss. His lips only followed hers. Clasping her hands around the top of his shoulders, she strained upward to keep her lips connected with his.

He suddenly rolled, taking her along with him. The bed was wide enough to allow him to settle all the way onto his back with her on top of him. Her thighs remained spread, her own weight pressing her down on top of him. He threaded his fingers through her hair, spreading the long strands out before gripping it around his fist. Tiny pricks of pain traveled along her scalp but it mixed with the need flowing through her blood, heightening everything again.

"Kiss me, Helena."

It was an order, but deep in his eyes she saw the plea. He was a proud man but not an arrogant one.

"Kiss me because ye want to, lass."

She touched one fingertip to his lips instead. He shuddered, the motion moving along his body and up into hers. His hands left her waist to cup the sides of her bottom. Male satisfaction burned brightly in his eyes.

No one had ever touched her bottom.

Not that she could recall.

Keir tightened his grip before rubbing slowly over each rounded cheek. He watched her while he did it. His gaze lacked the possessive look she would have expected. Instead there was an inquisitive look, a questioning slant to his eyes that sent color burning along her cheeks.

He chuckled, pressing a kiss against the finger on his lips. A look of experience settled into his eyes that chafed. There appeared to be so much that she didn't understand about her own body. She felt that lack keenly.

Leaning forward, she kissed him. It was nothing soft or hesitant. Holding his head with her hands, she angled her face so that their lips could fit together easily. Keir was finished being docile, too. He took her kiss and met her in the middle, demanding she open her mouth for their tongues to mingle. She shivered, that spot at the top of her sex throbbing harder. His tongue thrust deeply into her mouth and her passage ached for the same treatment, but from something harder.

Keir rolled her over again. This time he settled lower, his hips below her spread sex. She was acutely aware of her passage, in a way she'd never been before. But there was no humiliation. No raging concern for her modesty. Only a need to be closer to her lover.

He smoothed his hand along her inner thigh, spreading her thighs so that his fingers might trail into the moist center of her body.

She cried out, not able to form words any longer. There was too much sensation, too much pleasure. Her heart was racing and her breathing was harsh, trying to keep pace. The first touch made her arch, her entire back straining away from the bed. But his body wouldn't allow her to escape. She clawed at his shoulders, gripping the hard muscle.

But his fingers returned to her open folds, tormenting them with light touches that sent pleasure spiking up her passage. She ached for more. Her eyes slid closed because she just couldn't keep her thoughts on anything but the teasing touches of his fingers. The sound of her own heartbeat filled her ears. His skin felt hot beneath her palms.

He found the spot at the top of her sex that was throbbing. Her eyes opened wide as he settled one thick fingertip on top of it. His face was a mask of tension. She stared at it, both fascinated and apprehensive of the raw hunger displayed there.

"Aye, lass, you're testing me mightily. But I swear I'll no' hurt ye by rushing."

"I'm a maiden. It will hurt. I'm not afraid." No, she was achy and hot. Her hips lifted toward his hand and she gasped when the increase in pressure against his finger sent pleasure through her so sharply that she felt dizzy.

"Aye. But ye will learn to trust me because I didna claim ye the second the church gave me the right." His finger moved, rubbing her clitoris in a motion that nearly drove her insane. "First I'm going to show ye what delights marriage offers."

"I don't understand."

And her eyes closed because pleasure was twisting and tightening beneath that finger. Her hips jerked upward, grinding against his touch. The need intensified until it was the only thing that she noticed, that pulsing need to lift and grind against his hand. She pulled on his shoulders, desperate to get closer. Suddenly the tension broke in a burst of pleasure so acute, she cried out with it. The delight twisted down her passage and into her belly. She was held frozen in that moment. Time stopped as the pleasure consumed her.

"Now ye understand." A soft kiss pressed against her lips. It was so tender, she felt tears sting the corners of her eyes. His hand was back on her breast, gripping the soft mound and gently pinching the nipple.

But his cock was pressing against her opening, the hard head of it burrowing into the spread folds. She was slick with her own juices, making it easy for him to push forward. Her sheath was tight, the walls protesting his invasion. But her muscles were lax, allowing him to press deeper. Her passage ached and then burned. Her fingers renewed their grip on his shoulders, her back arching away from his possession.

He held her still. She sucked in a deep breath when he withdrew but it hissed through her clenched teeth when he thrust smoothly back into her. This time he gained more depth, her passage screaming against the hard flesh invading it. For a moment the pain ruled her. It was white-hot and blinding. She struggled to escape.

"Shhh . . ."

It was only a sound, combined with soft kisses against her temple. The pain vanished as quickly as it had come. She gasped for breath, trying to relax with his length lodged deep inside her.

Tears eased down her face. She lifted her eyelashes to see her husband's concerned look. It was a deep emotion that burned in his eyes. But she gasped when she realized that her fingernails had cut into his skin. Blood colored her nails and she jerked them away in horror.

"I'm sorry."

"I'm not." His voice was raspy now. All hints of control vanished. "Claw me."

His hips flexed and he drew his cock out of her body.

"Share it with me, Helena."

His eyes glowed and he thrust deeply into her spread body. Her passage took him with only a dull ache. She did as he commanded and dug her nails back into his arms. There was too much sensation to contain inside her. She couldn't remain still, her hips lifting once again to press up tighter against him.

His nostrils flared. It was a tiny movement but her gaze seemed fixated on it. She clawed at him and he snarled softly.

"Dinnae ever submit to me, Helena."

She answered him by meeting his next thrust. Hard and thick, his cock filled her, feeding that need that had gnawed at her since she met him. It wasn't romantic but it was true. She wanted him just like this, deep inside her. Her breath was rough and so was his. His hips flexed and bucked between her thighs. She clasped him to her, trying to hold onto him and keep him deep inside her. There was no reason to keep her eyes open. She wanted to immerse herself in the sensation, the fullness of his flesh filling her, the smooth sliding of their skin as he moved on top of her.

Pleasure tightened her once again. This time it was centered deeper, all the way inside her passage. She was straining up off the bed, striving to help drive his length toward that knot of throbbing sensation. A moan pasted her lips, followed by a second one. The pleasure peeked before it broke again, spearing through her flesh with sensation that was mind-numbing. She twisted in it as if a flame had been put to the bedding. Above her, Keir snarled and ground his cock into her. A series of hot spurts filled her, satisfying the last of her hunger. She didn't know why, only that satisfaction washed over her, leaving every muscle limp. Pleasure lingered as Keir hunched over her, his elbows keeping his chest from crushing her. His chest labored with hard breaths that rasped through his teeth.

He lifted his head, showing her an expression that touched her heart. It was so full of admiration and tender concern that tears eased from her eyes.

"Yer tears bring me to my knees, lass. Dinnae cry. It won't hurt so much again."

He rolled over, leaving her, and she shivered, feeling his withdrawal keenly.

"I understand. . . ." But she didn't understand why she felt deserted.

Keir didn't give her time to investigate her odd feelings. He rolled right out of the bed. The firelight bathed him in scarlet now that the flames had died down. He picked up his kilt while she tried to smother her tears.

Of course he was finished with her. . . .

But he returned to the bed, on the side that his sword was leaning against the wall. He lay back down and slipped an arm under her waist. Pulling her close, he nuzzled against her, kissed the tracks her tears had left on her cheeks.

"I always sleep nearest the door, Helena."

He pressed her cheek down onto his chest. The sound of his heart filled her ear. She sighed, grateful for the excuse to be silent. She noticed how lonely her bed had been. The scent of his skin brought a contentment that pulled her into a slumber that was deep and unburdened by any worries. There was only the embrace of the man holding her.

Nothing else mattered.

*   *   *

Keir didn't sleep immediately. He was too fascinated by the woman in his arms—the soft brush of her breath against his skin, the steady throbbing of her heart—all of the tiny details of life that he had never noticed in a bed partner before. Remaining awake to enjoy it was not a chore. Stroking her smooth shoulder, he closed his eyes. During the night he followed her across the bed. She wiggled out of his embrace and he pulled her back against his body. At dawn he was still tired but a contentment had settled over him that he'd only felt when his mother had been alive.

He did not know what it was, only that he'd kill any man who tried to take Helena from him.

She was his.

Chapter Nine

Helena awoke tired.

She looked at the canopy above her in confusion, the brocade fabric a stark contrast to the attic ceiling. She sat up and the covers fell to her waist. The morning chill hit her chest and her nipples instantly drew tight. She looked down, stunned by the sight of her own coral-tipped breasts uncovered in the morning light.

"Och now. That's nae a good idea, Helena."

The bed rocked and two very male arms reached around her to gather the covers up around her. Her memory returned but she froze when the shutters opened. The young maid pushed the large wooden window covers wide until she latched them to the walls. She dropped a curtsy when she noticed Helena staring at her.

But that wasn't the worst of it. Helena shifted her attention toward the door and found several of his men standing there.

"I suppose I cannae fault ye for nae being accustomed to waking up without a stitch on."

His own lack of clothing didn't seem to bother him in the least. Keir gathered her up along with the covers and carried her out of the bed. His men stepped closer, peering down at the sheets.

Of course . . .

It was a tradition so old no one really knew when it began. Dark stains marred the creamy surface of the sheet. Heat burned in her cheeks in spite of the fact that those stains were exactly what she wanted to see this morning. The maid pulled the sheet free, but one of Keir's retainers took it from her.

"I'll take charge of that, lass. It's going home to Red Stone, as it should be flown from the window there."

Home to Red Stone. . . .

She hadn't thought of that, either. A shiver left gooseflesh on her arms. Very soon she would be completely at Keir's mercy. He was the laird on his land; no one would challenge his word.

Just like Edmund . . .

She hated her mind's impulsive linking of Keir with Edmund, but couldn't prevent her thoughts from doing so. There were many similarities.

"The king expects us to hunt with him today."

Keir's men grinned. Several of them looked relieved as well. They tugged on their bonnets before quitting the room. Once they were gone she pushed on Keir's chest, gaining his full attention. Something flickered in his dark eyes that told her he didn't care for her desire to be released.

He put her down anyway.

"You shouldna be angry over the sheet being inspected."

"I'm not."

She spoke too quickly but didn't wait for Keir to take issue with her. She walking toward the fireplace, where she found her chemise and pulled it over her head.

"Are ye upset over nae having any of yer family members present? I dinnae think yer brother would attend even if I told me men to let him in. Which I'll honestly tell ye I dinnae."

"You've instructed your men to refuse my brother entrance?"

"Aye."

And his tone made it plain that he wasn't sorry about that at all. She couldn't blame him for that, but it left her feeling very alone as well as vulnerable. The sheet was stained, proving her a virgin and that Keir had consummated their union, but the only witnesses were men who owed their loyalty to him. He had never given her cause to distrust him, but that didn't stop her from feeling lonely.

"Does that truly displease ye? I planted my fist in his face the last time we met." Keir was already dressed. His kilt pleated and belted around his waist once again. He was an imposing sight, the lack of court finery somehow enhancing his strength.

He approached her and her belly tightened. It was an instant response and one that she could not control even after getting what she'd desired.

"Maybe he'll learn to be more forgiving with his own hands now that he's tasted what it's like to have someone stronger hit him."

Keir touched her cheek, tenderly stroking the healing bruise Edmund had left on her.

"I doubt it. Edmund is a law unto himself. Now that my father is ill, I believe that his arrogance will only increase. There is no one to dictate to him."

"Save the king."

Helena moved away from him. Her dress was lying over a table but the stays only laced up the back, leaving her helpless to dress alone.

"The king enjoys harmony amidst his nobles."

"Aye, well, ye willnae have to answer to him."

No, she would be in Scotland. . . .

It wasn't that she disliked the country; part of her was curious. But she couldn't shake the loneliness from her heart. Every effort had been focused on installing her at court. Now that she was leaving it, she was at a loss as to how to move forward.

The door opened and the maid reentered. Two of Keir's retainers carried a trunk into the chamber. Helena recognized it instantly. She smiled just because it was something familiar.

"Edmund gave you my things?"

She reached out and ran a hand over the wooden lid. One of the men tugged on his cap before offering her a mocking grin.

"His housekeeper did. Dinnae know what yer brother thinks o' it. We didna ask."

A soft sound drew her attention to Keir. He sent his men from the room with a jerk of his head. They nodded to her before leaving, and the maid went along with them, leaving her alone with her husband.

"I hope it pleases ye to have yer things, but I'll be happy to buy ye whatever else ye deem necessary." Uncertainty flickered in his eyes. She stared at it, wanting to see someone she might not call a stranger. The trunk was an offering, and one that she needed to meet with her own attempt at forging some sort of friendly relationship.

Tilting her head to the side, she sighed. "Well, I was eying some of those very large hair rolls. Many of the ladies at court wear them."

He scowled at her. But mischief lit his dark eyes. "Upon further consideration, I believe I like ye as ye are. In naught but that chemise."

"You want me to wear my chemise hunting with the king?" Helena opened her eyes wide. "I suppose I am expected to obey you as my husband, but . . ."

His expression darkened. He hadn't removed his whiskers yet and his chin was coated in a dark shadow, making him appear harder. He curled his fingers into the loose fabric of her chemise and tugged her forward. She tumbled into his body, her hands landing on his chest. Excitement surged through her as her senses filled with the scent of his warm skin. Everything about him was strong and male. It made her aware of the fact that she was female and fashioned to take him within her. It was a carnal thought, but one that sent heat racing through her veins.

"I'll be interested in seeing just how much obeying ye are willing to do when we are alone."

"I thought you enjoyed my boldness. Not submission." She moved her hands over his chest, teasing the ridges of his muscles and forcing her body to press up against his. She quivered, her bottom wanting to curl away from him, but she ordered her body to remain in place.

He threaded his hands through her unbound hair. " 'Tis a fact that ye are learning very quickly who I am." He placed his lips on top of hers. The kiss was hard and full of need. He pressed her lips apart, holding her head between his hands.

She kissed him back, eagerly allowing his tongue to tease her into a deeper kiss. But his whiskers scraped across her skin, drawing a quiver from her.

"I'm going to have to start shaving before dawn."

Confusion swept through her, and he chuckled before releasing her.

"Do ye think that the only time a couple may lie in bed is at night?"

"Well . . . I suppose . . ." She didn't care for the amusement sparkling in his eyes. "I simply have not thought all that much about being with a man. I avoided them to maintain my reputation, even if it is grossly unfair to expect purity from a bride but not a groom."

She was being too daring. Men never took kindly to women who didn't accept their authority. Or pointed out that they expected higher standards from their wives than they held themselves to. More than one bride had felt the weight of her husband's hand for daring to voice such facts. Keir might have treated her kindly but that did not mean the man would be any different from the rest of his sex. He'd won her in a game of cards, after all.

"I'm sorry, that was cross of me."

"Dinnae do that."

She bit her lower lip instead of answering. Annoying him was certain to land her in difficult circumstances. For all that they were strangers, the man was her husband and the law favored him in every way. She was his chattel.

"Dinnae hide yer spirit from me, Helena."

Her eyes narrowed. He drew in a stiff breath.

"I suppose we'd better get to dressing, or the king will be unhappy that we missed his hunt, because I'm going to take ye back to bed in another few minutes of this quarreling. We communicate very well in bed."

He turned and left in a swirl of wool kilt. Excitement tingled all over her skin, but her temper raised its head.

The man was far too sure of his ability to . . . to . . . well, to make her body perform as he willed. It was infuriating.

It was also exciting. . . .

She scoffed at herself. She took a step toward her trunk and shook when her passage gave a slight protest. But lust was gently throbbing in her clitoris again. Her gaze swept the room, taking in the details she hadn't yet committed to memory. Her emotions were tangled. Tears stung her eyes, but she ordered them to remain unshed.

She was a wife now. How many years had she been told about what was expected of her? Keir was not unkind, but he was a man.

And she would have to learn to live with his rule, and some-day his mistress.

Two tears eased down her cheeks. It hurt to think of him with other women. It shouldn't. No noble wife received fi-delity. But that didn't stop her from wanting it. More tears eased from the corners of her eyes. She wanted her gallant knight; wanted a childhood fantasy so badly that it hurt.

But that was only because she wanted something that a marriage could not provide. Such a thing was shattered by re-ality. Those who loved lost when they gave into lust. The two did not mix.

She could have loved Keir and she mourned that loss.

Rage was strength. Pure, undiluted strength.

Edmund Charles Knyvett, heir to the earldom of Kenton, drew a deep breath and gave himself over to the anger burn-ing inside him. He felt the flames licking along his limbs, burn-ing away everything else. His thoughts were consumed until nothing but white-hot rage filled him. It was perfection. He missed the sheer abundance of emotion when he didn't have enough reason to work himself up into a rage often enough.

Keir McQuade made an excellent target.

That bastard Scot had no doubt spent the night between his sister's thighs. The image of them fucking fueled his rage. The stupid bitch had no doubt raised her hips for his damned common cock. Her womb was now stinking with his less-than noble seed. It was like a disease, eating away at her well-born womb. It disgusted him.

But the rage made every muscle in his body hard. He grabbed a goblet sitting on a table in his chamber and swal-lowed the wine left in it. A snarl left his lips when he turned it all the way up and the wine was finished.

"Wine!"

He hurled the goblet at the door, his rage making his arm stronger. He smiled as the goblet clattered to the floor. The sound echoed throughout the chamber.

All of his senses were heightened. He felt every little thing more intensely when he allowed the rage to rule him. Self-discipline was overrated. All it did was mask the nature of what he might feel when he was unfettered by the bounds of right and wrong.

"Wine, my lord." Young Avis froze halfway into a curtsy. Her eyes widened when they saw his cock standing tall. His nightshirt was in shreds because his skin needed to be free when he let himself burn with rage. He laughed at her horror. He could smell the fear on her skin. Her gaze darted to the door but there was no way to avoid serving her master.

"Wine!"

She moved forward on hesitant steps, offering the tray with the fresh goblet up in front of her. She was pathetic, a coward like all females. Their whining sickened him, but his cock twitched, recognizing something of which it might make use.

He grabbed the goblet and reached over the tray to grasp her neck.

"My lord! I beg you!"

She whimpered, but the rage burning inside him made it hard to hear such a weak sound. Taking a swallow of the wine, he dumped the goblet behind him.

"I have need of a bitch."

He forced her across the table, yanking her skirts up. A bucket of water hit him square in the face. Edmund snarled and turned on the person responsible. Avis rolled over the table and ran toward the door, where Margery stood with a bucket in hand.

"Run, girl! The master's gone insane." The door slammed behind them.

"I am not insane!"

He wasn't . . . wasn't . . . wasn't . . . Edmund pulled his own hair, slamming his fist against the closed door of his chamber. He was in a rage—burning in the grip of anger caused by Keir McQuade!

Margery grabbed her cloak, as well as one for Avis. "Come on, girl. We've got to flee this house. The evil eye is here."

They had to run before the insanity touched them as it had their master.

"Run, girl! Run!"

"Now that is a fair nicer dress."

Helena's husband sounded pleased. In fact, his men looked pleased with her appearance as well. A little flicker of enjoyment warmed Helena when she stepped outside to join them.

"I must admit that I don't care for court dresses too much."

" 'Tis glad I am to hear that. Those things would have no place at Red Stone." Her husband stopped for a moment. "Unless ye wanted to wear them, I suppose."

He looked as though he couldn't understand why she would want to. Her hunting dress was far easier to move in. Constructed of lightweight wool, it had only a petticoat beneath the skirts. There was no cartwheel farthingale with stiff boning to keep even when she walked, just a hip roll to help support the weight of the cartridge-pleated skirts. Her arms didn't need to be bent and positioned perfectly, because she had on only one pair of sleeves. While they were not common, they were built to move with the natural motion of her body. She felt freer than she had in years. Her mother had put her into court dresses a full year before she arrived at court, dictating that she wear nothing else so that she would become balanced and poised.

And all of it didn't seem to matter because Keir McQuade

found her quite charming in her hunting dress. She couldn't help but enjoy the way his lips curved while he took her hand. It was the sort of honest admiration that she liked about him so much.

There was no carriage today. Keir's men had their mounts waiting in the small courtyard that sat in front of the town house—large, powerful beasts that snorted in the morning air. Keir reached for one, a huge, sable-brown stallion that tossed its head before allowing his master to stroke its muzzle. Man and beast shared a moment of true friendship that was evident in both their eyes. Helena watched it, staring at the way Keir stroked the animal.

She was jealous.

The emotion caught her completely off guard. She looked away to force herself back into a composed noblewoman who did not care about tender feelings. It didn't work. She was still biting her lower lip when her husband spoke to her.

"Do ye ride?"

He hesitated over the question, phrasing it simply as though he was a bit afraid to hear her answer. His men watched her, fear lurking in their eyes as well: a fear of getting the chore of hauling a pampered and helpless court lady up to Scotland.

Keir swallowed roughly when she didn't answer him quickly. She watched the muscles of his throat contract and his lips press into a firm line to conceal his true feelings.

"Of course I can ride."

She heard more than one sigh of relief. Her husband, on the other hand, eyed her suspiciously.

"Ye're toying with me."

She tilted her head slightly to the side. "I cannot help it if you believe all the gossip about English women. If I gave any attention to half the things I've heard about Scotland, I'd have fainted dead away the moment I met you."

His men laughed and a grin split Keir's lips.

"Ye were too busy staring at me to do that."

His men chuckled and her face burned. Her husband's gaze instantly touched on the blush brightening her cheeks.

"We mustn't be late. The king doesn't hold his hunts for anyone."

Everyone found something to do, their amusement dying quickly. She missed it once it was gone.

"Farrell brought ye a fine mare this morning."

One of his men brought the horse forward. "She's young and healthy. Built for endurance." Farrell pulled the bridle down so that the mare was close enough to touch, pride gleaming in his eyes.

"She's magnificent. You have a skilled eye for horses." The mare was a lighter brown than Keir's stallion. But its coat was silky and shimmered in the sunlight. Running a hand over its neck, Helena smiled.

"It was very kind of you to buy me a mount." She spoke quietly, unused to receiving gifts. Every fine thing she owned had been purchased with the goal of securing her a place at court. There was nothing in her trunk that she valued simply for the emotional enjoyment it gave her.

"I would have preferred to have you ride double with me." Her husband offered her a roguish grin. "Aye, but we wouldn't get a whole lot of hunting done if I had to feel ye clinging to my back."

She blushed again, but this time she reached out and slapped him on the forearm. It was an impulse, one that her discipline should have prevented. Horror gripped her when she realized that every one of his men had witnessed the impulsive, unpolished gesture.

Keir tossed his shoulder-length hair back and laughed. His men followed his example. It was such a contrast to everything she had been trained to expect. But her husband grinned at her, his eyes sparkling with enjoyment. He grasped her waist and lifted her up onto the back of the mare. His strength amazed her. She'd suspected he was strong, but he lifted her as though she were a child.

"I think we may be more compatible than you think, Helena."

He winked at her. She blinked her eyes because she had never actually had someone do that to her since she was a girl. The footmen used to do it, in a kindly fashion, to distract her from something boring she was being forced to attend, but coming from Keir, it was a very different thing. She tightened her grip on the reins and hooked her knee over the small handle that was placed on the sidesaddle. Her cheeks were still hot and she realized that she was flattered by Keir's approval of her. His amusement was something to be proud of. He was not a man who laughed with his enemies.

She watched him swing up into the saddle through her lowered eyelashes. Heat traveled down her spine to pool in her belly as she did it. Keir was magnificent sitting there, the powerful stallion suiting him because he was so strong himself.

A gallant knight . . .

She didn't chide herself for thinking it. She couldn't. He embodied it right then, from the way his dark hair curled down to tease the top of his shoulders, to the manner in which he had his doublet sleeves tied behind his back. Only his shirt covered his arms. He tossed his head and cast her an eager glance.

"Let's ride, lass."

He kicked his horse and grinned. Helena did, too. There was a freedom in riding that she hadn't known in months. Keir took the lead and her mare followed out into the street. It was congested by wagons and carriages but their horses cut through the mass of busy merchants and ambassadors with ease, many of them clearing the road when they sighted the party of McQuades.

No . . . not a gallant knight.

He was a worthy laird.

"The poor thing, wed to a Scot." Lady Philipa Fitzgerald stared at her and didn't lower her voice enough to keep it from drifting on the breeze. "Such a waste of blue blood."

The woman was a notorious gossip. Helena had learned that within days of arriving at court. Lady Philipa was dressed in the highest fashion with no care for the fact that the sky was overcast. The swollen mass of clouds was promising rain. Her silk dress wouldn't fare very well but the lady sat there in her lace and finery while gossiping with several other ladies. They all cast looks at her, some of them actually wrinkling their noses. Helena offered them a serene expression, refusing to let their sniping get to her. There was another thing she had learned early at court. Never believe what was said about you. If she had, she would have cried herself to sleep every night for a year.

The king arrived with a fanfare of trumpets. James Stuart swept the assembled group with a critical eye.

"McQuade, my friend! I'm happy to see ye and yer bride."

Heads turned and Helena felt the weight of more stares than she might count. The variety of their expressions amazed her. Some were merely curious, others glared at her with scorn, while still others smiled at the idea of a wedding. Lady Fitzgerald looked at her friends with a smirk and a shake of her head.

The king didn't allow them much time to pick at her. He raised a fist and the trumpets sounded again. His fickle court immediately turned their attention to following the king. Most of them did not care for hunting, but the king did.

Groomsmen encouraged the hounds forward, releasing them from leashes. The dogs sniffed at the ground, whining and barking with growing excitement. James leaned down over the neck of his horse, allowing the animal to gain speed. Helena tightened her hold on the mare but didn't pull the animal up. The wind chilled her cheeks and nose, bringing a surge of excitement to her. The party headed toward the woods that surrounded the palace. It was the king's private land. The party entered the woods and the birds fluttered in the treetops. The trumpets were silent now, the king searching for a buck or maybe a boar. The hounds yipped and searched for a scent.

Knight and lords jostled one another in their attempts to ride near the king. Helena allowed herself to be pushed back, as all of the ladies did. She searched their faces, disappointment filling her when she didn't catch sight of the queen's colors. It was to be expected that the queen would not be present in her condition, but she had still hoped to see her friend Raelin.

"I am so sorry to hear about your wedding, Helena. I knew your mother when she was serving the late queen." Lady Fitzgerald sniffed and looked down her nose at Helena, disdain evident in her expression.

"The king gave us his blessing." Helena needed to use all her years of practice to speak to the woman in a sweet voice.

Lady Fitzgerald scoffed at her. "You're very young and impressionable. The king is a Scot and obviously feels the need to give his fellow Scots what they want. That does not make it a good match."

The king's party had separated from the main group. Many

of the courtiers who didn't care for hunting had lagged behind and now clumped together to talk while the king ran
down his prize. Other ladies joined them, sly smirks on their
lips.

"Such a shame that your brother didn't perform his duty
better. I really am quite shocked to see a Knyvett doing something like gambling away his sister. That is so common."

The ladies all shook their heads. Lady Fitzgerald offered her
a sad smile.

"I don't want to be the bearer of bad news, but I do feel that
you should be warned about Scotland." The lady shuddered,
her face contorting with disgust. "I was forced to follow my father there twice, and I must say it is a godforsaken place. The
men are barbarians without a hint of knowledge of civilized
behavior. Their clans are constantly fighting and they actually
steal brides. Can you imagine? In this time? Barbarians! I really
don't enjoy telling you, but I couldn't help but notice the long
sword strapped to your husband's back."

"Yes . . . well thank you very much, Lady Fitzgerald."

The woman looked astonished and the ladies surrounding
her raised their eyebrows. Helena didn't care. She refused to
remain near them and their gossip.

She liked that sword.

No hip sword had ever struck her as powerful. It wasn't so
much the weapon as the way that Keir wore it—exactly like his
men. There was no fancy pommel on his sword, either—nothing to set him above those who served as his retainers. She
found that lack of pomposity a relief, not a sign of barbarism.

The sky had darkened. She rode out into a clearing without
realizing that the storm had thickened above her head. The
cloud mass was black, and thunder began to rumble in the
distance. The few people in sight were making their way toward shelter. Lady Fitzgerald and her companions were al-

ready on their way back toward the palace. Helena pulled her cloak over her shoulders to protect her from the wind. But she didn't turn her mare toward the palace.

She was quite unexpectedly alone for the moment, and that suited her mood. Leaning her head back, she closed her eyes and let the sounds of the woods fill her ears. There had been a time when she was allowed to run free in the afternoon once her studies were finished. Even if it was childish, she longed for a few moments of freedom from the constant criticism— just a few moments to enjoy the bite of the wind on her cheeks and the sound it made in the treetops.

Overhead the thunder cracked again, this time closer. The wind whipped up, bringing with it the first hint of rain. Not actual droplets, but she could feel it on her face and smell it. Her mare danced nervously, tossing her head.

"There, girl. It's only a bit of rain."

Helena reached down to pat the horse on her neck. The mare quieted for only a moment before her nostrils flared, and she danced in a circle. An answering snort sent the mare backing away from the stallion her husband rode. Steady and silent, he'd emerged from the woods behind her.

"Ye dinnae believe that. . . ."

Her husband was annoyed. His horse felt it and refused to remain still. The stallion pranced in a circle around her mare.

"Believe what?"

"That Scots are uncivilized."

Thunder boomed across the sky and her mare reared. Keir leaped from his saddle and caught the bridle with a large hand. The mare was not pleased; she snorted and dug at the ground. Rain began to fall in fat drops that pelted the tree limbs above their heads, filling the air with the sound of water hitting leaves. Helena dismounted as the first bolt of lightning seared across the sky. It was not safe to remain in the saddle during a storm—even the most well-behaved mounts might throw you under such conditions. Everyone would be seeking shelter until the thunder quieted. A quick look around showed Helena that no one from the hunting party was nearby. She and Keir were very much alone. Keir pulled her mare toward the thick trunk of the tree and tied her there. He led his own horse there as well, and knotted the leather reins with solid motions.

"Tell me the truth, Helena. I dinnae want to think ye fear going home with me. Red Stone is a wondrous place."

And he was proud of it. She heard it in his voice, in spite of the rain falling all around them.

"Well, I suppose I will be content to discover you are not uncivilized." She sighed, unable to resist the urge to tease him. His eyes narrowed.

"Are ye teasing me, Helena?"

"Possibly. You did appear to encourage such this morning."

His lips twitched and then rose into a grin that flashed his teeth at her.

"Unless you are going to prove Lady Fitzgerald incorrect and tell me to conduct myself with dignity, because you are not uncivilized, not even a bit. I suppose I shall have to endure if that is the case."

"Oh, I'm pure Scot, have nae doubt about it, lassie."

Heat filled his dark eyes. She was drawn to it, mesmerized by the flicker of hunger. Thunder cracked overhead and the storm raged. The elements heightened her senses, the smell of rain making her more aware of how Keir smelled pressed against her with nothing between them save passion. She licked her lower lip and his gaze instantly settled on the tip of her tongue. Excitement tightened in her belly. She repeated the motion, licking over the surface of her lower lip slowly this time. The skin was ultrasensitive, and little ripples of delight went down her spine from that simple touch.

"You cannot think that I believe everything I hear at court. Even if you are my husband. I simply must reserve judgment until I experience things firsthand."

It was bold. But empowering, too. She felt her confidence rise just by watching the effect of her words on his face. His skin darkened and his lips pressed into a hard line.

"Is that a fact?"

"It is best, don't you think?" She couldn't remain still. Too much sensation was building inside her. She could have sworn that she felt the energy in the storm through her skin. Her heart accelerated and her breathing grew more labored. "You wouldn't want me to believe what courtiers say, would you?"

He laughed. It was deep and husky and very male. "Of course not, lass. That would never do. Ye should experience things firsthand."

He tugged on the fingertip of one of his leather gauntlets, working his way across each fingertip until he slid the leather glove off. He placed it on his saddle and removed the matching one. The bare skin of his fingers sent a chill down her back. Even with the rain, she grew warm enough for sweat to dot her forehead.

She recalled in vivid detail what those bare fingertips felt like on her body. Behind her stays her nipples were hard and needy. He flexed his hands and her mouth went dry.

"Run."

His voice was soft but his eyes glowed with hunger. If she had ever believed the tales of wild men in the woods, he embodied such myths right then. He bent his knees and stretched out his arms with his hands curled into talons.

"I cannae chase ye if ye are nae running."

He dragged one foot across the ground like a stallion paw-
ing with impatience. Her hands tangled in her skirts, gripping
the fabric, before she really decided what to say.

"Keir . . ."

"I'm only going to count to five and then I'm going to run
ye down." He took one step toward her and she broke, turning and running out into the rain. Her heart raced as her mind
began keeping count.

One . . . two . . . three . . . four . . .

She didn't dare look behind her. She raised her skirts to her
knees and ran. The rain soaked her hair, cooling her skin that
had turned hot. The contrast sent more sensation through
her. The back of her neck tingled as though she could feel him
bearing down on her. It grew and grew in intensity until she
risked a look over her shoulder.

A shriek left her lips because Keir was almost upon her, his
powerful legs closing the distance between them on silent
strides. He didn't stop running; just captured her in hard arms
that tossed her up . . . up and over his shoulder.

He snarled with victory and continued on to a dense group-
ing of trees. She struggled, caught up in a storm of sensations
and feelings. He tossed her down but cradled her before she
hit the ground. Her cloak spread out beneath her and he
reached for the clasp to keep it from pulling against her throat.

"My prize."

He nuzzled against her neck, poised just above her. She quivered, her body shaking with need and hunger. She reached for
him, craving contact more than she ever had before. She
understood what the ache in her passage needed now and it
made her too hungry to be docile.

"My captor."

He lifted his head and stared at her. She reached up until
she found the skin above his collar, slick with rain. She pushed

her hands along the thick column until she reached his collar and pulled on the ties to open it. He didn't give her time to stroke the skin she bared. His mouth sought hers, demanding a hard kiss. She responded in kind, gripping his head to hold him in place while her lips demanded as much from him as he took from her.

He pulled her doublet open, the fabric groaning in protest. She didn't care. Her back arched and she offered her breasts to him. The lace of her corset popped when he pulled the knot loose.

"I'm going to ravish you."

"Yes!" She gripped his shoulders and cried out when he licked over the swell of one breast. His lips closed around the nipple, shooting fire into her chest. She arched with it, surging up off the cloak. More thunder echoed across the woods, and this time she felt it against her wet skin.

Keir pushed her back down, imprisoning her with his strength. His tongue teased the tip of her nipple, toying with it before he sucked it hard and deep into his mouth.

"Yes!"

There was nothing else in her mind save for that single word. She hit his shoulders, growling through her teeth as she repeated it. He pulled his head up and there was a faint pop when her nipple freed itself from his grasp.

"Yes?" He was demanding but she didn't care. She needed it, needed to feel his strength. He was part of the violent storm and she wanted to be swept up into it.

"Hard and fast, Helena? Is that how you want it?" He captured her wrists and pinned them above her head. The wind brushed across her bare breasts and nothing had ever sent hunger like it through her before. There was a wildness in the sight of him above her and the feel of his hands gripping her wrists, but there was the secure knowledge of how tenderly he'd taken her the night before to give her the faith to trust him.

"I'll toss yer skirts above yer waist and sink into ye. . . ."

"Yes!" She was demanding now, her voice full of expectation. "Do it!"

He released her hands and she reached for his hair, pulling the strands into her grasp. He hissed but enjoyment flickered in his eyes. Her skirts were raised with one quick motion of his hands. She spread her thighs eagerly for him, her knees bending, but he pushed them up above her waist and held them. He lowered enough of his body weight to pin her to the ground. The sky shook with another clap of thunder, this one centered directly over them.

The bolt of lightning that followed illuminated her lover. He was savage with bared teeth, but tender too as he slowly probed her open sex with his cock, merely shifting his kilt out of the way. He didn't push into her quickly. The effort cost him. The muscles on the side of his jaw twitched.

"Keir—"

"Nay!" he growled through clenched teeth. "You'll be sore from last night."

She bucked beneath him but he kept her pinned. His eyes burned into hers. "I'm your master and I said nay."

She snarled at him, but was helpless. His cock pressed forward in a slow thrust that made her whine with need. But he was correct. Her passage protested the penetration, pain snaking through her as he pressed deeper. It seemed forever that she waited to feel full. An eternity of needing and craving his flesh. When he pushed the last bit of length into her, his entire body shook.

"Sweet Christ . . ."

He said something else in Gaelic, something guttural and husky. She understood it somewhere inside her where words didn't have meaning. A moment later he was riding her, as quick and as hard as the swirling wind. He released her legs and she clasped him tightly, lifting her bottom to get closer to him, to take more of him into her. Rain filtered through the tree branches, the water hitting her face.

It was pure sensation—all of it. Keir surged forward, growling as he thrust into her over and over. Pleasure tightened under each stroke, pulling tighter and tighter until it burst. She erupted off the ground, crying out with her pleasure.

Keir pressed her back down, pounding his cock deeply into her. With a harsh cry she felt him empty his seed against the mouth of her womb, pumping the hot fluid deep inside her. Another spasm shook her, her passage gripping his length and pulling every last drop of seed from it.

The next clap of thunder was farther away. But she flinched, collapsing against the cloak in a heap of quivering muscles. Keir caught himself above her, his chest heaving.

"Sweet Helena . . . I cannae wait to take ye home to Red Stone, away from this place of false tales."

He trailed soft kisses over her jaw and down her neck.

"But you just proved that you are uncivilized."

He raised his head and showed her a cocky grin. "Aye, but ye enjoyed it. So I'm going to take ye home and ravish ye as often as possible."

"I will hope."

The storm was moving on, the rain subsiding into a soft sprinkle. A horn sounded in the distance and another one answered it. Keir groaned. He climbed to his feet and slid a hand beneath her waist to lift her up. Her skirts fell back into place, concealing their deviation from the prim and proper.

But little ripples of delight still moved down her legs, making her knees weak. Keir pulled her cloak from the ground and gave it a snap to dislodge the leaves that were stuck to it.

He swung it around her body while she laced her stays and buttoned her doublet.

His hands cupped her chin, raising her eyes to meet his. "Did I hurt ye?"

Concern filled his eyes and her pride rejected it.

"You really must stop believing everything you hear about Englishwomen. Some of us are quite hearty."

He grinned. "A good thing, too, considering how uncivilized Scotland is."

"You're insane."

Edmund slapped the table in front of him but kept his rage from flaring back up. Not now. There was a time and a place to allow the flames to control him. Now he needed to apply his wit to the matter at hand.

"If you aren't good enough to do the job, admit it and stop wasting my time."

The man in front of him flinched. But it was a tiny movement of his cheek, nothing more. His eyes didn't betray his emotions; in fact, the cold gaze coming from him fascinated Edmund. He had so much control; it was mesmerizing.

"I'm good enough. I know just where to stab you and make sure you live. I keep my knives sharp and clean. Only the best steel."

"Good."

"I didn't say I would take the job. You're a peer. I'd be tortured for attacking you if you are playing some sort of game. And my execution wouldn't be something as merciful as a beheading."

Edmund felt his confidence growing. Oh, he was plotting and he intended to win.

"It's about my sister. I have to get her away from a Scot before he breeds her."

The assassin raised one eyebrow. "How'd he get her?"

"The king has a soft spot for him and allowed him to wed her."

That did it. The man narrowed his eyes and leaned forward. "Even a king shouldn't play favorites. I've seen too many men dead in battles that were commanded by noblemen who had the ear of the queen. Good men. Friends of mine."

Edmund smiled. "Then we are agreed?"

The assassin fingered a long scar that ran down the side of his face. "Double the price and I'll make it fast and clean."

Edmund slid a folded parchment and a torn piece of Mc-Quade tartan across the table. "Don't forget to drop this on me when you stab me. And remember I'm hiring you to make sure you don't kill me. Be very sure that I'm leaving a letter with a reliable source should you make a mistake and kill me."

"I'm a businessman. You shall receive what you paid for: a wound that looks as though you were lucky enough to escape murder."

"Good. Drop that letter and plaid on me once the deed is done. It will pin the blame on the Scot. He'll be the one in the Tower and my sister will be a widow before next spring. Once I declare it was the Scot that tried to kill me, the king will have no choice but to have him executed."

Edmund looked around the tavern. It was the sort of place where men kept a sharp eye on anyone who walked too near them, but beyond that they ignored every face and expected the same in return. No one had names here, and no one was ever remembered being in the place.

It cost a pretty piece of gold to ensure it, too. Edmund didn't care. He dropped a full pound on the bar in front of the proprietor and never looked behind him. He was confident in the power of money.

* * *

The assassin watched him leave. He tapped the table with a finger, contemplating the job. Oh, it was nothing more than a job to him—one that would net him a purse that he could labor for a year and not earn at some sort of decent duty. It wasn't his responsibility to instill morality in the men who came to him looking for murder. He was just the instrument. He wasn't a murderer. The men who paid him were the ones stained with that crime. It was a truth that he was merciful to their victims. He killed them swiftly, most of the time before they even saw the knife. There was no fear, no terror. Not all of his clients liked that aspect of his service. God had blessed him with a steady hand and keen wit that helped him decide how to get the most profit. There was no killing if the silver wasn't there. It was up to him to make his way with the gifts his creator had given him.

It was only a job.

Chapter Ten

"Helena?"

Raelin McKorey gestured with her hand.

The courtyard was a mass of noblemen and servants. Intermixed with them were the royal guards, along with retainers. The king was happily showing off his downed buck while stableboys hurried to take up the reins of the noblemen who dismounted without any care as to what happened to their mounts.

Keir wasn't that sort of man. He took care of his own stallion and Helena's mare. His men were shouldering their way through the crowd to get the animals into the dry stable. Rain was still falling and the dark sky promised that it would not be a quickly passing storm.

"Helena?"

Raelin stood under an archway. She frowned at the sky and fingered her golden silk gown. It would spot if she ventured into the sprinkling rain. But Helena was happy to see her friend. She ran to join her, grasping her hands but being careful not to brush her skirts up against Raelin's maid of honor dress. It was a sure bet the gown was expensive and her family would not enjoy replacing it due to foolishness.

"I've been thinking so much about you."

Her friend searched her eyes but frowned when she looked at the purple bruise still marring her face.

"It's much better now."

Raelin narrowed her eyes and tugged her into the hallway to place some distance between them and the other nobles.

"Did your brother do that to yer face?"

Helena squeezed her friend's hand. "It doesn't matter now."

"Because ye are wed?" Raelin bit her lower lip. "I suppose ye are right about that. I do believe that Keir McQuade will not allow that brother of yers to lay his hand on ye now."

Helena heard the question her friend didn't voice. She offered her a genuine smile. The Scots girl relaxed.

"Och, I'm so happy for ye. I told him about ye nae coming to court. I hoped he'd be the man ye thought he was."

They had wandered far from the courtyard while talking. A pounding of boot heels on the stone tile drew both their attention. Helena looked up to see her new husband bearing down on them.

Keir was furious.

It was such an unexpected thing, Helena stared at him.

"Dinnae ever leave my men, madam."

His tone infuriated her. "Excuse me, Raelin. I do believe my husband and I need to have a conversation."

The Scots girl wasn't shocked; in fact she was slightly amused. "Aye, I can see he needs a thing or two pointed out to him."

Keir crossed his arms over his chest. Raelin curtsied low and very slowly in a mockery of his stern pose.

"Mistress McKorey, I believe I've already interceded on your behalf and that should have taught ye to remain where it is safe. Nae encourage others to make the same mistakes."

" 'Tis the light of day now." Raelin didn't seem impressed with Keir McQuade. She stood up boldly to the man. But she shifted her attention to Helena.

"Come to the queen's chambers later. Her Majesty would like to see you as well."

She swept past Keir and his retainers with her chin high. Helena envied the girl her confidence in the face of such stern disapproval.

"Ye cannae venture off on yer own, Helena. I willnae have it."

Keir wasn't bending. He glared at her, disapproval clear on his face.

"I warned ye that ye would nae be allowed away from my men."

She took a deep breath, searching for the face of her lover in the man standing in front of her now. "You said that the night before our wedding."

"I dinnae see what has changed, madam."

Hurt ran its claw across her heart. Where was the man she had just lain with? Try as she might, she could not see him. The pain stung.

"You are quite correct. Nothing has changed, husband."

She lowered herself. His eyes snapped with temper. "Helena—"

"I must pay my respects to the queen."

"Ye'll stay with me."

Helena straightened herself and stared at him. "Just as I had to obey the king and wed you, you shall obey the wishes of the queen to see me. It is my duty now that I have been told she wishes to see me."

Keir frowned. "I shall accompany ye."

Hard and unwavering, his eyes looked like obsidian.

She turned and began walking. The hair on the back of her neck stood up, tension knotting between her shoulder blades. She felt his distrust keenly.

It dropped her back into the swirling mists of loneliness that had assaulted her that morning. It slashed at the fragile happiness she'd felt around her since their afternoon tryst. She should have expected it. Their marriage might be ended if there was no child. Divorce was not uncommon. It was hushed up and muttered against by the church but it happened far more than anyone admitted. When inheritances and titles hung in the balance, even matrimony wasn't unbreakable. Keir would be wise to breed her often in order to plant a child in her womb. One living child would make it much harder for a divorce to happen.

She wanted to resist thinking that way. His men might simply be doing their duty in a world that was often filled with dangers for the unprotected. But emotions were fickle things that didn't listen to logic.

It was little wonder that affection of the heart was considered insanity. Her new emotions were playing havoc with her thinking and that was no mistake.

"You don't have to leave, Helena."

"There is no point in avoiding what is done." Helena hugged her friend, embracing her tightly. "He is not unkind to me."

Raelin nodded. "He has honor. And that is something that I nae ever thought I'd say of any McQuade, since his father tried to kill me only a year past. But I suppose neither of us should hope marriage to be anything except what it is."

"I will miss you."

Helena smiled at her friend in spite of the fact that her heart was filling with grief. It was likely that they would not see each other again for many years, if ever. She was wed and expected to return to her husband's home to see to the duty of producing heirs. Raelin would face the same fate herself soon. Letters would become their only means of continuing their friendship.

Keir and his retainers were waiting for her outside the queen's chambers. As strong and powerful as she had always thought him to be, today that strength represented the ability to keep her near him. Part of her rejoiced, but doubt teased her as well. She shook it off, refusing to behave like a child. He was certainly a better husband than Ronchford. It was best to show him how good a wife she might be.

"I am yours to command."

"No man ever truly understands the way a woman's mind works." Farrell's attempt to help gained him a hard look from his laird. The man tilted his head and returned his attention to the horse he was rubbing down. "Well, if ye figure it out, be a good lad and share the secret with me." Farrell added a shake of his head to indicate his lack of understanding when it came to women.

If he figured it out? Now there was a question if ever one was asked.

For the life of him, Keir couldn't understand why his bride had taken such exception to his insistence that she remain with his men. He was trying to protect her. Wasn't that his duty as a husband?

But there was no missing the fact that she was angry with him. It wasn't the temper that he had trouble dealing with; it was the resolution in her eyes that bothered him—that silent resolve to endure.

He did not want her to be unhappy.

He moved his hands along his stallion's flank, rubbing the

animal longer than normal. Keir stopped when he realized he was avoiding his wife. No matter what the trouble was between them, he was not going to tolerate distance between them.

Especially a distance caused by his own doing. He gave the horse a final pat and left the stable. Candlelight glowed from inside the house. It made for a cheerful scene, one that he slowed down long enough to enjoy before entering it. Anticipation was suddenly an enjoyable thing.

His wife was inside—the wife that he'd left McQuade land searching for. His clan name was restored to favor as well. He'd managed to do all the important things a laird was expected to do. All that remained was to go home and keep his lands running in good order. The town house itself was a symbol of his success. He scanned it from rooftop to front door. Satisfaction filled him.

A young face peeked through the front window. Two moments later the door opened wide for him. Keir felt one eyebrow rise. He was not accustomed to the staff waiting around on his pleasure and he was not planning on becoming so. The inhabitants of Red Stone had never scurried to please him and he would keep it that way. But as he walked through the open door, he was met by members of the house staff. They were lined up shoulder to shoulder to greet him, a few of them attempting to cover rapid breathing that betrayed the fact that they'd run to make sure they did not miss the master's entrance. They kept their eyes lowered and their chins tucked down in deference. The young boy had clearly been posted at the window to cry the alarm when he approached.

What surprised him was Helena. She stood at the head of the line, lowering herself neatly in a polished display of meekness. His temper ignited. He knew what she was doing. He knew it because he'd witnessed his sister putting on such displays when his father was alive. There was no truth in it. It was only a carefully rehearsed action that she performed to maintain peace by stroking his ego.

But he was not his father and did not care for false demonstrations of respect that were insincere. He moved quickly. His new bride had made an error by looking at the floor. He was already in front of her before she raised her gaze.

Helena gasped. The sound flew past her startled lips when she realized that her husband was only a foot away from her. Somehow she had forgotten how much larger he was than her. She had to tip her head back to meet his eyes. What she found there startled her, but not in a fearful manner. He was displeased, there was no missing that. But what drew her attention was the flare of determination that looked very similar to what she had witnessed during the thunderstorm.

Keir didn't give her time to ponder her thoughts. He swept her off her feet in a fluid motion that wrung another gasp from her lips. She grabbed at his doublet out of reflex but there was no hint of weakness in his embrace. He cradled her easily, striding through the dining room and toward the stairs without a single pause.

The cook stood near the table. Her apron was newly pressed and her linen cap starched so that the box-pleated edge stood straight. There were candles in the silver holders and in the wall brackets. All were lit and filling the room with a yellow glow. Fine dishes were laid on the table and the long cupboard set against the wall already held several platters awaiting the master's dining pleasure.

Her husband only swept the table with a quick glance before carrying her through the doorframe and into the back hallway. She heard the scamper of steps on the stone floor behind them and the unmistakable snap of the cook's fingers as she commanded the staff.

Her face colored because it was perfectly clear what her husband was in a hurry to do. For all that everyone expected newlyweds to spend time sharing intimacies, she did not appreciate her husband carrying her through the house like a captive.

But you enjoyed it earlier today . . .

Her thoughts annoyed her. She twisted in his embrace, pushing on the wide chest.

"Have done, husband. I can walk very well." She might have been mute for all the good her actions gained her. His embrace never changed. It remained solid and steady while he climbed the stairs.

"Aye, ye can, but I'm no' in the mood for rehearsed niceties."

He pushed the door to their chamber open with a shove from his shoulder. The hallway had been dim, with only the flicker of the lamps burning on the first floor to cut through the darkness. The chamber was very different. The staff were doing their best to make sure their new master didn't find any reason to begin replacing them. Candles were set into every holder on the tables and costly glass lanterns hung from hooks set into the walls. The colored glass filled the chamber with a surreal, reddish light.

"So now you are displeased with me because I show you good manners?" She hit his shoulder, completely exhausted with attempting to understand him. She struggled again, this time twisting her body and bucking without any care for how ungentle she appeared.

He released her but growled. It was a low sound filled with frustration. Helena tossed her head, refusing to lower her chin meekly. She didn't feel meek, not in the least.

"I do not understand you, *husband.*"

But she moved away from his imposing body—not because he was stronger but because she couldn't seem to stop think-

ing about how good he felt against her. Maybe it was the fact
that they were alone in the chamber, but her thoughts were
alight with flashes of memory from that afternoon. Her skin
grew warm and she had to shake her head to dispel the excitement that was beginning to swirl through her mind.

Keir stood with his arms crossed over his chest. He looked
as imposing as he had outside the queen's chambers, but here
she found it attractive, too. In the back of her mind all she
could think of was the large bed waiting for them with turned-
down covers.

He'd take her there—she had no doubt about it.

"I am nae yer brother."

Her mouth fell open in surprise. "Good God! I should hope
not, considering how we passed the after—"

One dark eyebrow arched in a mocking display. "The afternoon? Aye. I suppose that would nae be something a brother
and sister should be about."

It was sickening. Disgust travel through her. "Then what is
your discontent with me? I made no mention of Edmund."

He raised a single finger. "But you did, my sweet bride. Ye
stood there greeting me as he would have expected. All the
staff lined up."

And he didn't care for it. Helena stared at the discontent in
his eyes, confused by his mood. "Your men offer you respect."

" 'Tis different. I earned that from them by proving myself
with a sword just as I expect of every one of them."

"I can see that plainly enough. . . ." She was speaking without thinking again. Helena clamped her lips closed, frowning
at herself. Keir was the only man who swept her common
sense aside simply by being near her. It was as irritating as it
was exciting. But his lips twitched up at her words, a half grin
giving her a hint of his teeth before he shook his head and returned to glaring at her.

Helena felt her temper burn hotter. "Pray sir, do not leave me lingering in doubt and confusion any longer. For I have no idea what has annoyed you so badly that you felt the need to carry me up here instead of noticing how much your staff are trying to please you in the hope that you will not turn them out."

He winced, his arms unfolding. A flush appeared on his throat. "Och, well I dinnae mean to ignore their efforts. I am a wee bit new to being a lord."

Helena crossed her arms in response. Her husband looked stunned, his gaze moving over her for long seconds before his mouth rose into that roguish grin once again.

"Ye are too pretty when ye're mad for me to remember what we were fighting about."

A frustrated sound of fury escaped her lips. Her hands flew up as every lesson she'd ever mastered sailed out of her mind. "You hauled me up here like a sailor taking his dingy sack home, and now you claim you cannot recall what I did to annoy you?"

He surged. "Och, now I recall just fine, but I'm finding it much more enjoyable to dwell on yer sweet face than on what bothered me."

There was truly no understanding the way a man's mind worked. Helena waved her hand. "As well as that might be, I can only wonder what shall happen once the newness has worn away from our union."

"You think I'll turn mean toward ye? Why would ye think such a thing?"

His pride was wounded by the very idea. Helena heard it but it was that very pride that she expected to bring her grief someday.

"I did not say mean."

"But ye implied that I would not longer find ye sweet enough to blind me." He moved toward her, seeking the answer to his question.

Helena moved away from him, needing the space to keep her thoughts clear. She was treading on dangerous ground— that place where a man's pride might easily take offense over some truth spoken without thinking about the consequences.

"I simply am not vain enough to believe that I can expect to monopolize your attention forever."

Her words were still bold, in spite of how carefully she phrased the idea. But pain still drew its claw across her heart. A man such as Keir had a mistress, and it was likely that she was a beautiful woman. It was also likely that he would have more throughout the years and that she would be expected to be gracious in the face of his needs. Such was the lot of a wife.

He frowned again but this time he seemed partially annoyed with himself.

"If ye want to know something of me, Helena, ask yer question straight. I am nae a man that enjoys false displays of respect such as ye just offered me below. It's yer courage that I find irresistible, nae just the sight of yer face."

It was tempting. Helena chewed on her lower lip for a moment, but Keir didn't offer her anything else except for a challenge shimmering in his dark eyes. She felt her own pride rising in the face of that look. He was not a man who was easily impressed. Knowing that she had earned such from him filled her with confidence.

"Very well. I expect to be sleeping alone once we arrive at your home because you have a mistress there waiting on your return."

"Red Stone will be yer home, too, lass. Dinnae doubt it." Heat coated his voice and it tempted her to believe in that idea. A home. It was the truth that she wasn't sure what it felt like to be home anymore. The estate her parents lived on was run on tradition and schedule.

"But you didn't deny that you have a mistress waiting for you." She spoke quietly but kept her chin level. It would be better if he understood that she wasn't afraid of him.

He reached up to untie his sword. "I don't." The huge weapon was set on the table before he turned back to look at her. "But that is only because Gwen knew it was in the best interest of the McQuades for me to find a noblewoman for a wife."

His words hurt. Her gaze lowered to the floor to hide the pain slashing through her. Keir cupped her chin, following her backward when she retreated from his touch. She hadn't heard his feet on the floor—not even a tiny hint that he was closing the distance.

"She left me because she knew that I didna love her. At the time I argued with her. Even insisted that she would make a fine wife. But she would nae wed a man who didna love her."

His hand left her chin. He stroked her cheek and she turned to allow the touch. A shudder wracked her body. She felt his touch so much more keenly than anyone else's. Each fingertip brought her joy as they slid over the surface of her face.

"I didna understand at the time, but I do now."

He turned her face back so that their eyes met. Emotion flickered in his dark gaze. She didn't fully understand it, but neither did he.

"You cannot claim to love me."

"I know that no woman has ever upset me so much by giving me deference that I knew was false. Or that looking up to see ye gone put a bolt of fear through me that I swear I would have fallen to my knees and sobbed like a lad to escape."

He drew a stiff breath, his hand slipping away from her. She shivered at the loss, her entire body leaning toward his, seeking out the warmth she witnessed in his gaze.

"I didna know what love was and thought I could live very well without it. I swear that I would have married Gwen and never hesitated. But the first time I kissed ye, I understood the difference. There is no mistress waiting on me. No matter how much we quarrel we shall share a bed. I promise ye that."

Shock held her in its grasp. Her mind raced in circles. She expected a mistress but not one to whom she would be thankful. His promise was arrogant, but so sweet that tears burned her eyes. The distance between them was suddenly too great to endure. She needed to be in contact with him, craved to feel his skin against her own again. It seemed an eternity since the last time they touched. She ached with the need.

Helena reached for him. He drew a sharp breath when her hands made connection with his chest. But she was mesmerized by the look in his eyes. Heat filled the dark centers. She smoothed her hands over his chest, delighting in the hard ridges of muscles hidden beneath his clothing. She moved closer and inhaled the scent of his skin. It was warm and very male. She didn't pause to ponder why she thought he smelled male. For the moment there was only the way she felt and the fact that touching him filled her with happiness.

But she wanted to touch his skin. She cupped her hand behind his neck and pulled him toward her. He shivered when her lips made contact for the first time. She felt the delicate tremor running along his nape. It was a light kiss—only a soft pressing of her mouth against his throat—but the connection sent a bolt of awareness through her that did not stop until it reached every single one of her toes.

"Sweet lass." He cupped her face, taking command of her. "Ye have no idea how much I enjoy yer touch."

His voice was raspy with hunger. He held her head in place

and angled his own before pressing a hard kiss on her lips. Passion licked down her body, making her long to be rid of her dress and stays. She wanted to press against him, their skin bare to increase the sensation, the intimacy.

She reached for the buttons on his doublet, working them loose. He lifted his head and watched her for a moment. The hands cradling her face slipped down to her shoulders. He found the tiny button that kept her partlet closed and opened it.

A little sigh of relief crossed her lips.

"I couldna agree with ye more."

He turned her around, his hands seeking out the laces that held her dress closed. He was far more confident at the task than she was at removing his clothing. In a few tugs and pulls the bodice sagged. He pushed it right off her shoulders and down to her waist. The small hip roll that was tied around her hips didn't stop him, either. He reached down and pulled the tie loose. A moment later her dress puddled around her ankles. He lifted her up and away from her clothing. The night air brushed up her thighs beneath her chemise but was stopped by her stays.

"I want to undress you, too."

Her feet touched the ground closer to the fire. Its scarlet and orange light bathed them both. A carpet lay over the cold wooden floor. Her shoes sunk into it while her toes longed to be free to experience it. Her husband moved to face her. His face was alight with excitement. She reached for him and witnessed the way his eyes lit with anticipation. It was intoxicating. She was equally excited by the impact her touch had on him as she was by any stroke of his hand across her flesh.

She flattened her palms on his chest beneath the open doublet. It still hung on his wide shoulders. A shiver raced down her back as she felt his heartbeat. It was such a simple thing, one that her own body did, but that seemed to be so much more unique when she felt it through her fingertips. Slipping her hands up, she lifted the open edges of the garment over his shoulders. But trying to control it so far above herself proved awkward. He chuckled and shrugged to get the doublet to fall all the way down his arms.

"I swear the slowness of this undressing is about to kill me, but I'd nae miss it for anything."

She reached for his belt buckle, her cheeks brightening. It would have been far more demure to lift her hands toward his collar, but he enjoyed her boldness and she found that too tempting a prospect to miss. His hands slipped into her hair, hunting for her hairpins. He pulled them loose, one at a time, until her braid fell down her back. His belt was stiff but she pulled it back and the weight of his kilt took the carefully pleated garment down to the carpet.

"Undress for me, Helena." Keir's voice was rough with hunger. "I swear, the image of ye brushing yer hair last night is burned into my soul. I want to look at ye, the way ye were made."

The firelight turned his shirt translucent. She gained a glimpse of the way his torso tapered down to a lean waist, and then the unmistakable thrust of his erection. But he took one step away from her and removed his boots in quick, efficient motions. His attention returned to her. The fire crackled and gooseflesh raced along her arms. She was suddenly more aware of her own heartbeat, could hear it and feel it pulsing along her limbs.

The look on his face made her feel beautiful. She realized that nothing had the power to make someone attractive until someone else believed that they were. It wasn't about the color of her hair; it was about this moment and their need for one another.

"All right. But you shall promise to stay until I grant you permission to touch me, husband."

He frowned, but excitement flickered in his eyes. She offered him a look through her eyelashes, enjoying the moment of flirtation. It heightened the need that burned along her skin, deepening the pleasure.

" 'Tis a good thing I was no' playing cards with ye. I would have lost me shirt."

She slowly smiled, her cheeks burning hotter. He tilted his head and offered her a mocking look.

"I do believe I like that idea, husband."

He chuckled. "I thought noblewomen needed their maids."

There was a teasing note in his tone. It challenged her, making her bold. Reaching up, she tugged on the lace, keeping her stays tight. The moment the knot was free, the weight of her breasts pulled the lace so that the front sagged open. A little shiver traveled along her skin. It was a relief to be loosened from the constricting garment. Keir's attention was focused on her fingers. She toyed with the lace, gently pulling it through the first few holes. He swallowed roughly, filling her with confidence. She had never really taken any time to think about whether or not her body was attractive. All of the pads and supports demanded by fashion gave her a distortion of what in fact a man enjoyed in a woman's form.

Keir enjoyed hers. It shimmered in his gaze and his expression was tight. Her curiosity was piqued. She pulled the lace from the next few holes. It was curious to believe that he might enjoy her out of her stays more than he did while she wore the essentials of fashion.

Yet his face indicated that he was very pleased by the enlarging area opening down the front of her stays. She eased the lace through the last few holes and realized that she had been holding her breath. Her body shuddered when she exhaled, sensation tingling along her skin. For the moment she felt freer than she ever had. Keir moved toward her while she was lost in contemplation of his face. His hands cupped her shoulders and gently rubbed them. A little hum of contentment rose from her throat. Need was beginning to pound through her but it was a steady tempo and one that she was at ease enjoying tonight. Something had changed between them. She no longer feared allowing him to see her true emotions.

Keir caught the straps of her corset and sent them down her arms, the open garment sliding easily off her. The heat from the fire traveled up her legs and the fabric of her chemise billowed gently. She was now more aware of her breasts. They felt swollen and needy hanging free.

"Ye win, lass. I couldna wait any longer."

He took a single step away from her and pulled his shirt off his body. She bit into her lower lip as every inch of hard muscle was illuminated by the flickering fire. He looked surreal, like a legend she might envision yet never touch. Her hand stretched out in spite of that thought, seeking to touch the image of perfection.

She shivered when her fingertips made contact. The tremor raced through her, touching off a need that roared to life. Her nipples drew into hard peaks that poked against the sheer fabric of her chemise. The delicate skin covering her breasts begged to be stroked.

"No a bit longer," he said as he gently fingered the fabric of her last garment. She couldn't have agreed more.

Lifting her hands up above her head, she sighed when she felt him drawing the chemise up and over her. Her hands came down on his chest, trailing over the hard muscles. She didn't stop but stroked lower until she found his belly.

His hands cupped her hips. Pleasure swirled in her belly, making her breathing uneven. There was something incredibly intimate about his hands gripping her hips. It drew to mind the way he held her when he was deep inside her. It was a shockingly carnal thought, but one that she enjoyed. Her clitoris throbbed softly between the folds of her sex.

His grip tightened as though he was forcing himself to wait for her, wait to see how far she might trail her fingers, how low she might venture. Maybe it was the need filling her or the approval she witnessed in his eyes, but she sent her hand down until she found the base of his cock.

He muttered something in Gaelic that didn't need translation. The rough tone of his voice was enough to spur her forward. She closed her hand around his girth. His eyes narrowed with pleasure and the grip on her hips tightened. Confidence filled her, along with an insane delight at being able to affect him so strongly. She had been on the receiving end so many times that she was eager to affect him as strongly as he often did her.

Which brought to mind several dark whispers that she had heard at court. . . .

Seduction was an art perfected by many ladies of the court. They shared their knowledge and often shared the details of their liaisons. The fact that she was a maiden didn't deter them. They delighted in whispering torrid details of what went on behind closed doors.

Pulling her hand up his length, she didn't stop until she gripped the head. A thick ridge of flesh circled it but she only remained there for a moment before pulling her closed hand down to the base.

"Helena . . ."

He growled her name and she smiled. The thick carpet beneath her shoes offered a perfect place to try what she had heard whispered. Kneeling in front of him, she gained her first true look at his cock. Thick and long, it was crowned with a ruby head that boasted a slit down half its face. Maintaining her grip, she leaned forward and licked that slit.

"Holy *Christ!*"

Her husband pulled her back by her hair, his face betraying his shock.

"Where in the hell did ye learn to do something like that?"

His brogue was so thick she had trouble understanding him. But there was no mistaking the fact that she was affecting him.

"Court gossip." She worked her hand up to the tip and slid one fingertip through that slit. A muscle jerked along the side of his jaw. "I believe I may have just discovered the first good use of it. What do you think?"

His eyes glowed, anticipation burning in their dark centers. The grip that held her hair relaxed and she lowered her attention to his length again. She licked him again, this time running her tongue all the way around the crown. His hips jerked toward her and she opened her mouth to allow the first inch to enter.

"I swear to God I cannae believe ye're doing this."

There was no way she was going to stop, either. Moving her head in slow motion, she took his length in and out of her mouth, allowing more of his cock to penetrate each time she pressed toward him. He captured the back of her head and his fingers gripped the soft strands, sending little prickles of pain across her scalp. The portion that wouldn't fit into her mouth she stroked with her hand, keeping the same motion as her mouth. He shuddered and groaned, his large body drawn tight as a bowstring.

"Enough, lass! I'll be unmanned in another few moments."

He pulled her away from his cock, frustrating her. "And what is wrong with that?"

He sank to his knees in front of her, maintaining his grip on her hair. One hard arm encircled her waist, shifting the power balance between them. She was now his captive; his superior strength bound her against him. But she was a willing one. Her body eagerly soaked up the feeling of his skin pressed against hers. Pleasure washed over her, every warm ridge of muscle delighting her.

"A good lover doesna spill himself until he has satisfied his partner."

"But many a husband does not concern himself with his wife's pleasure."

He bent her back until she lay on the carpet. But he didn't lie on top of her. He sat back on his haunches, making her long for his body against hers again.

"I enjoy pleasuring ye."

Promise flickered in his eyes. He reached for one of her feet and stripped her shoe and stocking off. His fingers toyed with her bare calf, stroking the skin. The fire had burned down but the coals turned her skin scarlet. She was suddenly shy and pressed her thighs together.

"Och now. That willnae do at all."

He lifted her other foot and removed her last garment. He gently massaged her foot for a long moment before rubbing his fingers down over her ankle, working the muscles with soothing motions. A little hum of pleasure crossed her lips.

"Better, but I'm wanting that confidence back that ye had when ye so boldly sucked my cock."

Her cheeks burned but she couldn't stop the smile that parted her lips. His hands stroked past her knee, gently parting her thighs. He leaned down until she could feel the soft hair that coated his chest against her breasts. His breath teased her lips before he pressed a warm kiss onto her mouth.

"But I'm also wanting to repay the favor."

"What?"

He chuckled while keeping her back on the floor with his larger body. He gently cupped both of her breasts. Need spiked through her but there was no hurry displayed in his expression. He tilted his head and pressed a kiss against her neck while his thumbs toyed with her nipples. She arched beneath him, craving more contact. He kissed his way down her body until he found one soft mound. The skin drew tight with anticipation, her nipple aching for the touch of his lips. She had never wanted something so badly.

Keir didn't disappoint her. He licked his way to the top of her breast and closed his lips around the hard point. She cried out, unable to keep the pleasure behind her lips. She reached for him, gripping his shoulders and arching so that her breast was raised up for his mouth to feast upon. He cupped it, his grip holding the soft mound in place. She'd never have guessed that a mouth might feel so hot, but his lips burned across the tender tip of her nipple, the point of his tongue lavishing it with attention.

It all flowed down to her belly. Her clitoris throbbed and she forgot why she wanted to keep her thighs together. The folds of her sex felt swollen and she needed to open her legs to relieve that pressure. He smoothed a hand over her hip and down across her belly the moment she opened for him.

"Ah, exactly what I was hoping for. An invitation."

His fingers grazed over her mons. She jerked, too aware of every touch to remain still. He pressed her down with one large hand centered on the top of her belly. But it was a soft touch, his hand stroking and massaging, tempting her to relax and allow him to touch more of her. Her clitoris begged for attention.

"Better, lass. Much better."

His fingers ventured lower, stroking across her open sex. It was a mere whisper of a touch but she sent her hands into the carpet as her body contorted with sensation. It flowed through her like a living thing, all of the need combining into a passion that was consuming her.

Keir placed a soft kiss on the smooth skin of her belly before moving back to hover over her spread sex.

"Keir?"

He looked up her body, a wicked gleam in his eyes. "What, lass? Did the gossips never discuss how a man might repay the favor of having his cock sucked?"

"No. . . ."

He rubbed her belly with a firm hand, then stilled and pressed her against the floor.

"Well now, I'll be happy to introduce ye to what delight ye just gave me."

Her breath froze in her lungs, and even when they burned she didn't exhale. She was too shocked by the sight between her thighs. His shoulders kept her spread wide but he used a single hand to spread her further, exposing the little button of her clitoris.

"Keir . . ."

He didn't respond to her. Instead he leaned down and gently lapped her exposed slit. She would have rolled away if he wasn't holding her down. That single touch sent desire up her passage so quickly her vision blurred. Her neck muscles lost the strength to keep her head up and she closed her eyes when she collapsed against the floor.

There was nothing except the hot tip of his tongue. He licked her slowly, beginning at the opening to her passage and up her spread slit to her clitoris. He toyed with it gently until her hips arched toward him.

He seemed to understand her need. His lips closed around the little nub. Pleasure raked through her, drawing tighter. He began sucking and she cried out, her head thrashing from side to side. She was suddenly afloat on a rippling surface of sensation and need. Delight shot through her a hundred times a minute but it was always chased by need so acute she felt she couldn't bear it. Seconds became eternities in which she bounced between need and pleasure. It drew tighter and tighter, her body straining toward his mouth, seeking true satisfaction. He didn't grant it to her quickly. His mouth released her clitoris so that he could lick his way down to her passage. The tip of his tongue circled the delicate skin several times until she sobbed with need. She felt so empty, tears stung her eyes.

"Aye, lass, I've no more discipline for waiting either."

His brogue had thickened again but she didn't care. He closed his lips around her clitoris and this time he applied more pressure. She felt the promise of release coming closer and closer. Her heart pounded harder as the pleasure built to a crescendo and burst. It flooded her with blinding pleasure that tore away every pretense of who she was expected to be. There was only the way she felt and the man holding her throughout the torrent.

She lost track of time but gasped for breath when it began to subside. A moment later her husband rose above her. Hunger drew his features tight and the scarlet glow of the coals bathed him.

But he didn't cover her. One hand grasped her hip and

rolled her over onto her belly. He slid one arm beneath her body and pulled her back onto her knees. She felt him behind her, his hands gripping each of her hips just as she had enjoyed him doing earlier.

This time it was very carnal and that pleased her greatly. His cock pressed against her, easily sliding into her slick passage. Deeper satisfaction filled her along with his flesh. Ripples of delight were still moving through her and the hard pounding seemed to add to it. He wasn't gentle and she realized that she didn't want him to be. She wanted to feel his strength, enjoy the hard slap of his body behind her. His cock was harder than she recalled and he drove it deeply into her, all the time holding her hips in place, even pulling her back to meet each thrust. Lust and need sent soft cries past her lips.

"Aye, lass, let me hear ye whimper. 'Tis a sweet sound."

Her entire body was feeling so much more than it ever had. Keir grasped her hips and rode her with fast, hard thrusts. Her breasts swung back and forth with the motion, her hands gripping the carpet, but she began moving back toward each thrust. Her back arched, lifting her bottom into prominent display. A soft growl of approval came from her husband.

The fingers on her hips suddenly tightened and she heard a harsh intake of breath. A second later his seed flooded her. Hot and searing, he thrust a few final times before catching his weight on flattened hands that pressed down on either side of her. Her legs quivered but so did his body against her back. They both sank down onto the carpet, his arms pulling her against his body. He rolled onto his back, his chest rising and falling rapidly.

"Sweet Christ. Ye may be the death of me, lass." He pulled her close, pushing her head down onto his shoulder. "But I'll face me demise a happy man."

"You shouldn't tempt fate by saying things such as that."

He found the end of her braid and began working her hair loose with his fingers.

"Like what? Am I no' permitted to tell ye how much I enjoy lying with ye? Does the fact that ye're noble born mean we must be unhappy? Sharing a bed the minimum amount of times in order to produce children that will then grow up with parents who have no affection for each other? I dinnae agree with that. Ye make me very happy, Helena."

Her throat tightened. She didn't understand the strange reaction. "You simply should not tempt fate."

She tried to roll away but he held her still. "I'm chilled."

"Nay, ye are not. Ye're trying to escape so that ye can think yerself back into that model of proper behavior that yer parents sent ye off to court believing in."

He rolled over on top of her, pinning her down with his greater weight. "I'll nae have that, Helena. I have tender feelings for you, and I am stunned to discover such, too. The difference is I thought I could live without affection in my marriage and I'm happy to be proven wrong. 'Tis truly a delight to find myself proven wrong."

"Love is insanity."

He kissed her, hard and long. He didn't stop until she kissed him in return, the need inside her too great to ignore when he touched her.

"Than I am a happy victim of the disease."

He rolled over her but left her closest to the fire. The coals bathed her bare skin in heat and Keir kept her tight against his body to warm the rest of her. He was correct; she was not cold. He had her hair loose and began playing with it.

"But—"

"Hush now. Tomorrow will be time enough for us to return

to what the world outside those doors tells us is right and
wrong. For the moment, let us enjoy just being a man and his
woman, with nothing to worry us save when passion will demand more from us."

"You mean lovers."

He cupped her chin and raised her face so that their eyes
met. Approval coated his features and she found it too tempting to resist.

"Aye, lass. Now ye and I have something to agree upon.
Lovers is a fine word."

"It is nice."

Very nice. Her eyelids fluttered, suddenly feeling heavy. Her
heart slowed down and the night carried the heat from her
skin, but not the scent of her lover. She cuddled up closer,
seeking his heat, her legs sliding along his. She savored the
difference between them, his harder form and the way her
body melted against it so that they might lie so completely
against one another. It was perfection. He stirred, shifting for
a moment and reaching for something. She didn't open her
eyes to see what. But she sighed when his kilt wrapped
around her. He tucked the length of soft wool over her body
and his, stroking a hand through her hair to lie it in a straight
line. Her lips rose into a smile of contentment. Maybe it was
just fine that he was not what she had always expected of a
husband.

After all, he was a Scot.

Edmund smiled. It was a small curve of his lips, nothing too
large. But he was very pleased. Obviously the assassin was
good and worth the money he'd paid the man. Across the
great hall the man paused just long enough to make eye con-

tact with him before he blended back into the crush of courtiers.

It took a clever man to gain entrance to the great hall, the feat likely costing the man a good bit of his fee.

Edmund tipped his mug back without a care for the cost of the wine. His lips curled into a sneer as he considered the pain it would cost him to retrieve his sister. She would have to make recompense for that. He never forgot a slight. Not even from a family member. He was the earl, or would be, as soon as his father died.

And his only sibling was not going to be bred by a Scot. Even if he had to offer his back to an assassin. He handed the goblet off and strode away from his retainers. They hid their smirks behind gloved hands, assuming he was off to enjoy a quick fuck in the dark corridors of the palace now that it was well into the night.

Edmund grinned. He was off to set in motion a plan that was truly majestic in its cunning. He traveled the darker hallways, pinching out a few of the lanterns along the way. Outside the storm still raged, the wind driving heavy rain into the glass windows. It filled the hallways with noise, which suited him perfectly. He kept walking until he neared the dock. The royal barge was missing, no doubt taken to a safer harbor. Here the sound of the storm was loud because the river added to it. The water was choppy and speckled with debris such as tree limbs. He turned all the way around the corner but he was not alone.

"Now this is a surprise."

Raelin McKorey turned in a flutter of gold silk and wool cloak. Her eyes widened when she recognized him. Edmund stood in the opening that would allow her off the dock.

"Meeting a lover, are you?"

She scowled at him. "I am not. I sought a bit of peace from the hall full of men like ye."

Edmund toyed with the sword hanging from his hip. He stepped toward her and she backed away.

"I really am very happy to have this opportunity to settle our affairs."

She glanced behind her, but stepped even closer to the edge of the dock when she looked up to find him closing in on her. The water was so swollen, it ran over the edges of the dock.

"Stop this. I am in service to the queen."

"You are a bitch who doesn't know her place—"

"Sweet mercy!"

Raelin's eyes widened in terror. Edmund stared at her face, enjoying it. White-hot pain went through his shoulder, snapping him out of his mental obsession with watching Raelin suffer. He looked down to see the tip of a thin dagger protruding from his own body. The pain was so intense he felt almost in awe of it. His thoughts became sluggish, his heart thumping slower and slower. The dagger withdrew, sending a new stream of torment through his body. Hot pain felt as if it was melting his flesh.

"Good work. Exactly what I paid for." He turned to look at the assassin, his thoughts still moving slowly.

"Guards!" Raelin raised her voice so it could be heard over the rushing water.

"Kill her!" Edmund turned and lunged toward Raelin. "She'll ruin our game. I need McQuade blamed for this attack." He grasped a handful of her silk skirts. She dug her heels into the wooden deck to escape, but his strength was too much for her.

"Kill her!" Rage began to burn in him again. "I want to see her bleed."

The knife penetrated his own chest instead. This time his entire body went cold. His knees bent and slammed into the floor but there was no pain, only a growing chill. Every muscle drew taut, his fingers tightening on Raelin's skirts. The tip of the dagger was stained with blood. The moonlight reflected off it as water soaked into his hose.

It was a mortal wound. Looking behind him, he stared at the man he'd hired.

"I paid you . . . to wound me. . . ."

The man pulled his knife loose. "Aye, that you did, and I done my duty with the first thrust."

"But . . . what means this second one?"

Edmund felt his heart slowing even more. There were long seconds when it did not beat at all. His hands twisted in the fabric of Raelin's skirt, trying to hold onto the world of the living.

"Well now. Another man paid me to kill you. It's only business, you understand. I've a family to provide for. You paid me to wound ye and he paid me to kill ye. I done both jobs."

"Who?"

The assassin tilted his head and considered the question. He suddenly sniffed and shrugged. "Suppose it don't make no difference if I tell you. Lord Ronchford paid me. To kill you. Claimed you took his money and never gave him what he paid for. Seeing as how he's the man you left that letter naming Keir McQuade as the one that done the deed, it all works out rather well. To my way of thinking." Both of my customers will be satisfied.

"I am . . . a . . . peer. . . ."

"You'll be a dead peer soon, as will the girl. I'm sorry about that. But she's seen my face so I have to kill her. Pity, though. No one paid me to kill her. It's a waste, sure enough."

There was a rending of fabric. Raelin pulled the small dirk

her brother insisted she carry from her bodice, and cut her dress away. She fell backward, crying out as her body tumbled into the raging water behind her. It rose over her head, encasing her in darkness that was bone-numbingly cold. The cloak pulled on her throat, choking her as the heavy fabric was caught by the current. She went deeper as she tried frantically to fight against her clothing. Her lungs burned and her fingers refused to unhook the cloak.

Sweet mercy help her. . . .

Chapter Eleven

"Raelin?" Catriona McAlister called softly because the queen was sleeping. Several of her ladies had nodded off as well, their eyes closed even as they sat in their attendant chairs. Many times, that was the only sleep a lady of the bed-chamber got.

"Raelin?"

Catriona pouted. She wanted to slip out while everyone was asleep. The queen had spent most of the last few days abed while it was dark and gloomy. She was full of the need to do something—anything but sit and be still. She grabbed her cloak and slipped out of the queen's chambers. The dark wool garment was large enough to cover her golden gown. She reached for the hood and pulled it up to hide her blond hair. Excitement laced her blood like wine, slowly intoxicating her. She cast a look right and then left before hurrying down the long hallway toward the garden. With all the rain, the river would be wild. She missed Scotland. London had so many people and buildings. She longed for the view of a grass-covered hill with the sound of water. Now that the queen was pregnant yet again, all the maids of honor could expect to re-main inside with her. The lying-in would be the worst. All the windows would be covered with carved wooden screens to re-duce the light so that Anne might conserve her strength for the birth. For a full month, there would be nothing but whispers and careful steps.

That certainty made her walk faster. Raelin was probably already outside savoring the moment of freedom. She moved down a hallway that would take her to the water gate. The sound of the Thames reached her ears, tantalizing her with everything she had been shut away from for the last few days.

She froze before making it to the edge of the river gate. The storm clouds didn't allow much of the full moon's light in, only a dingy gray illuminating the choppy river water. It shone off wet spots on the dock, but they were beneath the roof, built to protect the royals from rain when they boarded the royal barge.

The rushing river filled her ears, but the scent of blood touched her nose. A frozen form lay on the dock. Her hand shook and she turned in a quick circle, searching the shadows for assassins.

"Help! Guards! Help!"

Her heart felt like it would break through her chest, every second taking longer than an hour. She heard the footfalls of the royal guard but it seemed to take forever for them to reach her. The first to reach her were naught but shapes in the dark.

"Look there!" She pointed at the still body lying unmoving on the dock. The yellow glow of lanterns came closer, casting light over the dismal scene.

Catriona gasped. The stone floor was covered in blood. It seeped out from the body, running into a growing puddle. The fine fabric of his clothing made no difference in the color of his blood. The royal guard turned him over and she smothered a horrified gasp.

Edmund Knyvett was dead. His eyes were still open but were glazed over. The guards shook their heads but Catriona followed their eyes toward the length of gold silk that Edmund's hand clenched. It lay stained with his blood, and hung over the edge of the dock.

It was the same gold silk as her own dress.

"Raelin!"

She ran to the edge of the dock. The guards tried to stop her, but she fought them. The silk dropped into the choppy water, but there was no sign of her friend. The guards pulled her back, refusing to allow her near the swollen river. She tried to resist the urge to look at the scene but couldn't keep her eyes from lowering to the blood once again. This time she stepped on another torn piece of fabric. Reaching down, she picked it up. Turning it toward the lantern light, she stared at the heather, tan, and green stripes.

McQuade colors.

She would know them anywhere. She opened the folded parchment and found the signature of the McQuade laird. Disbelief held her in its grasp, her fingers tightening on the paper until it crinkled. One of the guards took it from her, his face becoming a mask of fury.

"This is murder."

The fire had burned down, but Helena wasn't cold. Keir was too warm. His fingers were busy toying with a lock of her hair. She watched the way he stroked it, slowly running his fingertips over the silky strands. He'd pulled his kilt over them both while he kept her close against his body. Her legs tangled with his. Her head rested on his chest.

"I cannae wait to lie with ye like this at Red Stone."

Neither could she. The desire was growing inside her. Even though she had never seen it, the tone of his voice enticed her to want it as much as he did.

A pounding on the front door shattered the moment. Keir was on his feet before he heard his men arguing with whomever was at the door. He shrugged into his shirt while reaching for his sword. That single garment was the only concession he gave to his modesty.

"Stay down, Helena."

Hard authority edged his voice. A fist landed on the chamber door. She gasped and rolled onto her knees, holding the wool close. Keir opened the door, the tip of his sword aimed at whoever was on the other side.

The uniformed royal guard stood there with Farrell in front of them.

"What the devil is this?" Keir glared at his man.

"They claim the king demands yer presence."

Helena gasped. The king did not send his personal guard to make sure that someone showed up unless there was trouble. Grave trouble.

Keir lowered his sword but didn't set the weapon aside. The guards looked around the chamber, stopping when they spied her.

"I'll thank ye to keep yer eyes off me bride."

"His Majesty wishes to see the lady as well. We will wait outside."

The captain of the guard offered Keir a nod of respect but he swept the room one more time, looking for exits. He pulled the door shut with a firm hand.

Keir cursed. His body was tight with rage.

"I detest this city."

"I agree."

He jerked around to stare at her. Anger held his expression tight but there was a flicker of appreciation in his dark eyes. Pushing to her feet, Helena shook out the length of McQuade wool.

"I suppose I had better learn to fold this correctly."

"Being wed to you, I might need to keep a second one about so that I don't get caught in me shirt as I just did."

He was trying to be playful but there was too much tension in his voice. He hesitated over releasing his sword, finally gritting his teeth and placing it aside. He took his plaid and began laying it across the table in neat pleats.

"I'll teach ye later, lassie. It seems Jamie needs something settled. Ye'd best get dressed."

She turned to obey, her stomach becoming queasy. She couldn't help but suspect that her brother was yet again attempting to regain his hold on her. The sounds of clothing being donned filled the chamber. Her husband dressed quickly and moved across the chamber to help her. He touched her carefully, as though he was worried that she might vanish. Lifting her rebraided hair to his lips while she buttoned her doublet, he closed his eyes and inhaled, enjoyment breaking through the tension on his face. She quivered, tenderness flooding her.

She must have made some sound because he opened his eyes and stared into hers. His hand tightened around her hair, his face drawing tight once more.

"I swear, Helena, that no matter what scheme is afoot tonight, I will nae give ye up. Nae while I draw breath. I swear it."

She reached for him, her hands landing on his shoulders. He wrapped an arm around her waist, pulling her against his body.

"I will trust in that, Keir."

"Och now, lass, that's the sweetest thing I've ever heard."

He pressed a hard kiss against her lips. It was a promise of many more, a declaration of his intent to keep her. She rose onto her toes to press herself tighter into his embrace. Desperation was beginning to rake its claws across her, dark fore-boding filling her thoughts. She kissed him back and sighed when he broke away. Firm resolve filled his dark eyes.

"Pin yer hair up now. I've a mind to be finished with this court business."

There was so much courage in him. She took solace in the firm resolution she witnessed in his eyes. Reaching for her hairpins, she coiled her braid while her husband retrieved her cloak.

Whatever it was, they would face it together.

"That's a bloody lie." Keir didn't add any title onto his state-ment. He stared at his king, his body seething with rage.

James Stuart rubbed his jaw. "Your signature is on the letter ordering his death, man."

"But nae my seal."

Lord Ronchford looked at his king. "This man comes from a family of violent men."

"Violent? I'll tell ye what is violent. You trying to kidnap a woman on the street because you and her brother had some manner of arrangement."

"I don't know what you are trying to insinuate, Scot."

Keir pointed at the man. "I'm saying it plainly enough. You tried to steal Helena away the night before I was set to wed her. It was my men that beat ye off her."

"So you admit to setting upon men in the street now?"

"Enough!" James slapped the arms of his throne. His guards already held their pikes in a lowered position, most of the points aimed at Keir.

The English lord fumed, but what drew Keir's attention was the look on the faces of the king's personal guard. In spite of their position of duty, you could see condemnation of him in their eyes. It was English against Scot, as it had been for hundreds of years. He forced his rage down, searching for diplomacy. He might be a Scot but he wouldn't prove to be a barbarian. Sometimes, using your brains was more important than winning the fight.

"Anyone could have written that note, sire."

"And the wool?"

Ronchford sounded too arrogant, making Keir's fist itch to knock the man down. Keir raised an eyebrow. He pulled on the end of his belt before Ronchford figured what he was doing. James understood and a hint of suspicion entered the monarch's eyes.

"There's my kilt, man, there is nay an inch missing. Nor a single repair. Kilts are woven in one length, never cut. Never sewn." Keir held it up and watched the guards' eyes shift to it. Ronchford flushed, his eyelids fluttering. Keir stared at the telltale action. The man was covering something up.

"That proves nothing. You might have a dozen kilts."

"My wife was with me every second since I left the queen's chambers."

Several guards nodded, but Ronchford drew in a stiff breath.

"She likely conspired with you so that her sons might inherit the Kenton earldom!"

Keir sent his fist into the other man's face. The guards didn't react fast enough and the other man went rolling over his own body. The pikes appeared inches from his throat but he remained still and looked at the king.

"Leave my wife out of this. I'll nae listen to any man blacken her name. Ye want to fight, man, ye fight with me."

Ronchford stumbled to his feet. A trickle of blood marred his chin. Fury flickered in his eyes but the king held up a hand.

"I was not aware that you and Edmund Knyvett were such good friends that ye would stand in front of yer king and demand blood so passionately."

Ronchford's eyelids fluttered once more. Keir crossed his arms over his chest.

"He was at the table the night I won Helena's dowry. He left once Edmund ran out of coin." Keir turned his attention to his king. "I stayed."

"That is correct. Edmund was my friend and fellow English peer. I will not stand idle while his murderer goes unpunished!"

"We do not as yet know who that is."

"My king . . . we have the order and the piece of kilt!"

James stood. "Yet we do not have the witness. Believe me, this matter shall be investigated. We shall begin a search for my queen's maid at dawn."

"She's another Scot."

James was not amused. "Enough, Ronchford! Being a Scot does not mean McQuade is guilty of murder."

"His father tried to murder you and he has the most to gain."

Keir flinched. It was the truth. "I didna kill that weasel. He was kin by my marriage."

Ronchford snarled. "So much your kin that you did not allow him to be present on the morning after your nuptials to inspect the wedding sheet? Oh yes, Lord Hurst. Everyone at court knows that."

"Is that true, McQuade?"

The king's voice had dropped in to a deadly tone. Keir stared him straight in the eye.

"Aye. I didna want him anywhere near his sister, seeing as how he seemed to enjoy hitting her." He turned to look at Ronchford. "Everyone at court saw proof of that on her face.

But the man never appeared at my door, nor did he send any of his men to see the wedding sheet. I'll be happy to have it displayed."

"Of course you would. Consummation of your wedding only furthers your case to claim the Kenton earldom for your sons."

"I'm nae ambitious enough to gain what I want through murder."

Ronchford laughed. "You are a Scot. Raiding is in your blood. I am not the only one that can see the blood on your hands."

"I'll be the judge of that." James Stuart sat back in his throne.

Ronchford spread his hands out. "I am not the only English nobleman who is now fearing for his own life."

The king snorted. "Ye're nae quivering in yer lace stockings, Ronchford, so dinnae try to tell me that ye are. Ye're mad as hell that ye didna wed that lass, which gives ye as much reason to be viewed suspiciously as McQuade. And how many times must I remind the lot of ye English-born nobles that I am *Scots*?"

"Majesty . . ."

The king held up his hand. "I am nae making light of the matter. A peer has been murdered in my own palace. It will not go unpunished. But I shall not watch the blame be laid too easily on any man. There will be careful study of the facts, not what rumors try to form into truth."

The king stared at Keir. Keir returned it without flinching. His monarch shifted his attention to Ronchford and the man did not hold up as well. He sniffed and shook his head.

"This is preposterous. Edmund was my friend."

"Then you should be relieved to know that I intend to make sure his death is investigated."

Ronchford fell silent, his body becoming still. His face lost some of its color and the room became a compressed space full of tension. The guards looked at both men, uncertainty in their eyes. The king held his emotions behind a mask that spoke of too many similar times in his past.

"Convey both of these men to the Tower."

"But sire!" The king flicked his fingers toward the blustering man, and Ronchford found himself hauled away by the royal guard. They dragged him from the room even as he shouted at the king to hear him out. His boots skidded on the stone floor.

Four guards surrounded Keir but they merely held their place while he waited for Ronchford's yells to fade down the hallway.

The king stared at Keir. "I've no choice, McQuade. Ye must be placed in the Tower if I am to maintain peace between English and Scots in this court."

"Aye. I see the way of it."

The king's expression lightened. A ghost of respect lit his eyes. Keir ground his teeth together to keep his temper in check. The idea of being confined sent his entire body into revolt. He wanted to fight, not to stand there agreeing that it was for the best. But the king was nae in the mood to be challenged.

"May I have a few moments with me bride?"

James nodded. "Aye." He pointed at his captain of the guard. "Allow McQuade to bid his wife good-bye."

The captain removed his hat and bowed before turning toward Keir. His gut tightened but he forced his body to bend in deference to his monarch.

"I bid ye good luck in yer search for young Raelin McKorey."

The king's eyebrow rose. Keir straightened and stared at James Stuart.

"That's correct. I have no fear of the lass being found alive.

But I think ye should find her a husband soon. That lass seems to attract trouble here at court."

He turned and left, unable to maintain his poise any longer. Each step took tremendous amounts of discipline to force his feet to move. Every instinct made him want to smash his fist into the guard nearest him and escape.

But he was laird and the McQuades could not suffer another disgrace. He would go to the Tower and hope against hope that Raelin McKorey proved as strong as her Scottish blood, and was found alive.

If she wasn't, he might be joining her in death very shortly.

Helena wrung her hands. She didn't seem to have enough poise or control to remain in one place. She paced back and forth in an alcove outside the king's receiving room. Something was wrong. She could feel it permeating the air. Even in the dead of night the palace felt devoid of joy. Death's icy claw was creeping through the hallways. She saw it on the faces of the few people who passed. That gray cast to their skin and the way they looked at the ground the moment they recognized her. Keir's retainers stood nearby, their faces growing tighter and more tense with every turn she made.

She suddenly stopped. Footfalls echoed on the stone tile. They were extremely loud, echoing in the silence. She turned to face the most horrible sight she had ever beheld—her husband flanked by the royal guard. There could only be one reason for such a thing. The air grew even colder around her. She was certain that the cries of other unfortunates echoed from years past—such as Queen Catherine Howard, who had run screaming through the hallways to beg Henry the Eighth to spare her life.

He hadn't.

She suppressed a horrified whimper, forcing it down her

throat lest she disgrace her husband in front of his retainers and the royal guard. She was a noblewoman. Her mother's lecturing voice grew louder than the icy screams of the condemned ghosts of the past.

Keir came to her, grasping her hands in a grip that hurt. The overuse of strength confirmed what she already knew.

"I'm sent to the Tower."

"Why?" Her voice was a mere whisper. All eyes were on them but she couldn't waste the opportunity to touch him. Even so simple a touch as palm against palm was too sweet to forgo. His men glanced at one another, their bodies becoming tenser. The guards gripped their sword pommels and the tension grew even thicker.

"Yer brother was murdered."

"Sweet mercy."

The air rushed out of her lungs so fast, spots danced before her eyes. The only thing that kept her alert was the near-crushing grip in which her husband held her hands. Pain shot down her fingers but she did not wiggle them.

"A letter with my signature and a piece of McQuade plaid was found near his body."

Her horror doubled, the screams of condemned ghosts growing louder in her head. She clamped her hands tightly around his, trying to hold onto him.

"Lies! English lies!" Farrell snarled.

"Be still." Keir shot the two words toward his men in a tone that she had never heard before. It was solid steel and sharp with authority.

"My time is brief so I must be blunt." His eyes swept his men before he returned his dark gaze to her; it was filled with the need to fight. She witnessed the battle he waged to conduct himself with noble bearing, thinking of his people instead of his own needs.

"I understand."

"Yer friend, young Raelin McKorey, was swept away by the river. A piece of her gown was found in yer brother's grasp. Let us hope she is found alive and makes it here to the king, still able to testify as to the truth of the matter."

Or he would stand accused of murdering a peer . . .

Helena fought back her emotions. She had to be as strong as he was. He looked past her shoulder at his men.

"I charge ye with keeping my bride safe. Even if she deems it unnecessary."

There was no leniency in his gaze when he looked back at her. "Forgive me, lass, but I cannae suffer knowing ye are unsafe. Whoever killed yer brother did it to get to you. I have nae doubt."

He kissed her, refusing her the chance to reply, his mouth taking hers with no concern for the eyes watching them. Time stood still for that moment, his kiss pulling her into a world where nothing existed but the joy that touching him produced inside her. It was a perfect utopia, but fragile, too. A harsh grunt shattered it, sending everything down to the ground in a shower of silver rain. Keir released her hands and she shivered. Bitter cold clamped around her as she watched her husband give a final look to his men before turning in a swirl of his kilt. The royal guards fell into formation around him, the light glittering off the deadly tips of their pikes. Their steps bounced between the stone walls, merging with the ghosts of other men and women who had been taken off to the Tower, so many of them noble, so many of them losing their heads.

She stiffened her resolve and walked down the hallway as gracefully as her mother had taught her. She didn't do it for her parents or their idea of what she should be to benefit the family name.

She did it for Keir, for the laird that he was and the man

who refused to place his own desires above those of his clan. She was his wife, so she kept her chin level even when she crossed the great hall and heard the whispers begin.

She was Lady Hurst, and would not be seen as anything but worthy of that name.

News travels quickly, and bad news even faster still. The servants lined up for Helena's arrival, even in the dead of the night. Their lips bloodless from being pressed so tightly together, they cast their gazes toward the floor. Farrell didn't remain in the stable. The man followed her along with another at whom he snapped his fingers when she walked toward the front door.

"You must begin looking for Raelin."

Farrell's eyes flickered with approval. But he shook his head. "I cannae. My laird charged me with yer well-being."

"Very well. I shall accompany you."

Farrell looked more approving but swallowed roughly. "I cannae take ye into harm's way. Wherever that poor lass is, there is sure to be trouble."

"We cannot leave this to chance."

Her voice rose and she shut her mouth to regain her composure. Farrell agreed with her. She could feel the man's impatience radiating off him. He looked at the walls of the house like a cage.

"I cannae place ye at risk. My laird charged me with yer safety, my lady."

Plenty of people had called her *lady*. As far back as she could recall the title had been used by everyone, save her immediate family. She had learned to detest the word at court, but tonight it was different. Farrell spoke it out of respect and she had no doubt that she had earned it.

"Yes, you are correct. He did say that."

Her mind was racing and her feet moving as she tried to think of some solution. She climbed the stairs to the second floor, one of the maids hurrying past her to open the door and light the way with a lantern. The candles in the chamber had died down and the fireplace was now cold.

A shiver raced down her spine. The room was as unwelcome as a cell. In fact it was a prison now that Keir didn't share it with her. Her belly tightened until it ached, the horror of the night digging into her like iron spikes.

The maid lit the candles and light flickered over the turned-down bed. Nausea sickened her when she looked at it. Understanding filled her, Keir's words replaying in her mind. She hadn't really grasped what she felt either, not until it was taken from her.

That was love.

The gripping claws raking along her belly at their separation was that most elusive emotion, the thing that playwrights tantalized their audiences with and physicians treated with bitter tonics. It was the thing that noblewomen were warned against because their marriages would not be forged on the rhythm of the heart.

Yet every now and again, fortune smiled on some. She was in love with her husband and it was a treasure that she had not the wits to see until treachery snatched him away.

Oh, Edmund . . .

Try as she might, there was no remorse in her for her brother—only a sense of pity that he had wasted his life on schemes that bore no true gain, not the sort of gain that truly mattered. She didn't think he had ever been happy, and that sent two tears down her cheeks. No one would weep for him sincerely; only out of noble duty.

"Shall I fetch you something warm from the kitchen, my lady?"

Her belly was in knots. Helena shook her head but glanced toward the door to see Farrell and the other McQuade retainer standing on either side of the doorframe. Each of them had a large sword tied to their backs and the lanterns were lit to illuminate the passageway. Their bodies were tense and set to stand guard just as their laird had charged them to do.

How very much like the Tower . . .

She was as imprisoned as Keir by this foul scheme. The only difference was the uniform of her guards.

She suddenly stiffened, an idea forming in her mind. The maid was still waiting for an answer, the girl fingering the edge of her apron.

"No. I am not hungry. If there is a chest somewhere, have it brought up."

"Yes, mistress."

She was gone in a rustle of wool skirts. Helena glanced at the bed. She would never be able to sleep in it but she moved toward it with determination.

Farrell wanted to know what she was doing. Helena avoided the burly Scot's eyes and hurried down to the kitchen. There were too many things to do and each task felt as though it took twice the time to accomplish. Her frustration grew as dawn turned the horizon a lighter shade of gray. The storm showed no signs of breaking. Rain fell on the city, and those who ventured out into the street huddled beneath their cloaks.

"I need a bath."

The housekeeper looked at her strangely. "In this chill?"

"Aye. Here in the kitchen, it is warm enough."

The housekeeper didn't agree but she snapped her fingers at two maids and Helena stepped into her bath within the hour. She forced herself into the tub, refusing to quibble over the lack of privacy. The two boys who helped in the kitchens were banished by another sharp snap of fingers, but the cook was busy watching her while she baked bread. The house-keeper brought her a piece of soap that was kept locked in the store cabinet. Only she held the ring of keys that unlocked the cabinet where valuable items were kept. She might be dis-missed if even one linen was found missing. As the new mis-tress of the house, it would be Helena's duty to oversee the counting and marking of figures in the household books.

At least it would if she were not planning on departing.

Taking up the soap, she scrubbed herself from head to toe, even lathering up her hair before leaning over so that the maid might pour fresh water through it. She kept her mind on the task at hand, standing up before the water was completely cool. Now was not the time for soaking.

In the stormy weather her hair was slow to dry. She lost pa-tience with it and had it braided while still damp.

"My lady, you'll catch a chill."

"I must see the king before he retreats to his privy chamber and his council begins to bend his ear."

Edmund's insistence that she study the court was finally going to be of service. The king kept a pattern to his days. Even with the matter of her brother's murder, the monarch would attend his private chapel for services before going to see his privy council. She would wait for him in the hallway or risk being one of a hundred waiting for the chamberlain to call her name in the outer hall. It was one advantage to being a woman. The royal guard would not stop her as quickly as a man. They would assume that she was on her way to the queen's chambers or running some errand for one of the ladies.

But it was a dangerous game that she played. James Stuart ruled absolutely. If the king was annoyed by her presence, his wrath would fall on Keir. But she squared her shoulders and finished dressing. She ordered spices and soap packed in the two trunks the staff had found in the stable. Both were difficult to close when she finished adding everything that she could think of.

The Tower was not known for its refinements. Many a prisoner had found himself at the mercy of guards who only fetched them what they wanted if there was a large bribe attached to the request. Farrell eyed the trunks with suspicion.

"What are ye planning, my lady?"

"To begin acting like a wife."

The Scot raised an eyebrow. He planted himself in front of her, his hands settled on his hips. None of the McQuade retainers moved to pick up the trunks. They waited on his command. Farrell stood silently staring at her.

"Do you think your laird is being treated any too well in an English stronghold?"

"I'm trying nae to dwell on it or I'm likely to find myself run through when I charge the bloody bastards with keeping an innocent man prisoner."

"There are other things that might be done."

The Scot raised an eyebrow again and his fellow clansmen shifted closer to make sure they heard what she said.

"Noblemen have rights in the Tower of London. I plan to ask the king to allow me to take these trunks to my husband."

"And do you think Jamie will be agreeing to that?"

"Only if I catch him in the hallway after morning prayers and alone."

Several throats cleared. Farrell narrowed his eyes. "Nae alone. You will nae be alone while it's my duty to see to ye."

"The king will bestow many things on a weeping bride that he might not grant to a woman who is surrounded by men."

Helena abandoned her stiff composure and widened her eyes. She wrung her hands and allowed her lower lip to tremble. Farrell's complexion darkened. Alarm flickered in his eyes before she shook it off and regained her poise.

"Och well, now that's a low bit of trickery." Relief coated his voice. "But it just might work."

A gleam entered his eyes. He glanced at the horizon to judge the hour.

"We'd best make our way to the palace."

The men behind him picked up the trunks a moment later.

"And you shall leave me alone?"

"It will look that way." Farrell aimed a solid look at her. "But I swear on my mother's sweet head that McQuade eyes will be on ye at all times."

The palace was already filling with nobles. Another day of competing for the king's favor showed on their faces. Helena tightened her resolve and resisted the urge to turn her head when the whispers began around her.

Her thoughts were on her plan and she hurried past the great hall and into the maze of corridors that connected the palace buildings. Each monarch added to it, and newcomers often became confused.

She glided easily to where she knew the king would pass. A shadow of guilt descended on her as she recognized that her brother was the one who had taught her the hallways.

Well, she would use something of Edmund for a good purpose. There was only the living to consider and she was all too aware of how quickly her husband might join Edmund in the afterlife. Without proof to clear his name, Keir might face the headmen's ax. Someone's blood would be spilled over the murder of a peer. Every lord on the privy council was no doubt anxiously awaiting the king to demand it.

They needed Raelin. Helena refused to allow herself to think about how she wanted her friend found. The idea of her death was too difficult to consider when she needed her composure.

Pain raked across her heart. Helping her friend was going to prove a difficult task, but she would do it. Helena cast a look around and discovered that Farrell was a man of his word. There wasn't a McQuade in sight; only the shadows of the early morning. But every corner might conceal someone. Her heart accelerated and her senses became acute. She heard the king and his entourage before they drew close enough to escape the gloom of the stormy morning.

The royal guard was not amused by her presence. They rushed ahead of their king to lock their pikes in front of her.

Helena sank into a deep curtsy.

"Your Majesty, I beg your permission to visit my husband."

It was all too common a request from a wife who was soon to be a widow. Helena allowed the fear to bleed out into her voice. The king strode forward and eyed her. He waved his guard back. The men hesitated, earning a frown from their monarch.

"What do ye think the lass is going to do? Slay me with her tears?"

They withdrew but the king shot her a hard look. "Which I noticed ye do not have any of in yer eyes."

Helena recovered, standing firmly in the face of her king. "Weeping is for the guilty."

One of the king's eyebrows rose. "McQuade claims he was with ye every moment of last evening. Is that a truth?"

"It is."

She held the king's stare. It was intense and she couldn't tell what the man was thinking but she refused to lower her eyelashes. Confidence burned inside her too brightly to pretend anything but solid belief in Keir's innocence.

"Why did ye run away the night before yer wedding?"

The question surprised her. It seemed so long ago that she allowed the answer out without hesitation. "Edmund told me I was to wed Ronchford by your command."

"So ye ran away from your king's order?"

Her cheeks colored but she maintained her level chin. "Yes, I did."

Everyone was silent. Helena heard the rain hitting the glass in the windows but the king suddenly chuckled.

"Ye're a better match for McQuade than I ever imagined. God grant me patience to deal with the children ye will give him." His amusement vanished. "Providing we can discover the truth of this mess."

"Raelin McKorey will prove it."

"The girl is likely drowned." The king's tone was hard with authority. "Which leaves me with a dead peer and a pair of lords who were fighting over you for the gain ye would bring them."

Helena shook her head but the king held up his hand. "Ye may visit yer husband. Once."

James Stuart resumed his progress down the hallway. Helena didn't bother to lower herself. The man wasn't looking at her but many of his entourage did and she refused to show them anything except confidence.

"Well now, I'm impressed." Farrell moved out of the shadows to grin at her.

"Don't be. The difficult challenge is still in front of us. The king may have two lords in the Tower, but the one who wed me shoulders more suspicion."

The sort of suspicion that cost lives. Helena shivered, unable to suppress her foreboding any longer. It grew inside her chest every moment that she waited for the parchment that would allow her to enter the Tower. When the king's royal guard returned with it she took it with a hand that trembled.

"Let us go to the Tower."

The McQuade men closed around her, escorting her toward the yard. Every set of eyes in the great hall turned toward their progress. But Helena's attention was focused on the journey in front of her. It was one many had traveled on their way to their deaths.

One that led to the Tower of London.

Chapter Twelve

The Tower of London was a fortress that struck fear into those who entered it. Helena decided that the dark weather fit the moment. The outer walls were protected by a moat, and somewhere along the stone walls was the traitor's gate. The storm had likely saved Keir from entering the Tower through that infamous opening.

But that wasn't much mercy.

The walls rose up above her, sending a shaft of fear through her. The solid stone and iron was inhabited by too many ghosts to name. Past the outer walls and towers there was another entire set of walls and towers before you reached the tower green where the scaffold stood. At the very heart of the fortress stood the white tower. Its walls rose ninety feet into the air, built to impress Norman rule after Britain had been conquered.

Black-uniformed yeomen stopped them. Helena felt the rain splatter on her cheeks when she stretched her neck to watch Farrell hand the parchment over to one of the yeomen. He looked up, his gaze settling on her face.

"Bring the lady closer."

She climbed down from her seat at the front of the wagon that hauled her trunks before any of the McQuade men offered her a hand. She didn't blame them. They were uneasy and watching what was coming toward them. Her own stomach was twisted into a knot. The sight of the outer wall sent terror through her. The Earl of Essex had lost his head not a full two years ago.

And now her husband was imprisoned inside it.

Helena moved closer to the yeomen.

"Push your hood back and open your cloak."

Farrell protested but the yeoman silenced him. "It wouldn't be the first time someone tried to sneak in wearing a dress."

"I am a woman." Helena did as instructed and the rain quickly soaked into her hair. She opened the wool cloak wide. Heat burned in her cheeks when she watched the man's gaze settle on her breasts.

"All right then." He waved his hand and there was a groan from the iron gate. It creaked and moaned while it was pulled up. "The lady may enter. Only the lady. Her escort will remain here. My men will take the trunks and deliver them once they have been searched."

Arrogance and authority edged his words. Helena bristled beneath it but she knew the way the Tower worked. There was only one way to survive inside its walls. She reached into her doublet, the yeoman's eyes following her motions. A hint of lust flickered in his eyes but it quickly changed to greed when she plucked a pound coin from her bodice. He licked his lower lip with anticipation.

"I place my faith in you, sir."

The coin disappeared in his gloved hand in the blink of an eye. The rain continued to fall, drenching her dress. The cloak became heavy with water, pulling on her shoulders. Walking across the drawbridge, Helena shivered when she passed beneath the raised gate. The yeomen sent men into the rain to pick up her trunks. They hurried back across the length of the bridge on their way to shelter.

Helena stopped just on the other side of the raised gate. Farrell and the other McQuades looked more at ease in the weather than any Englishman in sight. They had a portion of their kilts pulled up over their heads but there wasn't a miserable expression among them. They looked strong and invincible, exactly as she recalled from the first day she had laid eyes on Keir.

"We will be waiting on yer return, my lady. Right here."

"I will not be leaving until you have found Raelin."

Farrell scowled at her. He stepped forward but the yeomen instantly lowered their pikes to keep him on the outside of the tower.

Helena raised her voice so that the men behind him heard her.

"You promised Keir that you would not leave me unprotected. Look around; there is no more secure place than the Tower of London."

"That is nae what my laird meant and you know it." Farrell cast a look at the pikes, judging the men who held them. Helena stepped back and he frowned at her.

"Come back here."

"Do you mean to tell me that you plan to place your faith in the English to recover Raelin McKorey?"

Several of the retainers behind him scoffed at her words. Farrell pressed his lips together.

"Ye're trying to confuse me." He dug into his own purse and produced a silver pound. He held it up. "One of ye be a good lad and give me mistress a push this way."

"I have the king's permission to see my husband."

The captain of the yeomen gripped her arm. "You do, and you shall see him. That is my duty."

Farrell snarled. "Be a good fellow and bring her back here."

Another pound appeared in his fingers. It was a large

amount of coins and a few of the yeomen looked at the grip the captain had on her.

"Farrell, stop it. Can't you see that this is the only way that I can help? Keir is your laird. You must go looking for Raelin."

The burly Scot was torn. She witnessed the battle in spite of the rain. The other clansmen frowned, clearly divided between loyalty to Keir's last order and the need to do something other than stand watch over her.

Farrell replaced the money. He reached up and tugged on his cap. Approval shone from his eyes and it humbled her to see it.

"Are ye sure ye are nae a Celt, my lady? You have a very clever nature."

Relief flooded her. "I am a woman. No matter where we are born, we females need be clever to survive."

"See that ye do that, ma'am."

There was a groan as the gate began coming down. So close to it, she flinched at the harsh metal-on-metal sound of the chain grinding against itself. The black iron gate shook when it connected with the drawbridge. It was such a final sound, one that shook her to her soul. How many nobles had listened to that same sound and never lived to cross back over the drawbridge? Farrell turned and took to his horse in powerful motions. She could see the impatience in every motion. Smiles split the lips of the other McQuade retainers, many of them turning to offer her a quick tug of their bonnets before they dug their heels into their mounts and galloped into the afternoon gloom.

It gave her hope. She clutched it tightly against her heart as she turned to look at the inner wall of the tower. The captain of the yeomen led her through a maze of stone corridors and walls. She shivered, but it had nothing to do with the rain—it was the emotion rising from the walls, all of the suffering that had happened between their hard surfaces. A raven called out and others answered. The black birds swooped down from the sky to land beneath the eaves of the tower roofs. They stared down at her, looking sinister with their feathers slick and shiny from the rain. Their steps echoed on the cobblestones and she swore that she heard the faint sounds of drums echoing from an execution.

"We gave Lord Hurst a decent room. Not bad at all." The captain pointed up at one of the round towers that was built into the inner wall. "That's the bell tower. Our good queen Bess was staying there when she was just a princess. It's got a view of the Thames."

And the scaffold on Tower Green . . .

Helena swallowed her horror. "Thank you for your kindness."

"Well now, we appreciate the noble behavior of your husband. That Lord Ronchford made quite the fuss. We stuck him somewhere where we don't have to listen to his bellowing."

There was a sick enjoyment flickering in the yeoman's eyes. But Helena imagined that it was the sort of thing that kept a man sane while living and working within the Tower.

"You'll have the use of the wall up there once the weather clears up a bit. Of course, your husband is Scottish, so I imagine a little rain doesn't bother him any too much."

"How nice."

The yeoman's lips twitched, almost as though he was enjoying her struggle to maintain civility while they moved deeper into the fortress.

"Right up these stairs. You understand that you have the right to leave, but once you go, you may not return."

The stairs were narrow and dark. Wind blew down them but it was still musty. None of those things deterred her. Keir was there, up the last few steps and behind a locked door. The rattle of keys bounced between the sides of the stairway as the yeoman pulled a ring from his belt.

"Do you understand, my lady?"

Helena lifted her chin. "I do, sir. I will not be leaving until my husband does."

He didn't believe her. The look on his face showed her a man who had seen too many prisoners deserted by their spouses when the years began to pass. Helena stared straight back at him, unwavering in her determination.

"Well then. I wish you well, lady."

He fit the key into the door and turned it. A grinding sound issued from it before the latch opened and he pulled the door wide. The chamber was dark, with light coming only from the fireplace. She stepped boldly inside, seeking the man for whom she longed. He was sitting in a chair, staring at the embers of the fire. Wood was stacked up near the hearth but he had not fed the fire; it was only a faintly glowing bed of coals.

Her husband swore.

His eyes glowed and he cursed even fouler than the first time. His body rose in a powerful motion that made the yeoman next to her reach for his sword.

"Easy now, my lord."

Keir stepped forward, his anger clear on his face.

"The lady has the king's permission to visit."

Keir froze. "Permission to visit?" Suspicion darkened his features. His attention shifted to her and she felt her throat tighten.

Her husband was not pleased.

"Are ye telling me that ye asked to be here?"

His brogue thickened with his anger. He looked at the yeoman. "Would ye excuse us, man?"

The door of the chamber slammed shut. There was the sound of the key grinding in the lock that made her flinch. It sent another shiver down her spine but she did not regret her choice. Even angry, her husband was the dearest sight she had ever beheld. The first true smile lifted her lips since they had been interrupted in their chamber.

"Now dinnae do that." Keir shook his head, even raised one finger and pointed at her.

"I am not allowed to be happy to see you?"

He closed his eyes and groaned. His face lost its stern expression. It was replaced by a need so fierce it drew a gasp from her. His eyes opened and she stared into eyes that hungered for her.

He scooped her up and she wasn't even sure when he crossed the distance between them. Helena didn't care. She clung to him, her arms trying to pull him even closer. She wasn't near enough, couldn't seem to hold him tightly enough to drive the chill out of her heart.

"Good God, ye're freezing and soaked to the bone."

"But I'm with you. That's all that matters. We've time aplenty for my dress to dry." Her feet touched the floor but she kept her hands on his shoulders. Her husband frowned and picked her up once more, depositing her in front of the fireplace. She trembled when the heat touched her chilled skin. She hadn't noticed the chill, hadn't allowed herself to be concerned with such things as her own comfort. What was a bit of rain compared to the possibility that the Privy Council might well be urging the king to sign an execution order even as she had her reunion? Keir tossed a log onto the coals. It began to snap and pop almost instantly.

"How did ye give Farrell the slip?"

"You assume he did not agree with my choice to join you."

He unlatched her soaked cloak and hung it on the wall. Keir slid his arms around her without a care for how wet she was, placing his body against her back to warm her.

"I know my man. He's going to blister me ears when I see him again, isn't he?"

"Perhaps. Yet he did tell me I was clever."

He muttered something in Gaelic. "More like irritating, madam. I told ye to stay with me men."

She turned, pushing at him and frowning when she had to glare at him and wait for him to decide to release her. The hands she had planted flat on his chest were no real inducement when pitted against his strength.

"And I believe your men are far more needed to find Raelin. Since I am with you, they may begin to search for the witness that will clear your name. You see? Very logical."

He growled but his face told her that he agreed with her. Reaching up, she smoothed one of the creases from the side of his face.

"Don't be angry with me, Keir. I couldn't stand being away from you. It hurt too badly."

He captured her hand and held it against his lips. He turned it over and drew a deep breath, inhaling the scent of her skin. Heat flickered to life, a tender passion that sent tears into her eyes.

"Aye, lass. I understand what ye mean."

His eyes opened and she gasped. So much need shimmered in their dark centers. It cut deep into her heart, laying her emotions open to his keen gaze. She loved her parents because they were her parents, but she loved him because she could not resist. The tears spilled over onto her cheeks.

"I cannae stand the sight of yer tears." He caught them with his thumbs, easing them across her cheeks.

"I only cry for you, Keir."

He stiffened. "Ye cried the night afore our wedding and the slash of that still pains me. Tell me why." His voice was raspy with need. The hands cradling her head suddenly held her more firmly. "Tell me."

"I was half in love with you and I didn't want to see reality shatter it."

Surprise flashed through his eyes. "You mean to say that you believe all this nonsense about love nae belonging in a marriage?"

"Well, you told me that you didn't think that you would ever fall in love when your mistress was leaving you."

She tried to shake off his hand but he held her head firmly. A grin offered her a flash of his teeth.

"I keep telling ye, Helena. I am a Scot and we do things a wee bit differently."

She scoffed at him. "You cannot say that you expected love from your marriage. Admit that you are as surprised as I."

"Right after ye tell me ye love me."

Determination flickered in his eyes. Hunger and need was there as well, making her heart ache. He was so powerful, so full of strength that her love seemed a pitiful thing to offer to such a man.

But it was the only thing that was truly hers to give. It was unique because she knew that he was the only man she would ever say such words to. That gave her words luster. She felt it shinning in her eyes.

"I love you, Keir McQuade, and I don't care how angry you are about my joining you here. I would wither away without you."

She reached up and pulled one of his wrists toward her lips. Closing her eyes, she drew in a deep breath, exactly as he had done. The scent of his skin filled her senses, triggering a flare of passion that licked over her skin. His other hand opened and the fingers cupped her neck. She felt him move closer. Felt the way his body loomed over hers, surrounding her with strength.

"I love ye too much nae to be cross with ye, lass. This is nae a place that I want to see ye in. Even if I longed for ye so badly I thought it might kill me."

She opened her eyes and stared into his dark ones. "Any place we are together is perfect."

"I'll nae argue with being together, but I do wish it were on me own land."

He kissed her and she rose up to meet his lips. Conversation had lost its appeal now that she could smell his skin, feel his warm embrace. Her wet clothing chafed, irritating her skin. She wanted to return to the security the king's guard had interrupted. The kiss was hard with need, his lips moving over hers and pressing her to open her mouth for a deeper kiss. The tip of his tongue slipped along her lower lip until she complied and allowed it to tease her own tongue. A shiver went down her back and her husband lifted his mouth away from hers.

"I should paddle yer bottom."

Helena frowned at him. "I'll overstarch your shirts."

He chuckled and reached for the top button of her doublet.

"No."

"No?" One dark eyebrow rose in question.

Helena stepped back and noticed that she left a wet smear on the stone floor. She reached up and unbuttoned her doublet. The wet wool was difficult to manage with chilled fingers. But she finished and opened the garment herself. It was too stiff to slip down her arms. Instead it stuck to her shoulders.

"Perhaps ye'll reconsider."

He didn't wait for a response. His hands gripped the doublet and swept it down her arms. "I'm nae sure what I find more attractive—the idea of ye disrobing for me or the satisfaction of doing it with me own hands."

He wasn't wearing a doublet and his shirt was wet. Helena reached for the ties that held it closed at the neck.

"I confess that I don't care how it happens, so long as we both rid ourselves of these clothes."

"A point I find myself agreeing with ye on."

Her clothing didn't make it an easy task. It took his greater strength to unknot her corset tie. The log he'd placed in the fire had caught and heat radiated out toward her. Keir pulled at her corset until he freed it, gaining a soft sound of delight from her.

"Och now, there's another thing we can agree on. I prefer ye without all these layers, as well."

Her breath caught on a gasp. An amused chuckle rumbled form his chest. "Is this the lass who just offered to disrobe for me?" He opened her waistband and reached inside to find her bum roll. His hands pushed the entire wet mess down her legs in another few moments.

Her cheeks warmed. "I am still becoming accustomed to your way of saying things so boldly."

"Good."

He leaned toward her and pressed a warm kiss against her neck. It sent a delicious ripple of sensation over her skin that traveled down to her breasts. Freed from her boned stays, the delicate skin rose into goose bumps. His gaze dropped to her chest and she realized that her chemise was translucent in its wet condition. The thin fabric stuck to her every curve, the coral tips of her nipples showing plainly through.

She stepped out of her skirts and enjoyed the way his eyes remained on her. It was empowering, the way his face changed, his features becoming tighter, his eyes narrowing. She turned in a slow motion and paused with her back to him while peeking over her shoulder.

"Ye're beautiful, lass."

She believed him, actually felt her confidence rising. He pulled off his clothing, his motions rougher than they'd been on her. She turned back around, watching his skin being revealed. It was the most erotic thing she had ever witnessed, and the most tender. Unlike her wedding night, she was completely at peace. More than eager for the coming union but also content to enjoy the motions that would lead them to intimacy. There was a subtle seduction in the way they watched each other, something that words wouldn't translate. It was in the slant of his eyes and the way his nostrils flared ever so slightly. Her body responded, her nipples tightening into hard pebbles. His dark gaze swept down to them and his lips thinned.

He opened his belt but didn't allow his kilt to fall to the floor. He caught it in a firm hand and laid it over the chair in which he'd been sitting. Pride flickered in his eyes when he looked back at her, pride in who he was and the clan colors he wore.

That was the man that she loved enough to give her trust to.

She pulled the wet fabric from herself. It resisted for a moment before leaving her skin with a soft wet sound. He stood still. A muscle twitched in the side of his jaw, betraying the fact that it cost him to do so. But he remained where he was, allowing her to look at him. His body was sculpted into ridges of muscles, all covered in smooth skin. His torso was lightly covered in dark hair that thinned at his waist but also grew around his sex. His cock stood at attention, confirming that he wasn't in the mood to wait. Her own body slowly heated up until the warmth from the fire was almost too much.

He moved toward her, cupping her breasts in gentle hands. "I treasure yer trust, lass."

She quivered, lifting her chin to stare into his eyes. Love shone there. It was sweet and tender, and was everything that she had foolishly believed did not exist in reality. She was grateful to be humbled by discovering it.

"I love you." Her words were a whisper but they broke through the still of the moment, shattering it.

His arms slid over her body, one going down over the swell of her hips to hook beneath her knees. He lifted her and cradled her against his chest.

"I hope so, because I love ye too much to ever let ye leave me side."

He carried her to the bed that the chamber provided. It wasn't as wide as the one in their town home, nor as comfortable, but it was clean. Keir followed her down onto the sheets, his mouth seeking hers. She wasn't sure of all the touches. His hands slid over her, almost desperate to trace each curve. Her own hands were just as determined not to miss one part of him. It was the only way of truly healing the hurt that had tormented her from the moment she had watched him leave her. She reached for him, stroking the powerful shoulders by which she had first been mesmerized. His kiss was demanding but sweet, his tongue thrusting into her mouth in a slow imitation of what her body craved. She opened her mouth to accept the penetration, her thighs parting to allow his hips to move between them.

He didn't rush toward taking what she offered. Instead, one firm hand slipped between their bodies to tease the top of her sex. She shuddered and arched up toward that touch, need beginning to twist into her. A soft whimper broke through their kiss and Keir lifted his head. There was meager light on the side of the room where the bed was. But the shadows only heightened her awareness of how his skin felt pressed against her own. It was as though she had never known exactly what her body was capable of until she was bare against him. It was a treasure, something rare and uncommon.

He rolled onto her, pressing her back to the surface of the bed. His hands tangled in her hair, pushing into the braid to hold her still. His wounded pride made him crave submission from her, but she lifted her hips, refusing to be docile. She breathed deeply of his scent and felt the rapid beating of his heart. Surrender was the furthest thing from her mind.

For once the chamber was filled with the sounds of plea-sure. Her husband thrust deep and she whimpered with de-light. No grisly facts surfaced to intrude. There was only the rapture building between them, the pleasure tightening be-neath each stroke of his length. The hope that his seed might take root and bring them the joy of a family with which to share their love. Everything built into a moment that stole them both away from all things except each other. Helena clung to her lover, clasping him with her thighs while her body clasped his length to pull his seed deep into her. The pleasure was blinding and she surrendered to it gladly, basked in the warmth. Ripples of delight continued to move along her limbs long after Keir had ground himself into her for the final time. She held him, her hands smoothing over his back. He caught his weight on his elbows but didn't roll off her quickly. Instead he pressed small kisses along her forehead, over her cheek and down to her neck. His heartbeat slowed to normal before he drew a stiff breath and moved.

He hooked an arm under her waist and pulled her over so that her head rested on his chest. Reality broke through her joy as she looked around the room, truly seeing it for the first time. There were three windows, but she would have to stand on a stool to see out because they were set so high in the wall.

Since it was a tower room, the chamber was round but the windows were thin to make it harder for arrows to enter. It also served to keep prisoners inside.

Only the bare essentials furnished the camber: two X-framed chairs that looked many years out of date and a small table that was scarred and etched with knife marks. There was no carpet on the floor, only the dull stone with a coat of dust. The pile of firewood along the wall was the most luxurious thing afforded her husband. If the yeomen were angry enough, they would have forgotten to bring up such a comfort.

There was a second doorway that led to a short walk along the inner curtain wall. The young princess Elizabeth had used it during her incarceration within the Tower. The doorway was narrow and low, built to Norman standards, and she guessed that her husband would have to duck to clear the top of it.

The bed was nice enough. Keir had his noble blood to thank for that. Along with the fact that he didn't stand accused of treason. Murdering a peer was no small crime, but it was considered something that might allow him to be kept in the Tower according to his station. Those incarcerated for treason against their monarch would discover just how miserable the Tower's dungeons were. If she had felt horror permeating the air when she entered, it no doubt rose from those places where torture was employed. She shivered and a warm hand smoothed over her shoulder.

"Tell me about the home you plan to take me to."

The hand on her shoulder paused and gripped, betraying his emotions.

"Red Stone? 'Tis a fine place. The heather will bloom in a few more weeks. . . . Have ye ever seen heather? Or inhaled its scent when the sun is warming the blossoms?"

Helena listened to his words. She used every bit of selfdicipline she had ever been forced to cultivate to focus on the picture he painted of a place she made herself believe she would someday go with him. There was no other option to consider. She refused to think about the Privy Council or the demands of other noblemen for Keir's blood. She wouldn't think about his head being displayed on the bridge as a warning to others.

She would immerse herself in his words, the rich sound of his voice, and believe as she had never believed in anything else that faith would deliver them both to Red Stone.

"Curse this rain!" Farrell glared at the sky. The swollen clouds were black, promising more rain, not reprieve. His feet sank in the mud up to his ankles, wringing another curse from his lips.

There was nothing but swollen ground to find. The Thames was flooding and sweeping debris along in its powerful current. He studied the way it rolled large tree limbs under the surface with ease. There was power in the current, the sort that may have made easy work of sweeping a lass to her death.

He grabbed the thick neck of his horse and fit his foot into the stirrup. With a pull and push, he swung up into the saddle. He didn't bother to notice how wet it was. That didn't matter.

"We're going to split up—half of ye go to the opposite bank to search for the girl. See if some silver buys us the information we need."

None of his clansmen looked any too hopeful. It was an opinion he shared, but there was little point in dwelling on it. He was a McQuade, after all. Keir McQuade had taken the name he was born to and restored more luster than most of them had believed possible in the short time since the last laird had tarnished it. Now it was his turn to serve Keir, and

Farrell didn't plan on losing faith just because the odds didn't look favorable.

He'd face defeat only when he was forced to and not one minute before that.

"A peer is dead."

James Stuart wanted to crush Lord Bramford's neck, but settled for gripping the arm of his chair. More than half his council was calling for retribution and he couldn't truly blame them. If one murder was allowed to go unpunished, it would be their own throats they would be worrying about come next month. There were always rebels who believed noblemen needed to die for some cause.

"I agree that it is a grave matter but that does not help us decide upon a clear course of action."

"Put the man to trial by the barons."

James held his emotions behind a mask. The rest of the council pounded on the table in agreement.

"The man? I believe I have two who had reason to do this deed, and the next man who accuses McQuade because he's a Scot is going to be reminded very solidly that I am done hearing that the country I hail from is beneath yers."

There was silence at the table, many of the men pulling their hands off the polished surface.

"Make no mistake, I am very interested in discovering the truth of this deed. But there will be no assumptions. No use of torture to gain a confession."

Lord Bramford leaned forward. "Sire, I suggest a baron's council be convened to try Lord Hurst by a company of his peers."

The others nodded. James could see the quest for vengeance burning in their eyes, but his own temper ignited.

"Lord Hurst?" He rose out of his chair and planted his

hands on the table with a loud smack. "Dinnae ye mean Lord Hurst *and* Lord Ronchford? Or does being English mean that the man is guiltless by blood alone?"

"Lord Ronchford did not marry—"

"Because he was beaten off the girl. But my fine-blooded Lord Edmund Knyvett told his sister that she was to wed Ronchford. I am suspicious that there was an agreement between Ronchford and Knyvett that would have led to the man being angry that he didn't get the bride he wanted. Or possibly paid for, since the girl's dowry ended up on a gaming table."

His councilors did not speak, but their eyes were full of brewing discontent. James sat down, forcing his own temper to cool. Balance was the key to maintaining power. Elizabeth Tudor had taken England from a penniless country and built it up into one of the richest kingdoms in the world by maintaining balance.

"They will both be tried. Bramford, I wish a list of noblemen to be presented to me for consideration. We will be fair with an eye for justice, gentlemen. I suggest Lord Warwickshire be placed on that list, since his daughter is married to a Scot."

"An excellent plan."

Lord Bramford didn't care for it but he masked his displeasure well enough. James looked around his Privy Council, his gaze resting on each man for a moment. Most were placated by his plan. For the moment, it would keep the discontent from boiling over.

Yet it would not hold forever. Someone's head would have to rest on a pike for Knyvett's murder. That was a shame. The man had been an arrogant fool upon whom fate had taken its vengeance. James didn't mourn him and he doubted that any of his Privy councilors did, either. No, their insistence for justice was about protecting their own skins. Many of them were not the most likeable men, either. They had abused those around them and taken far more than they had given in return. They craved knowing that the masses had an example made to them to keep them in their place, with them remaining on top.

He just hoped that he didn't have to do that at Keir McQuade's expense. He frowned, dark thoughts settling over him. Being king came with a burden. Sometimes it was so heavy, he believed it might crush him. Now was one of those times. He didn't want to sign Keir McQuade's execution order, but he very much feared that he might have no other option.

Aye, heavy. Too heavy.

Chapter Thirteen

Catriona McAlister knelt behind the queen during morning service. She couldn't pray, couldn't force even a silent one through her mind. Three weeks after Raelin had gone missing, the queen had ordered the morning prayers to be said for her soul.

Catriona knelt but could not pray for her friend. Every fiber in her resisted accepting the idea that she was dead. There was no body, no one coming to the palace to say they had found a noblewoman drowned by the surging storm waters. There was nothing except time passing and everyone whispering about what had happened on the dock.

I won't let you go. . . .

The service ended and she followed the queen, still denying that her friend was dead. They made their way through the palace hallways and it felt surreal. How could someone so dear to her vanish so easily?

She suddenly froze. A group of Scots were bowing to the queen. Their laird was a dark-haired man she recognized well. Alarik McKorey stood back up to his full height, in which he towered over Anne of Denmark. He wore his clan colors proudly, the kilt around his waist a combination of maroon and lavender on a gray background. He still wore his riding boots, which were laced up to his kneecaps. The tops of his socks were visible, as was a hint of bare thighs when he moved and the pleats of his kilt shifted. His long sword was strapped to his back and every man with him looked the same.

"Forgive me, Yer Majesty. But may I have a word with young Catriona?"

Anne glanced at her and she immediately sank into a curtsy. Appearances were important at court, but she fluttered her eyelashes, telling the queen that she was not against speaking with Alarik McKorey.

"She has my permission. Lady Gibbs shall wait for her."

Alarik swept the queen another bow but it was short and quick, his attention clearly on what he wanted. The man must have ridden hard to make it to London in the three weeks since his sister had gone missing. It would have taken the messenger more than half of that time to travel to McKorey land. Rage flickered in his eyes as he closed the distance to where she stood. It was not personal and still she shivered. This was not a man to cross. He had been a laird since he was a lad of ten, and the duty had hardened him. That told her something about him. Men like Edmund Knyvett became arrogant with their station, but some, like Alarik, became forged steel when duty was yoked on their young frames.

She decided that Edmund was lucky to be dead, because she planned to tell Alarik exactly what had happened to his sister—beginning with Edmund's attack on her person.

Being dead was going to prove very fortunate for the English lord today.

"By the king's permission, you have a visitor." The captain of the yeomen announced his news in a clear voice. Helena hurried to shrug into a dressing robe while her husband dealt with the Tower guard.

Keir lifted one eyebrow. "Who is it?"

Alarik McKorey walked into the chamber before the yeoman could answer. The door shut behind him and the key ground in the lock. He swept the chamber before speaking.

"Damn miserable place."

"We've recently made improvements, thanks to my wife's knowledge of these English yeomen and their enjoyment of bribes."

The two trunks had arrived and thick bedding now adorned the bed. There was a writing desk and candle holders on the once-bare table.

"Is that a fact?"

Keir stood and studied Alarik. His father had raided McKorey lands. He was unsure what to make of the man. Alarik stared at him in silence.

"Ye've brought honor back to the McQuade name. 'Tis a welcome thing, I'm thinking."

Alarik offered him a grin and his hand. Keir took it. "What news?"

The grin faded from Alarik's face. Helena moved to the bed and sat down, leaving the two chairs for the men. She chewed on her lower lip, awaiting what Alarik had to say. There had been no word from court, only a simple letter informing her that Edmund had been sent home for burial.

"None that is good."

"Well, ye're nae a bishop, so I'll take that as a sign that I'm keeping me head, at least for the moment."

Alarik rubbed his jaw. "A trial has been agreed upon. A trial by yer peers."

"Barons . . ." Helena clamped her mouth shut when she realized she'd spoken. Alarik looked at her.

"Nae quite. The king has made sure to place a few earls among them, yer brother-in-law Brodick McJames among them."

"That's sporting of Jamie."

"It is. He wasna so kind toward Ronchford." Alarik smirked. "I'm set to judge him."

The attempt at humor didn't work for Helena. A trial was double-edged. So easily it might lead to the word *guilty* being placed on Keir's name. There was much to condemn him and little to clear his name. Fear dug into her, raking its claws across the fragile hope she had kept cradled against her heart. As more days had passed, it had become harder to keep her hopes kindled against the amount of time that passed without Raelin being recovered.

"When, McKorey?"

"Tomorrow. I figured those English wouldn't tell ye until ye were standing before them."

Keir scowled.

"I didna do it."

Alarik shrugged. "Of course ye didna. Ye're a Scot. Ye'd have snapped his neck with yer own hands, or I'll rip that kilt off ye myself."

"It's a relief to have someone who understands me at last."

Both men chuckled, making Helena shake her head. Men did not make sense. Their humor was incomprehensible. But that left her with nothing to ponder but the coming trial.

Keir tried to kiss her the moment Alarik left.

"Don't."

She pushed past his arms and he frowned at her.

"'Tis good news."

She turned on her husband. "How can you say that? Without Raelin, there is no witness."

"Ye're assuming the lass will have something to say that will point the finger at the man who paid for the crime."

Helena frowned.

"'Tis most likely that yer brother was slain by an assassin that those English lords will say I paid. A trial has always been the only end to this."

He crossed his arms over his chest in a pose that she recalled too well from their first few days together. The man was fixing to be immovable.

"I am strangling in this waiting noose, Helena. I'll face every peer they line up to judge me and gladly."

"They may return a guilty verdict." Her voice trembled in spite of her effort to contain it.

"Better some decision than this." He opened his hands to indicate the chamber. "I willnae live like this just to hold onto life. 'Tis no life, Helena. I want to take ye to Red Stone, nae babble about it like some old man who is too broken by age to step outside any longer. Time will do that to me soon enough. What is the point of growing old if I have nothing to talk about except these walls when I get there?"

He meant it. Rage flickered in his eyes but it was the frustration that punctured her own temper. He nodded and closed the distance, reaching out and pulling her into his embrace in spite of her protests. They were only halfhearted ones. In her heart she understood that the man she loved was dying in front of her eyes.

"I cannae bear to think of ye growing round with my babe in this place."

And he wouldn't tolerate her thinking him coward enough not to face what was to come. Of course not. That gallant man she had first been attracted to could never hide in a prison because it allowed him to draw breath.

"I love ye, Helena. But I am nae content to hide."

She reached up and placed her fingers against his lips. "Let's not speak."

He kissed her fingers, agreement shimmering in his eyes. But there was also a glimmer of anticipation. He was eager for the battle. Of course he was. So she would be as well. Instead she reached for him, her fingertips far more familiar with his form now. For all the horror that the chamber might have seen, in the last month it had been a place where they had become lovers, where they laughed and teased, doing all of the things that time had not allowed them to do.

Keir threaded his fingers through her loose hair, pleasure lighting his eyes. Here she left it hanging down her back because she knew he loved it that way. He pushed the dressing robe off her shoulders, leaving her in her chemise. He bent his head, angling it so that his lips might be pressed against her throat. He kissed the smooth skin and she gasped at the heat. It rippled over her skin and down her body. Only a loose chemise covered her and she made a little sound of delight when he pulled her against his own shirt-clad body. Her breasts were free to enjoy the way they compressed against his harder body. His cock was hard and it pressed against her belly.

But her husband lingered on the column of her throat, teasing her with unhurried kisses before gently biting her. It was a soft nip but it sent pleasure surging through her. He licked over the bite, a low rumble vibrating his chest and throat. Her hands curled into talons on his biceps.

"Ye make me impatient, lass. Like a lad without a beard."

"Patience is overrated as a virtue."

Her voice was raspy with need. Keir slid his hands over the curves of her hips, gripping them and lifting her up onto the tabletop.

"I agree."

He pushed her chemise up to bare her thighs, his hips

pressing them apart. He gripped her hips again, holding her firmly as he raised his kilt and moved his body until the head of his cock pressed against her. For all the rush to penetration, neither of them hurried the pace. He rode her gently, keeping each thrust smooth. He lingered deep inside her, letting her feel the way her body stretched around him. Helena reached for his hair, tangling her fingers in it. Her senses were full of his smell. Pleasure tightened slowly until it became unbearable. Her husband sensed it and abandoned his lazy pace, his body working fast and hard to push them both over the edge into a pulsing rapture that wrung a cry from her.

He held her, remaining deep inside her as their bodies quieted. His hands smoothed over her. He plucked at her chemise and finally moved back enough to pull it over her head.

"I think I shall keep ye nude."

"I'll freeze."

He grinned and scooped her off the table, walking across the floor toward the bed. He settled her among the bedding and joined her there, his hands cupping her breasts while he trailed kisses over their soft skin.

"I'll keep ye warm, lass, and that is a promise."

The Chapel of St. Peter-ad-Vincula was silent. Keir walked down its center aisle, making the only noise, and that was minuscule. His fellow peers sat waiting for him. It was the same place that others had been condemned, the same aisle that Anne Boleyn had walked down before her head was struck from her body. Had she been as full of life? Helena watched her husband and couldn't help but marvel at the way he moved. It was powerful and striking without a hint of hesitation.

He reached the end of the aisle and stood firmly in front of the assembled lords. The trial commenced and each moment felt like a dagger being poked into her skin—small torments that produced an agony that lasted for an eternity. When the last question was asked, they both watched the lords retire to a chamber for deliberation.

Helena wondered if it would, in fact, be a true verdict of their opinion on the facts. So many times the guilty verdicts pronounced were given in response to the king's whim. Anne Boleyn's had been. The large doors shut, preventing her from seeing what transpired. She stood with two yeomen of the guard. Their faces were like stone while they guarded her. Soon enough she would be called to answer to the details of whatever the lords wanted to know. But she smiled because her husband would have at them first and Keir McQuade was no fool.

The nine lords sent to judge her husband were quite intimidating. Helena faced them without fear. Her husband was gone now, so that her testimony might be kept from his ears. A test of their honesty, to see if their accounts matched. Lord Warwickshire sat among them along with his Scottish son-in-law, the Earl of Alcaon. Brodick McJames was dark-haired like Keir and he wore his kilt proudly. They were the highest-ranking men present. True to his word, Alarik McKorey sat among the English barons but that was only three votes against the others that she felt sure would judge the situation fairly. Lord Bramford rose and began questioning her the moment she stopped in front of them. His voice was coated with disdain, and he peered at her like one might a rodent. Helena refused to be intimidated. She answered his question but the man became bolder.

"Come now, Lady Hurst, do you intend to maintain that

your brother lowered himself to striking you because you did not defend him in the presence of the king?" Lord Bramford said as he pointed at her. "Admit that you were Lord Hurst's lover." He spoke it so calmly, as though it was the most common truth. She lifted her chin in the face of his accusation. She had no shame to cast her eyes at the floor over.

"I was not. We'd barely met. I was pure on my wedding night."

"Is that why there was no witness to your wedding sheets? No inspection by a midwife before the wedding that we may call upon to prove you a maiden at that time?"

"I held no control over those matters." Helena tried to keep her voice even. Anger might so simply be considered a sign of guilt. "I was ordered to wed by the king and my brother. The queen herself brushed out my hair. I obeyed."

Bramford glared at her. "Obeyed? You ran from the king's will, madam."

"Enough, Lord Bramford. I have a few questions myself." Brodick McJames, the Earl of Alcaon, silenced the blustering English lord with one hard look. He was not an easy man to read. When he returned his dark stare to her, she felt the intensity of his gaze.

"Why did ye flee into the night?"

"My brother told me I was to be wed by royal command to Lord Ronchford, but that he would spare me that and sneak me to the country if I braved the three blocks to make it appear that I had fled on my own. Edmund promised me that his carriage would be waiting."

The earl's brows lowered, and Helena stared straight at him. She was finally grateful to her parents for teaching her to stand so perfectly. Today, she would not crumple in the face of questions designed to smear her with guilt. The church was lit with hundreds of flickering candles, but she did not feel comforted by their light. For a house of worship, it was tense and filled with dark suspicion. A queen of England had been condemned here, as had other men who had been as guiltless as her husband.

"Ye trusted yer brother to have a carriage waiting for ye when he had used yer dowry for gaming debts?"

Her cheeks colored. She couldn't help it. It was still a shame, long after becoming happy in her marriage.

"I did not know the details. Edmund told me I was to wed because Raelin and I were out of the queen's chamber without escort. I knew nothing of the gaming bet."

"Preposterous." Lord Bramford scoffed at her.

"I would like to question Lord Ronchford." Lord Alcaon cut a quick look at the assembled lords. Several of them nodded, but Helena was more concerned with how many of them sat in sullen silence. Their minds were already set. She lowered herself and turned to leave. The aisle was suddenly too long and the sound of her own footsteps piercing.

Keir stood in front of his peers. His patience was thin and that was no lie. His father had spent his entire life berating him, but it appeared that he seemed only to tolerate such from his sire. Today, this group of peers was treading on his last bit of goodwill with their prying questions and dishonorable insinuations.

At least it appeared it was nearing an end. He stood at the front of the church, waiting for their verdict. It was Brodick McJames who stood up to pronounce the lords' decision.

"We have no verdict."

"What is that supposed to mean, man?"

The earl maintained his somber expression except for one

corner of his mouth that twitched upward. "We are evenly divided on the issue, with the exception of one man who refused to cast a vote. Hence, we have no decision."

In another time or place Keir might have laughed—chuckled at all the wasted effort, or at the ironic twist of fate. But instead he crossed his arms and stared at the lords in front of him.

So close.

Yet not close enough. He'd failed to do everything he set out to complete in London. That knowledge stung. The stain of this trial would remain on the McQuade name long after he'd departed. It would haunt his children when they came to court.

Brodick tilted his head to one side. "We'll send our findings to the king for his consideration."

"Aye. And I'll be right here awaiting his pleasure. No mistake about it."

The earl did smile; he just couldn't help but enjoy Keir's humor.

Lord Bramford, on the other hand, turned red with rage. "Your humor is quite misplaced, Lord Hurst!"

"Is that a fact?" Keir unfolded his arms and pointed at the man. "I'll tell ye what is misplaced. I am. Being laird means I've people and land to be seeing to. I came to London to find a bride who was educated in the ways of running an estate and she is nae helping a soul locked up in this fortress. Nobility is nae a thing that should be used to mask laziness. If Edmund Knyvett had learned that lesson I believe he would still be among the living today. Instead he was a boy in a man's body, who managed to keep inflicting his shortcomings on the living."

"Disliking him did not give you the right to have him murdered."

"I didna pay for his death, man. If you cannae see that I have what I want, ye're a blind man. Do I look like I'm eager to join the court?" Keir reached down and pulled on his kilt. "I'm a Scotsman and I plan to finish me business and go back home. There are crops to plant with a care to how it's done, or there will be suffering on my land next winter. It is a duty my father charged me with while he was off seeing to the glory of his own gains and it is one that I intend to continue doing since I've no care for dancing around the king day in and day out. That is nae to say that I didna see that some of ye work hard with our monarch to keep this country running, but it is nae something I crave."

Keir offered them a nod of his head before turning his back on them. Discontent filled him as he covered the steps that would lead him back to his tower chamber. Every fiber of his being resisted. Rebellion burned in his gut and it was getting hard to remind himself that his actions would fall onto his people's shoulders should he act on his impulse to fight his way free.

Damned diplomacy.

"I have decided on my vote." Roan Lawley, Baron Heaton, spoke up.

Brodick turned to stare at the man. He had kept his thoughts to himself throughout the proceedings and had been the one lord who refused to pass a verdict. He was a large, burly man. He wore only a wool suit, cut in the English fashion, but lacking lace and baubles. The finest thing on him was his boots. Brodick admired them for the workmanship. They came up his legs and the top of his pants tucked into them.

"Innocent. That man is innocent."

Bramford sputtered but Roan Lawley turned to glare at him.

Bramford snapped his jaw shut instantly, upon which Brodick raised his eyebrow. There was something there. Something a plain wool suit hid.

"Do you wish to change your ruling on Lord Ronchford?"

Baron Heaton fingered his chin. "If my silence vexes you gentlemen, so be it, but I have stood before a panel of my peers and it is no light duty in my opinion. I will not cast my vote without firm conviction in my conscience. I still find insufficient evidence to condemn Lord Ronchford. Or to find him innocent."

"But enough to set Lord Hurst free?" Bramford asked the question. It annoyed Lord Heaton. He rose and towered over his fellow English lord.

"The man didn't come to court expecting a title."

"But that does not mean he didn't marry with an eye on gaining one."

Lord Heaton frowned. "I doubt you understand, Lord Bramford, but I do know what it is like to be locked up while my responsibilities go unattended. Lord Hurst is not a man who places his position above his honor. If that were so, he never would have spoken as he just did, without a care for the egos sitting in front of him."

Lord Heaton turned his attention to Brodick. "He reminds me of you."

Brodick chuckled. For all his English blood, the man was likeable.

James Stuart smiled—at least, inwardly. His gut had been clenched most of the day while he waited for word from the Tower.

"McQuade is judged not guilty."

Several of his advisers frowned. His temper itched to slap

them down, but that was the sort of thing that made for short-lived kings. The world was not as it had been at the time of Henry the Eighth. Elizabeth had known that and left him a mighty nation, thanks to her ability to walk down the center of every hot issue laid before her.

"But this leaves the matter of murder of a peer unresolved." His Privy Council was not as happy as he was. James couldn't blame them. His own life might be the next taken if the masses believed that they might get away with murder.

"The rack would gain the name of the culprit."

James stared at Lord Brampton. "Would ye have me behaving like Henry did? Signing execution orders for innocent men and women? Every man has his limit and the rack was designed to take them to it quickly. I could send anyone of ye to its backbreaking grasp and I believe ye would confess in spite of the fact that none of ye are suspected of the crime."

"I would have justice, Your Majesty."

"Hear! Hear!"

Hands appeared on the tabletop once again. That was another sign of the times. None of Henry's councilors would have dared slap the top of the table in the face of the king's displeasure.

A pounding began on the doors, snapping the last of his patience.

"Who dares interrupt?" James roared his question, finally having an outlet for his temper.

The last person he expected to see appeared when the doors opened. The queen lowered herself in deference to his tone.

"Forgive me, my lord husband."

She was breathless and flushed, her eyes flickering from the floor to his face and back again as she waited for him to receive her. Anne was a most suitable queen in that way, always preserving the image that she considered him her master.

"Rise, Anne. What brings ye here?"

"The Marquis of Wyse has arrived." She stood up, clearly agitated. Her face was flushed and her normally perfectly folded hands were plucking at her pearls.

"Demetrius? What dragged him out of his tower?"

Anne lifted one hand and made the sign of the cross over herself.

"He has word of Raelin McKorey."

James stood so quickly his guards had to dive out of his path. "Fetch McQuade and Ronchford. I want to see their faces when we hear what fate has befallen that girl."

"No, I don't want time to dress." Keir was in a foul temper. He scowled at the royal guard and the way they turned up their noses at his clothing.

"I'm a Scotsman, nae an ambassador. I'll wear me kilt."

Helena sighed. She didn't argue, but carried her husband's doublet to him. He jerked his attention off the royal guard who waited to stare at what she held. Frustration flickered in his eyes.

"Well, I suppose I shouldnae show up in just me shirt."

He stuck one arm into a sleeve and then the other. Helping him into it, Helena moved in front of him to begin working the buttons.

"Leave us."

The guards didn't need any more urging; they withdrew, leaving the chamber. Keir cupped her chin, his fingers wrapping around her jaw easily. She clamped down on her emotions before raising her eyelashes to allow him to lock stares with her.

"I suppose every honeymoon must end."

He smiled at her words. "Och now, dinnae be so quick, lass. I think we can still collect a fair number of bottles of honey mead from our friends."

"I don't much care for it."

He stroked the side of her face. "That leaves more for me."

"I will enjoy watching you drink it."

She had to rise onto her toes to finish the last few buttons. Her fingers lingered on his warm skin before carefully completing her task. Her emotions surged, too much of a tangled mess to understand. Fear and relief that the moment was finally at hand battled against her poise.

"I do believe I shall miss having you completely to myself, husband."

"I'll have to do me best to see that ye dinnae go lonely in spite of all the duties life will expect of us once we make it home."

Helena broke the contact between their eyes, turning to pick up her gloves. Hope—it was a magical thing. She heard it edging her husband's voice and the deep tone beckoned to her. His arms came around her, enclosing her in an embrace that was too tender to remain calm in. A soft whimper escaped her lips.

"Sweet lass. Never wonder if I regretted coming to London. I don't. I found ye here and ye taught me what love is. That is worth every struggle that has landed in me path. I swear it."

He pressed a soft kiss against her temple, his arms tightening one final time before opening.

"But let us get on to the palace and see what Jamie has to say."

There was no hint of wavering in his voice. It was eager, and when she turned to look at him, she saw the man who had boldly appeared in her path in spite of being told to leave her alone.

Confidence was exactly what Keir was full of.

"I am ready, husband."

Whatever came, she was ready. He was correct—this was no life, but it had been a time that she would always treasure, for it gave her time to become lovers with him.

Chapter Fourteen

The king didn't plan on them slipping out of his grasp. Keir and Helena walked to the outer courtyard to find a full forty men waiting to escort them to the palace. They were still mounted, telling them that time was short. Two carriages waited in their ranks, the drivers still seated with the reins in their gloved hands. These were royal guards, not the yeomen who had charge of the Tower.

"I told you to unhand me!" Lord Ronchford's voice rose in the early evening. His tone was haughty and the yeomen pulling him along didn't look pleased with their duty. Only after they delivered him to the ranks of the royal guard did they look pleased. Ronchford drew himself up with an arrogant sniff. His gaze landed on them. He sneered at her.

Keir bristled beside her. Helena raised one gloved hand and gently laid it on his arm behind her.

"He isn't worth it."

"I disagree, wife. The man needs a good thrashing and I am more than in the mood to give it to him."

"There will be none of that." The captain of the guard stepped forward. "The king is impatient."

Keir tilted his head but shot Ronchford a look that sent the other man back a pace. "Well then, we'll nae keep Jamie waiting."

Another guard pulled open the door of one carriage. Keir raised an eyebrow at the captain.

"Your pardon, Lord Hurst, but for the moment I cannot allow you the freedom of being mounted."

Keir grumbled something in Gaelic but followed Helena up into the carriage. He had to sit on the very end of the seat and curl his back and neck. His knees rested against the opposite seat. Constructed to maintain warmth, the inside of the carriage was quite small. For a man of Keir's size it was very confining. Helena pressed up against the side of it to make as much room for him as possible, but he continued muttering.

"I believe I shall have to learn Gaelic," Helena said.

He straightened and cracked his head on the top of the carriage. She didn't need to understand the language to grasp the meaning of the next word he spoke; his tone was clear enough.

"I hate carriages."

But Ronchford didn't. Helena watched through the open door as he climbed into the second carriage and propped his boots on the opposite seat without a care for the mud clinging to his heels. Instead he tugged on his lace cuffs to make sure they were sitting exactly the way he liked.

How like Edmund.

How very much like court. The door shut and the horses began pulling them almost in the same moment. She wore only her hunting dress and was perfectly content. A bit of finery would be nice from time to time, but she held no desire to follow fashion too closely. Nor did she want to see her husband sporting lace and silk slops.

She heard the iron gate open and peeked out the window to see it rising and clearing the drawbridge. A smile lifted her lips even while her gut twisted with apprehension.

"Dinnae fret, lass." Keir captured her hands, which she hadn't realized were twisting in her skirts. He lifted one to his lips and kissed it before gently massaging her fingers until they relaxed.

"I cannae stand the sight of ye when ye fret."

Helena fluttered her eyelashes. "Everything shall be well; I am very sure of that."

He frowned at her. "And I cannae stomach those false courtly manners. Have a bit of pity on me and spare me."

She allowed her expression to reflect her true feelings. The sounds of the city street drifted in and she realized that she had missed them. The inner tower had been so quiet, so secluded, that time almost ceased to pass. It felt like their magical sphere had shattered and the pieces were raining down around them, allowing them to see the harsh face of reality. It was so strange how the Tower had become a haven from which she was sad to depart.

But there was anticipation burning in her belly, too, a flame that gained strength as the carriage made its way toward the palace. They pulled right up to the main stairs and the door was opened again. Keir gratefully left the carriage, shaking his shoulders. The royal guard flanked them with pikes held straight up, but there was no missing the keen attention those men gave to where Keir moved. When he walked, they countered by keeping just out of his reach.

It was not something they did to Ronchford. He alighted from his carriage and stormed up the stairs without a care. His face was flushed with temper and the guard remained very close to him, obviously not fearing his ability to lay them low.

The great hall was hushed. Helena heard the whispers rise in volume when they entered. Every set of eyes turned to look at them. Many raised fans to mask their mouths, as if that canceled their gossiping. She walked quickly, trying to keep up with her husband. Keir set a determined pace, intent on reaching wherever the royal guards were taking them. They increased their strides, the sounds of boot heels echoing in the quiet hall.

James Stuart sat on his throne, and Anne was seated on the raised dais as well. The queen sat straight up and her hand held a rare folded fan that she tapped against her loose gown. The guard closed the doors behind them. Helena scanned the other men in the room. All of the King's Privy Council was present and they were along the sides of the room near the dais, watching Keir and Ronchford. She had never seen so many facing down the receiving chamber. James normally sat on the dais and whoever was in his presence remained facing him.

Alarik McKorey was also in the room. His face was stern but rage flickered in his eyes. She could feel the man's impatience. He stared at the only other men in the room. There were three of them behind her. Lowering herself, she took the moment to look at them closer. They were dressed rather plainly but their clothing was made of the finest wool, not the coarser sort that was often used by the middle class. Yet it was not dyed any fashionable color. Nor was it black, such as the Puritans chose to wear in order to avoid committing the sin of vanity. Instead they wore a rather pleasant shade of green that was complemented with gray edging.

"We are at an unforeseen crossroads, my lords." James spoke slowly, shifting his attention between Keir and Ronchford. "Neither of you were found guilty."

"I should hope not," Ronchford scoffed.

The king stared at him for a long moment until a slap of the fan against his queen's skirts broke his lapse.

"It seems new information has surfaced to help us discover the truth of this grave matter."

James flicked his hands and a servant moved forward. It was difficult to tell what the boy carried until it was closer. The fabric was mangled and filthy, bearing rents and dark smears of dirt so that it was almost impossible to tell that it had once been the golden silk that Queen Anne's maids of honor wore.

"The most interesting part is that the piece of silk found in Edmund Knyvett's hand fits up with it almost perfectly."

Another servant brought the piece forward. He laid it against the soiled dress and the ragged edges met. The hem was stained with Edmund's blood, which was now dark.

"McQuade has two murders to answer for now." Ronchford raised his voice and pointed a damning finger at Keir.

"That's interesting." One of the men behind them spoke. He moved forward on powerful steps. He was a large man and he kept one hand on the pommel of his sword. Unlike most of the men in court, he didn't stand poised on one leg with the other placed in a pose of unconcerned relaxation. This man stood like Keir and Alarik, his body weight even and his attention keen. He had dark hair but eyes were as green as spring meadows.

"Interesting in that Raelin tells a story that is different. She says the assassin named Edmund as the man who paid him to wound him and you as the man who paid for his death."

"Preposterous! Where is the lying wench? I would like to see her say such a thing to my face!"

"Edmund paid his own assassin?" Helena covered her mouth with a hand. Horror flooded her, but she suddenly realized what the man had said. "Raelin is alive?"

He nodded. "Aye, and some place removed from all this evil."

"More likely she is hiding for fear of not being able to utter such lies in the presence of her betters!" Ronchford had turned red. "Who would believe that Edmund would pay an assassin to attack him? It is ludicrous!"

But something her brother would do. . . .

Helena shook her head, her eyes closing in horror. Edmund and his schemes. It sickened her, but she knew it to be the truth. She lifted her eyelids to find the king's eyes on her. Every Privy councilor watched her and there was no concealing her emotions.

"He told me not to consummate my marriage, that he would not allow me to be wed to someone he did not deem noble enough." She shook her head. "Edmund swore that it was not settled."

Greed must have driven him insane. There was no other reason.

"*He promised you to me!*" Ronchford's voice was shrill and his eyes glowed with rage. He lunged toward her, his hands grasping for her neck. "Mine! Do you hear? Mine! The Earldom was to be mine! *Your creamy body was to be mine!*"

Keir swung his entire arm out and flung Ronchford onto his back with the blow. The guards swarmed over the fallen lord but he fought them with unnatural strength. He suddenly laughed, an insane sound that bounced off the walls of the chamber.

"It will be mine! Do you hear? The king will set me free and I will claim what I paid for. You shall see! You will be my wife and warm my bed. . . ." He babbled on while the guards carried him from the room.

"Remain, McKorey!"

"Yer Majesty!" Alarik McKorey turned in a swirl of kilt and rage. The man shook with his desire for blood. His hands curled into fists with white knuckles.

"The man is insane. Ye cannae challenge him in such a state. I cannae even have his head removed."

"What of my sister?" Alarik looked at the torn rag of her dress. "How fares my sister?

"Your sister is recovering on my estate."

Alarik stepped toward the Englishmen. "And who are ye?" He tempered his tone, trying not to growl at the man who had given his sister shelter.

"This is Demetrius Wysefield, the Marquess of Wyse." The king supplied the information. "And we are in yer debt, my lord."

"Good. Then I expect to be allowed to return to my lands." The marquess was bold. He shot a hard look at his monarch along with his words. James began rubbing his chin.

"Ye're a fine man to have near, Wyse."

King and marquess faced off, the two men attempting to buckle one another by sheer force of will. The king finally waved his hand, breaking the standoff.

"Enough. We'll continue this quarrel later, Lord Wyse. How is my queen's maid?"

"Extremely lucky to be alive. I had a bishop sleeping in the adjoining chamber for a full week after fishing her out of the river."

"Why didna ye send a letter?" Alarik's voice still shook with rage. "I thought me sister was dead."

The marquess turned his head in a motion that was lightning quick. "She was babbling about assassins intent on killing her. I thought it best to hear the entire tale before penning a letter that might have landed in the wrong hands and ended with someone coming to my land to finish what the river failed to do. She burned with fever for an entire week and she needed her rest after escaping that, not an interrogation."

"But she is alive and well?" Helena couldn't remain silent any longer. She was bursting with joy. She had hoped for such an ending, but found it difficult to absorb. Both Keir and Raelin were safe. At last her brother's grip was truly broken.

"She is recovering. She is still not fit for travel. My physicians tell me that her bones will have to heal for several more weeks before the jostling of horses will be bearable for her. Longer if you wish to consider her comfort."

"I certainly do." Alarik drew in a stiff breath. "Ye have my gratitude and that of every McKorey. I will glady pay for her care."

The marquess raised one eyebrow. "Keep your coin, man. I don't run an inn. Your sister is my guest." Something flickered in his eyes. "Even if she stubbornly insists that she would rather suffer the road."

Alarik looked angry for a moment but his lips began to curve up into a grin. "Well now, that's me sister for sure. Arguing, just to make sure no one tells her what to do."

"I'm relieved to hear that is normal for her." His lips twitched. "I did wonder."

The marquess turned his attention to Helena for a moment. "You are Helena Knyvett?"

"Yes."

He flicked one finger toward his escort. One man opened a satchel and pulled a letter from it.

"She wrote to you." Several letters emerged from the satchel. "And to Her Majesty. And this one was to be sent to her brother, although she wasn't sure where you might be."

Helena took the letter, staring at its wax seal. It was such a simple ending to weeks of waiting. Her lips trembled but she smiled a genuine smile of relief and thanksgiving.

"Go on, Lady Hurst, and read yer letter."

The king's voice startled her. Helena snapped her attention back to him, her cheeks burning with a blush. But James Stuart smiled at her and waved her off. It was her husband who curled his fingers around her arm to keep her beside him.

"Relax, McQuade, yer retainers are here as well, but I was wanting to see Ronchford's true reaction to this news, so I had them kept out of sight when ye entered."

The king gestured to the grooms standing silently at attention near the doors. They opened them without a sound from their polished shoe heels. Farrell stood there with Keir's men all at attention. He inclined his head before looking straight at Keir.

"I'll be happy to see to the lady, my laird." Farrell's tone implied that he had not forgotten his frustration at being outwitted at the Tower.

Keir smiled at Helena. A sinking feeling hit her belly but she lifted her chin in the face of it. With a quick curtsy to the king and queen, she left. Keir's men closed around her the moment her foot touched the hallway outside the receiving chamber. But today she enjoyed the feeling. They were McQuades, and so was Keir. Instead of trapped, she simply felt secure.

Sitting down in an alcove, Helena broke the letter's seal.

Dearest friend,

Be most assured that I do not harbor any contempt in my heart for your blood. Your husband's father was a horrible man and yet I discover myself admiring his youngest son. Keir McQuade is a fyne man and I hope you are happy in your marriage.

I pray that we shall forever be friends for it is a rare thing to discover so true a heart in another.

Raelin McKorey

Tears stung her eyes, but they were joyful ones. Helena read the letter twice before folding it and tucking it into her sleeve. She looked up to find Farrell's eyes on her.

"Did you find her?"

The burly Scot tilted his head while a grin split his lips.

"After all the trouble ye went to in order to send me on my way? It was a point of honor to discover the lass. You were correct, my lady—those English never would have found her."

"Careful, Farrell, my wife is English and she told me that you called her clever." Keir sounded amused. He looked at his second in command. "Clever enough to slip out of yer grasp."

"Och well, that simply means she's going to be a fine mistress for Red Stone."

Keir held out a hand, palm facing up. "I couldn't agree more."

Helena placed her hand in his, watching as his fingers closed around her own. It was so simple and yet so perfect. She raised her gaze to his, feeling that little jolt of sensation that looking into his dark eyes always sent through her.

"Are you going to take me home?"

Keir pulled her close. "Aye lass, I am."

Spring spread its warmth over the land, the last of the cold winter weather melting under its power. Farmers returned to their fields and English and Scot alike emerged from their homes to bask in the warm sun.

Keir and his men were anxious to return home. Helena hid her smile as they tried not to look impatient to begin the journey. Keir checked the saddle on her mare with his own hand. The courtyard in front of their town home bustled with activity. The servants helped to tie bundles to horses that would serve as baggage carriers. Helena watched it, smiling with joy, the tension of the last month finally leaving her. She had slept deeply, groaning when her husband woke her at first light in his eagerness to be on his way out of London.

Not that she could blame him for that. She wouldn't be looking over her shoulder, either. The cook came hurrying from the kitchen with a bundle of freshly baked bread. She had tied it up in a cloth, but the scent still filled the air. It filled Helena's senses and a moment later her belly cramped with nausea. The urge to retch was overwhelming and stronger than her will to maintain her dignity.

Poise deserted her completely. She yanked her skirt up in a fist and ran toward the garderobe.

Her entire body quivered by the time her stomach stopped heaving. She only had enough strength to move a few paces out of the necessary closet before sinking to her knees.

"Helena?"

She moaned softly, humiliation flooding her. Keir reached down and plucked her off the floor. She pushed at him, gaining a grumble of annoyance from his wide chest.

"I don't want you to see me like this." She sounded on the verge of tears and didn't know why. Everything was wonderful, every hope that she had cradled bearing fruit. But tears trickled down her cheeks in spite of all that.

"I'm taking ye back to bed. Ye're sick."

"I am not."

She slapped his arm. "Put me down now." The tears evaporated as her temper flared. "Immediately."

Keir set her down and stared at her in confusion, his dark brows lowering. "Ye're as pale as a new moon. Ye are going to bed right now."

Helena held up a hand to keep her husband away. The weakness left her limbs as though it had never been. "I feel fine."

The cook came into the room and walked right past Keir with only a nod of her head. "Drink this, mistress. It will ease the ache in your belly."

"I am not ill. Why will no one listen to me?"

"Yes, ye are, Helena, and I will no' take ye out onto the road where ye cannae be cared for."

The cook turned her head to look at Keir. She drew herself up in a manner that Helena had never seen the woman do. She normally tried to be invisible.

"Forgive me, my lord, but I believe the mistress is correct. She is not ill."

The goblet in her hand smelled of peppermint. Helena looked at it and sniffed again. New spring herbs filled her senses and it was much more to her liking than the bread had been.

"What are ye saying, woman?"

The cook cast a look toward Helena. "Did you bleed at the Tower, mistress?"

"No . . ."

Helena almost dropped the goblet. She tightened her fingers around it before it fell from her surprised grip. The cook offered her a small smile of knowledge from one woman to another. She curtsied with a satisfied look.

She wasn't ill—she was with child.

"I'll bundle up some herbs from the still room for your journey. You'll be wanting those in the mornings for a few weeks."

Helena lifted the goblet to her lips. Her belly protested but she forced a few swallows down her throat. When she lowered the goblet her husband was preening, his face a mask of arrogant male satisfaction and enjoyment.

"Oh, go and check your horse."

He plucked the goblet from her hand instead and set it aside. A moment later he bent his knees and wrapped his arms around her waist. When he stood up her head was above his. He swung her around in a circle while nuzzling her belly.

Tears returned to her eyes. He held her there, placing a kiss against her flat body. Her hands tangled in his hair, playing with the dark strands. He let her slide down to her feet but kept her in his embrace.

"I love ye, Helena. I promise to love ye my entire life."

They were the gallant words she had always believed were only spoken in sonnets and tales of long ago. But the arms holding her were real. They were warm and strong and she loved being held by them.

"Take me home, Keir." She stroked the side of his face. "Take *us* home. A McQuade should be born on McQuade land."

"That's a fact, lass. It is indeed."

D r. Walt Arnold took slow breaths to keep from freezing his lungs. At thirty below, he was accustomed to the staggering temperatures, but it was hard to regulate his breathing when he was lifting sixty pounds of pipe and ice. He wrapped the core sample in plastic, then, with his assistant, levered it onto the transport, its metal shell intact. The temperatures were in their favor to keep the core sample from relaxing, as well as maintaining the chemical isotopes in prime condition.

His team took care of transporting the sample to storage as he returned to the drilling. He adjusted the next length of pipe, clamped the coupling, then glanced at the generator chugging to drive the pipe farther into the ice. The half dozen random samples would help correlate the data from the deeper drills. He watched the meter feed change in slow increments. Nearly three hundred meters. It was the deepest he'd attempted on this patch, and he was eager for data. His report wasn't due for a year, but making the funding stretch took hunks of time he needed for the study.

When the core met the next mark, he twisted, the wind pushing the fur of his parka as he waved a wide arc. His assistants jogged across the ice and he warned them again about exerting themselves unnecessarily. They brought it up, the sample laid out in sections. Overstuffed with down and thermal protection, his colleagues rushed to contain it in the storage trenches dug into the ice to keep the sample from relaxing or their measurements for chemical isotopes would be screwed to hell.

The drill continued and out of the corner of his eye, Walt watched the computer screen's progress. The nonfreezing drill fluid flowed smoothly and he could kiss the scientist who'd perfected it. Pipes locked in the ice meant abandoning valuable equipment. The crew transported the next length into storage below one degree to maintain the specimen. The rest gathered around the equipment housed over the site with a windscreen that would protect them, yet not change the temperature of the core samples. Walt ached for hot coffee.

Suddenly the core shot another twenty-eight feet and he rushed to shut it down. *Shit shit shit.* Not good, he thought, his gaze jumping between monitors. A pipe had come loose, he thought, yet the readings were fine. There wasn't a damn thing wrong with the equipment. That meant there was a gap. An air pocket in the glacier. His brows knit, his heartbeat jumping a little. The core depths so far were a sample of the climate eight hundred years earlier, give or take a hundred.

"All stop, pull up the last sample."

It was useless anyway. The inconsistent drill would change the atmospheric readings of gas bubbles if the core relaxed and lost its deep ice compression. Holes under pressure were usually deformed. The technician went back to securing the steel pipes. Walt switched on the geothermal radar, lowering the amplifier, then waited for the recalibration. The picture of the ice throbbed back to the screen, loading slowly. He didn't see anything in the first half that shouldn't be there. The feed showed an eerie green of solid glacier ice. Then it darkened, a definite shape molding from the radar pulse. Bedrock already? Or perhaps a climate buoy. Thousands of those were getting trapped, yet never this far below the ice flow.

A graduate student moved alongside him, peering in. "There's something in there."

Walt didn't respond, waiting the last few seconds for the pixels to clarify. "Yes, Mister Ticcone. There definitely is."

And try THE FALCON PRINCE by Karen Kelley . . .

She needed to clear her head. Nothing in life mattered when she was out running. This was her time. She didn't have to worry that people thought she was a little mentally off-balance. She didn't have to . . .

A hawk swooped down, landing on the trail in front of her.

She came to a grinding halt, feet still running in place, and then stopping altogether.

What the hell? Hawks didn't just land in front of people. And it should have taken off as soon as it spotted her.

Ria stared at the bird as she tried to catch her breath, bending over and resting her sweaty palms on her knees.

The hawk was magnificent, with a creamy white breast and speckled, dark-brown wings that blended into black tips. The bird was so close she could see its sharp talons. Talons that were made for catching and holding prey. Something about this wasn't good. Probably because the hawk still hadn't moved. It stared at her as though it were silently trying to communicate. This was weird. No, it was more than weird.

Almost as weird as the thick fog rolling in. She straightened, her gaze flitting from tree to tree until she could no longer make them out. An icy chill raced down her back as if someone had run an ice cube over her spine.

Fog wasn't that unusual. Right? It was early morning, and

the trail behind her house was in a low spot. Except this fog wasn't like any fog she'd ever seen. Kind of *Friday the 13th* creepy.

Alrighty, maybe this was her cue to leave.

Someone groaned, but the fog was so thick now she couldn't see a thing. Ria hesitated. What if the hawk had been trying to tell her that his owner was hurt? That . . . that . . .

It had finally happened. She had completely lost her freakin' mind.

But the fog began to dissipate enough that she could make out a man's face. A very tall man. At least six-two. With short dark hair. Strong chin. Green eyes that studied her. Tanned skin. Muscular chest . . .

Her assessment came to a screeching halt.

Muscular *bare* chest.

The man stepped forward. "I'm Prince Kristor, from New Symtaria. I'm here to take you back to my planet," he said in a deep, commanding voice.

The fog vanished.

The man was totally naked.

Who wants to be good?
THE NAUGHTY LIST is much more fun!
Try this sexy anthology from Donna Kauffman,
Cynthia Eden, and Susan Fox, in stores now.
Turn the page for a sneak peek at Cynthia's story,
"All I Want for Christmas."

The strains of Elvis's "Blue Christmas" drifted in the air as Christie Tate tried really, *really* hard to disappear inside the women's restroom.

"Did you hear?" The more-than-slightly-catty female voice asked from a few feet away.

Christie hunched her shoulders and stared at her heels.

"Charles Donnelley is already seeing Vicki from accounting. I mean . . . what's it been? A week? Two? He and Christie were—"

"I think he was seeing Vicki on the side," another female voice chimed in, oozing sympathy.

Fake sympathy.

Christie stared at the gleaming black door, aware of the heat building in her cheeks. Was this what she'd become? A thirty-year-old woman hiding in a bathroom stall?

She knew those voices. Marsha Chad, a marketing assistant, was the one with the fake sympathy. And the other one—

"I heard Charles thought Christie was just . . . boring," said Lydia Clyde. "I mean the woman's a genius, but when it comes to men and sex, she's . . ."

Enough. Christie's spine shot up at the same instant her hand slammed into the bathroom door. The door flew forward and she caught the sound of two feminine gasps.

Her eyes narrowed as she took in the two women. "Lydia. Marsha." So what if her cheeks were flaming? She wasn't going to hide in the bathroom another second.

Not thirteen anymore. Not the nerdy girl.

"Christie." Lydia's blue eyes bulged. "I didn't realize you were—"

Christie jerked the faucet on and washed her hands. "For the record . . ." she lifted her head and met her own gaze in the mirror. *Backbone, girl, backbone.* How many times had she heard her mother say that over the years? *Don't ever let them see you break.* "Sex with me is never boring."

She saw their jaws drop. Good. Great. She kept her chin up, kept her back straight, and with really fast steps, she was able to escape that hell-hole.

And to trade it for another one.

Christie burst from the women's restroom and walked straight into the full-on madness that was the Tate Toy Company's annual Christmas party. Bright lights. Elaborate bows. Mechanical toys—trains and soldiers—that marched across the floor. And Christmas trees. So many giant, colorful Christmas trees. Normally, she would have loved this site but right then—*just want to escape.*

She sucked in a sharp breath and tasted pine. Christie glanced to her left and found her ex, Charles, arguing with Vicki under a giant piece of mistletoe. The pretty redhead's hair tumbled down her back as she shook her head at Charles, then she jabbed a finger into his chest. Trouble in paradise?

I think he was seeing Vicki on the side.

Jerk.

A waiter sidled by her. She grabbed a glass of champagne and drained it in one gulp. Elvis kept singing.

Can't get much bluer than this, buddy.

She marched forward, putting more needed distance between her and Charles. *Can't attack.* Because, no, that wouldn't be classy. A lady couldn't go up and jump on her ex's back as she started to pound the crap out of him. A good girl wouldn't do that. She'd been raised to be a *good girl.* Good girls became ladies, right?

But she was damn tired of being good. Damn tired of being gossiped about. Damn tired of it all right then.

Even tired of Elvis. And she loved the king.

Christie marched through the crowd, only stopping to pick up a few more glasses of champagne. Oh, but that bubbly went down nice and fast. Some folks tried to talk to her, but if they didn't have a tray of champagne flutes near them, she kept going.

Kept going until . . .

Until she reached the giant black chair that waited in the middle of the room. Santa's chair.

Presents wrapped in red and green paper surrounded the massive chair. Small surprise gifts for all the staff at Tate Toys. Santa would be coming soon. He'd be there to hear all their Christmas wishes. There to make those wishes come true.

Christie's fingers tightened on the champagne flute.

Then she caught a glimpse of Santa, and she spilled the rest of her champagne over the front of her red reindeer shirt.

Wow.

Santa was a stud.

She swallowed as she got a good look at the jolly old elf. Santa stood just inside the doorway of Tate Toys, a thick sack flung over his left shoulder—and what a nice shoulder it was. Actually, Santa had *two* nice shoulders. Nice, wide, broad shoulders that stretched the red coat he wore.

Her gaze tracked slowly down his body. No shaking like a bowl-full-of-jelly there. Oh, no, that man—*Santa*—was built. Tall, strong. His muscled thighs stretched the red pants and his powerful legs disappeared into a pair of knee-high black boots.

Santa stalked toward her. A fluffy white—and fake—beard covered his face and a bright red hat hid his hair. All she could see were sparkling green eyes and high, tanned cheekbones.

"Have you been a good girl?"